VINEET BAJPAI

SECRET OF THE BLACK TEMPLE

TreeShade Books

KASHI

SECRET OF THE BLACK TEMPLE

www.VineetBajpai.com

DISCLAIMER

This novel is a work of pure imagination and fiction, written with the sole intention of entertaining the reader. While the content has several references to various religions, historical events, institutions, beliefs, persons and myths, it is all presented with the only purpose of making a fictional story richer and more intriguing. The author is a believer in all faiths and religions, and respects them equally and deeply. He makes no claim to the correctness and veracity of any historical or mythological or contextual references used in the story.

STORY SO FAR – PART 1 –
HARAPPA

Harappa, 1700 BCE – The *devta* of Harappa, the mighty Vivasvan Pujari, who has been revered for decades as the *Surya* of Harappa, is ambushed in a ruthless betrayal. His trusted friend and brother-in-law, the wise Pundit Chandradhar, succumbs to the malicious greed of Priyamvada - his beautiful wife, the Princess of Mohenjo-daro. Three blind black magicians from Mesopotamia, Gun, Sha and Ap arrive in Harappa at the invitation of Priyamvada and her evil man-at-arms, Ranga. The dark wizards poison the water sources of the city with their concoctions, driving its entire populace insane and violent.

In the midst of the chaos, Vivasvan Pujari is indicted in a

false accusation of the murder of Nayantara, Harappa's most famous exotic dancer. The devta of Harappa is condemned to the *mrit-kaaraavaas* or the dungeons of the dead. His valiant son, the young Manu, joins forces with Pundit Somdutt, the chief architect of Harappa and the last remaining friend of Vivasvan Pujari. In the battle that ensues, Manu kills the vile Ranga in a spectacular duel. At the same time, the River of the Wise, the Saraswati, rises in unnatural and ominous spate, threatening to devour the whole of the Harappan civilization. Astronomers predict imminent doomsday. The devta's gracious wife and Manu's mother, Sanjna, becomes the target of the arrows of manic Harappan soldiers and breathes her last on the battlefield, dying in her son's arms. At the behest of Somdutt, and his closest friend, the beautiful Tara, Manu rides out into the mist with his mother's body in his lap. But even as he gallops into the haze, poison tipped arrows tear into the handsome Manu's back and neck.

The devta of Harappa is dragged and tortured like an animal in the Great Bath of Harappa. He is skinned by the mad soldiers, pelted with stones and spat upon by the maniacal citizens of the once glowing metropolis. The devta, the Surya of Harappa – Vivasvan Pujari - swears vengeance. A man once known for his glowing and God-like appearance now looks ghastlier than the Devil himself. He looks up at the sky and screams out his last, bloodcurdling words to the masses of Harappa -

'Listen, you who are already dead. Listen, you congregation of corpses. Listen, you fools.

I am half-human, half-God!'

Banaras, 2017 (present day) – Dwarka Shastri, the 108 year-old mystic leader of the *Dev-Raakshasa Matth* (God-Demon Clan) located in the ancient city of Banaras, is on his deathbed. He summons his highly successful, unusually handsome and supremely talented great grandson - the magnificent Vidyut to the matth. Before his departure from Gurgaon, Vidyut confesses to his beloved partner Damini and to his best friend Bala that he hails from an ancient and mystical bloodline of devtas. Upon reaching Banaras, Vidyut discovers that his arrival had been awaited for centuries. Among other loved ones like Purohit ji, Balvanta – the war General of the matth, and Govardhan - the clan's physician, Vidyut also meets his childhood friend Naina. Naina has grown up to be an indescribably beautiful young woman, and Vidyut feels an inexplicable, magnetic attraction towards her.

The great *matthadheesh* Dwarka Shastri reveals to Vidyut that their bloodline was the bearer of a primordial curse. And that Vidyut was the last devta, the prophesied saviour – not just of his own bloodline, of the matth or of Banaras – but of all of humankind. Just as Vidyut sets foot in Banaras, a mysterious man called Reg Mariani has a meeting in Paris with someone who is known not by his name but by his title – the Maschera Bianca. Reg hands over a note from his own superior, the Big Man, to the Maschera. The note has five words inscribed on it –'*Kill that bloody Aryan boy!*' The Maschera Bianca or the White Mask is Europe's most dreaded crime-lord. An innocent looking yet masterful assassin named Romi Pereira arrives in Banaras.

The great Dwarka Shastri narrates the haunting story of Harappa to Vidyut, along with how a dark conspiracy hid the truth of the metropolis forever from Indians. He elucidates how the East India Company blew up the most precious remains of the lost civilization and deprived the sub-continent of its true, ancient glory. But most unexpectedly, the matthadheesh reveals to Vidyut that he is none other than the great Vivasvan Pujari – reincarnated 3,700 years later... to fulfill his ultimate destiny.

Events unfold rapidly including a daring but failed attempt on Vidyut's life, a magical moment where Naina presses her lips on those of a smitten Vidyut, the bubbly arrival of Damini at the matth, and an open invitation to the last devta by Romi - for a final confrontation on the Dashashwamedh ghaat. Ridden with suspicion directed at Naina, Vidyut unleashes himself on the mercenaries sent for him by the same veiled overlords who had hired Romi. Vidyut vanquishes the mercenaries singlehandedly, but not before getting shot at by his most trusted friend – Bala. Bala is captured, and the devta then goes after Romi across the dark ghaats of nighttime Banaras. The sophisticated assassin is held captive by Vidyut and bites into potassium cyanide – in his dying moments informing Vidyut that a force called the New World Order was coming for him...and for all of mankind.

STORY SO FAR – PART 2 – PRALAY

Harappa, 1700 BCE – The *devta* of Harappa, Vivasvan Pujari, miraculously survives the torture at the Great Bath. He is rescued in a daring, violent raid led by his last friend and the erstwhile chief architect of Harappa, Pundit Somdutt, along with the valiant Tara. The rescue attempt results in a legendary battle that would be remembered for generations as the Rain of Blood. Vivasvan Pujari emerges from captivity looking like a demon, gutting through the entire body of a Harappan commander with his bare hands.

Burning with the desire for revenge and unaware that his son Manu still lived, Vivasvan Pujari, the Surya of Harappa, is consumed with hate. He rides alone to join forces with his once sworn enemy, the great King Sura – emperor of the mighty *Asuras*. The devious Sura and his able war-general Prachanda succeed in poisoning Vivasvan Pujari. In return for retribution against the Harappans who spat upon and tortured the devta, against the city that took away everyone and everything he ever held dear – the Surya promises something that would blacken his pious soul forever. He promises the heads of the eternal protectors of Harappa – the divine Saptarishi.

Meanwhile, Manu manages to escape the battlefield where he had slayed the bestial Ranga, and rides away with his beloved mother's body on his lap. Mortally wounded, as Manu rides eastwards towards what Somdutt had suggested – the Black Temple – he finds a strange fish-man in a half-dead state, pleading for a few drops of water. The mystical man who wore fish-scale robes and whose skin radiated a strangely captivating blue, slowly grows to become Manu's mentor, friend, philosopher and guide. His name is Matsya. Manu comes to believe that he is none other than an avatar of Lord Vishnu himself.

As Matsya leads Manu to an ancient Black Temple, he shares with the son of Surya that the temple is just one in a series of such shrines. And that the Black Temple guards mankind's most precious secret. He informs Manu that Manu's father was a guardian of the Black Temple, and that now the mantle rested on Manu's shoulders.

Matsya then announces the onset of apocalypse – *'PRALAY...ESHHYATI...!'*

'The Great Deluge is coming!'

As Manu reunites with his beloved Satrupa, lovingly called Tara, and with Pundit Somdutt – Matsya christens him with the name of Satyavrata, and commands him to build a gigantic Ark.

An Ark that would emerge as mankind's last refuge against the onslaught of Pralay.

Vivasvan Pujari crushes Harappan troops and seizes control of the mountains of brick and bronze after a stunning display of battle prowess. He leads the vile Sura to the secret abode of the holy Saptarishi. What follows is a fierce battle, as Vivasvan Pujari tries, in vain, to protect the seven sages. The near-vanquished devta's sword, the great Ratna-Maru, is burnished in the blue fire that burns the sages to ashes, and the Surya of Harappa kills the demon-king Sura.

But it is all too late. The seven sages are the proverbial sons of the Saraswati, who erupts in rage at the cruel murdering of her children. The Blood River curses not just Vivasvan Pujari and his descendants, but all of mankind to eternal strife, violence and hatred. She and her burning sons prophesize that every son of Vivasvan Pujari's bloodline would die suffering the same brutality that the Saptarishi had endured in this night of the blue fire.

Eventually, the last Saptarishi blesses the devta of Harappa. Before the abode of the Saptarishi is engulfed by a devastating avalanche, the last sage assures Vivasvan Pujari that his son Manu would prevail over the curse, as well as over the great deluge.

That Satyavrata Manu would be the deliverance of mankind

against the cataclysmic cleansing unleashed by the Gods.

The last sage then speaks of Vivasvan Pujari's own cosmic destiny –

> *"Your name shall become immortal, O Vivasvan Pujari. You will be born again, thousands of years from now - to fulfil a destiny greater than anyone to have ever walked this planet.*
>
> *You will be reborn to protect the secret of the Black Temple in its final hour. It shall be you who will unfurl it in the Rohini Nakshatra of a particularly pious purnima, millennia from now.*
>
> *You are the chosen one, O great devta."*

Banaras, 2017 (present day) – Vidyut is breathing his last as he is rushed from the ghaats of Banaras to the infirmary of the Dev-Raakshasa matth. Recovering spectacularly, Vidyut discovers how his great grandfather, the phenomenal Dwarka Shastri, had fought a deadly battle of exorcism to save Vidyut's soul from being sucked into the dark depths of the netherworld.

Still reeling under the betrayal of his best friend Bala, who had shot at him at the ghaats, Vidyut goes to meet the traitor in the prison cells of the matth. Bala is remorseless and mocks Vidyut for being ignorant to the realities of the world. He informs Vidyut that the New World Order had kept the devta (Vidyut) alive and wanted him so till the prophesied Rohini Nakshatra. Their conversation is disturbed by the arrival of a dreaded *maha-taantric* called Trijat Kapaalik, at the Dev-Raakshasa matth. Known a *Masaan-raja* or the Lord of the Cremation Grounds, the feared occult-emperor taunts Dwarka Shastri and observes Vidyut closely. The two deranged, murderous killer-twins accompanying him disappear into the crowd of the *aghoris*.

Bala's decapitated head is found on the very table where he sat talking to Vidyut. The last devta is shaken up by the inhuman brutality. His great grandfather, the mighty Dwarka Shastri, then narrates the chilling tale of the New World Order to Vidyut. He describes how the genesis of the morbid global vision began on the side-lines of the historic Council of Nicaea. He reveals how their valiant ancestor Advait Shastri tried to dissuade Constantine the Great from unleashing this monster, and how the 12th century Knights Templar were the Order's first significant success. He also elucidates to Vidyut how this once-sincere vision convoluted into a dark brotherhood of the world's most intelligent, ambitious and powerful men.

In between all the bloodshed and intrigue, Vidyut and Naina come closer than either of them had ever expected. Enchanted by Naina's striking beauty, Vidyut is unable to hold himself back and ends up kissing the breathtakingly lovely girl from Banaras.

The Big Man from Rome sends his emissary yet again to the green-eyed Italian don known as the *Maschera Bianca* or the White Mask. Now a trusted ally for the Overlords of the secret brotherhood, the Mask had risen meteorically, leaving behind a blood-stained trail - from being a screwdriver wielding killer on the streets of Milan, to becoming the un-disputed boss of Europe's organized crime.

Vidyut and Balvanta seek help from a wise teacher of the Banaras Hindu University, Professor Tripathi. As this reluc-tant *taantric* of the past joins Vidyut's fellowship at the matth, Dwarka Shastri welcomes the Professor as Brahmanand. Purohit ji informs Vidyut that both Trijat and Brahmanand were once disciples of the great Dwarka Shastri!

Brahmanand recommends an attack on the Masaan-raja's priory on the night of *amaavasya*. Interrupting the macabre *Raktbeej Anushtthann* is an imperative as per him. If not dis-rupted, the haunting anushtthann would make Trijat invin-cible.

A battle ensues, when Vidyut, Balvanta and Dwarka Shas-tri raid the vile *yajna-shaala* of Trijat Kapaalik. Stunned to his soul as he witnesses the corpse-ridden ritual-grounds of the Masaan-raja's sanctuary, Vidyut is drawn into *paataal*...the cavernous stronghold of the *mahataantric*.

Trijat wakes the dead. Two *daakinis* begin to emerge from his ritual-pit, when Dwarka Shastri intervenes with the all-pow-erful *Shiva-Kavach* chant, sending the ethereal beings back into the dark realm. In a shocking betrayal, Brahmanand strikes Vidyut on his head from behind. The devta loses conscious-ness. When he opens his eyes, he finds himself hanging di-rectly above Trijat's burning ritual-pit, the devta's arms and legs chained to four stone-pillars of the underground cave.

Upon the one-eyed monster Brahmanand's evil coun-sel, the Masaan-raja instructs his two female killers to behead Dwarka Shastri. This audacious move makes Vidyut erupt with rage. As the devta smashes one of the stone-pillars and sets his arm free, he makes his chilling pronouncement -

'You made a big mistake, O Masaan-raja!' cried Vidyut, his voice splitting with pain, rage and hate.

With this the last devta broke free his right leg as well, now swinging like a flying God just above the bed of fire.

'You forgot, Trijat!

I am half-human, half-God!'

PROLOGUE

November 1991, Fisherman's Wharf, San Francisco

He knew he would not be able to hide for long.

There were too many of them.

They had succeeded in tracking him down right from the banks of the Ganges to the freezing waters surrounding the infamous Alcatraz prison. He knew he was being hunted by the most dangerous men in the world…and there was no stopping them.

Not for now.

Not until the prophesied Rohini Nakshatra.

I must find a phone.

I must call Baba.

·‖ॐ‖·

He was shivering as much from the drenched state he was in as from the anxiety a battle-hardened warrior experiences when he knows his time has come. When he is clear that the odds are insurmountable and senses death approaching fast under the tightening grip of a winning enemy.

But this was no ordinary man. And he was not going to be defeated easily. He threw his long brown hair back from his handsome face and shut his deep, almond eyes for a few moments. He was summoning his consciousness into his *kundalini*, as most advanced practitioners of Vedic yoga do to prepare their mortal bodies for the final departure.

The scion of the Dev-Raakshasa *matth* then clenched his teeth and stepped out from behind the counter of an open-air restaurant into the darkness of that ominous night. He walked in the shadows, close to the walls of the shuttered down shops and clam chowder stalls. The torrential November rain lashed against his face and his shining black raincoat as he hustled towards a pay phone. He *had* to make that one last phone call. He *had* to say goodbye.

Before he took on that pack of rabid wolves.

All by himself.

·‖ॐ‖·

The giant African-American man, who appeared out of nowhere, towered at nearly seven feet. He was as broad as a bull and the heavy rain did not seem to bother him, as he drew out an enormous blade from his belt.

The dashing young man from Kashi was unfazed. He charged towards the monstrous man, diverted his own route in a flash towards a tall grill on his right, ran up the iron bars and used the elevation to twist his muscular body, landing a crashing kick on the American's massive head.

The man staggered like a crumbling mountain, swinging his gleaming knife blindly. The scion of the matth then shot another expert kick and knocked off the blade from his adversary's hand. He was going to go for the winning blow into the American's gut, when he heard an unnerving tear right on his back, followed by unbearable pain.

He turned to see that seven or eight beastly looking men now surrounded him in the dark, rainy night. The extraordinary man could see the red glimmer of the Golden Gate bridge far in the backdrop of his assailants. One of them had already slashed him with a fatal wound using a machete. Two others carried rusty, whirring chainsaws.

Blood seemed to be pouring out of his body like water from a torn balloon. His eyes started to black out. He knew the end was near. But he braced himself, shook his head to rid himself of the cold sweat and took a stance to combat them all at once.

But he knew.

This is how I am going to die. On this rainy night. Far away from my loved ones.

A brutal death. Like the ancient curse had prophesized.

·‖ॐ‖·

'Babaaaaa…!' he screamed into the phone, sobbing with grief and unbearable agony. 'It is me…Baba…'

He was leaning against the glass panels of the phone booth. The walls of the booth were smeared with the sacred blood of this noble soul, this profound yogi and this astonishingly skilled warrior.

'Yes, my son, I know it is you…I know it is you!' cried back the grand old Dwarka Shastri.

The *matthadheesh* knew what was happening. They had caught up with him. Finally, after all these years of battling the darkest force on earth, one more of the Shastri bloodline was going to fall prey to the black curse.

'I am going, Baba…' he gasped. 'But I fought them long, and I fought them fearlessly…Baba…'

He now crashed to the ground unconscious, the phone receiver dangling by its spiral chord right next to his ears.

'Say something…say something…*mera beta*!' yelled Dwarka Shastri into his phone, as he broke into sobs of indescribable anguish.

He stirred. The man from Kashi was not going to die so easily, so quickly.

He summoned his last reservoir of energy and reached out for the phone again.

'I did not reveal it, Baba…I did not give away the secret of the Black Temple!' he whispered with all his remaining strength.

Dwarka Shastri ground his teeth, as tears rolled out from his aged eyes.

'You make me proud, my son. You make us all proud.'

'Baba…look after her, Baba. And look after my little boy… Baba! Don't let him stay in Kashi. Promise me, Baba… promise me you will keep him safe. Only you can keep him…safe…Bab…'

The anguished, suffering voice slowly faded away.

'I promise you, my son…' said Dwarka Shastri, his voice choking with grief.

He whispered again.

'I promise you…O mighty Kartikeya!'

Banaras, 2017

'NAAAAAGG!'

He clambered down the dim, stone staircase. His tricky passage down the crooked, steep flight of stairs was lit solely by the *mashaal* or flaming wick-torch he carried. Despite having spent decades as a senior resident of the mystical institution at Kashi, this secret chamber was something he had actually descended into for the first time only in the last few days.

Every step he took echoed in a loud and unnerving boom in the deathly silence and hollow darkness that enveloped him. His *khandaau* or flat-sandals clapped jarringly, adding to his anxiety. He wiped his sweat every now and then, and kept muttering a prayer to Lord *Vishnu*. He could not believe how deep into the heart of the earth this underground *tehkhaana*

19

was built. He had heard about it many times, but never in his gloomiest nightmare could he imagine a place so haunting, so mysteriously charged.

As he finally touched the floor of the cellar, he was not relieved. Now was when the hardest part of his ordeal would begin.

·||ॐ||·

With nearly trembling hands he lit two torches that were perched on the cellar's walls. Slowly the dark chamber came partly to life, glowing a dull red under the light of the flames.

It was only now that the real expanse of the *tehkhaana* became visible. The secret chamber was built of black stone, with beautifully carved figurines depicting the conquest of Lord Shiva and Lord Vishnu over *puraanic*, ancient demons. It was the presence of these sculptures that gave him the courage to carry on. He warily turned towards the long, dark passage that lay ahead of him, leading deeper into the inner core of the vast, underground chamber. He felt a lump in his throat. Fear was gripping him again. And why not?

He now had to walk through the dusty, dark passage.

The passage that led to the *creature*.

Despite all the reverence he tried to muster for this mystical, all-important guest, there was no better term he could find to describe him.

Or *it*.

·‖ॐ‖·

Halfway into the passage he saw the spine-chilling green glow from a distance. Once again, his heart skipped several beats. It was his second visit to the secret cellar and he could still feel the impact of the first trip on his nerves. The distant glimmer then moved, the green radiance gleaming off the surface of their celestial guest.

And then he heard it. The sound that seemed to emanate from the walls, the ceiling and the statues of the black cavern itself. It was a nerve-shattering hiss.

The hiss of a monstrous, primeval serpent!

He did not know from where this otherworldly sound came. But it seemed to forcefully announce the presence of the scale-skinned guest of the Dev-Raakshasa matth. In a sound like that of a cold, swooshing breeze over a medieval graveyard, it seemed to declare *who* was in attendance…

'NAAAGG…'

'NAAAAAGG…'

'NAAAAAAAGG……'

The icy hiss percolated into every particle, every grain of dust in the underground cellar.

And like a cold arrow of horror, it also tore into the soul of Purohit ji.

·‖ॐ‖·

With both his hands, he scooped up milk from the bucketful that Purohit ji had brought him. His long hair covered his face completely, and from twenty feet away the old priest could make out that their guest was enormous in size, perhaps taller than eight feet. While he was human in his silhouette alright, his skin was scaly like that of a reptile, of a snake. And even under the spell of mortal fear, Purohit had to admit that the scaly skin of the guest radiated a dazzling green, something he had never seen before.

His mouth went dry as one of the cobras slithered over his foot. He did not dare look down as he knew what he would behold. Dozens of poisonous King Cobras seemed to be serving this *snake-man*. Never once did they bite him or anyone that enjoyed his grace – Purohit ji for now. They glided over his shoulders, his powerful, almost giant arms at all times. It was clear they served his will.

Purohit ji felt an urge to fold his hands in veneration to this human serpent. Something was magnetic about him. Moreover, if the great Dwarka Shastri had asked Purohit ji to take care of the guest like he would take care if Lord Shiva arrived in person, there must be good reason.

But the primal fear that even a man of his spiritual accomplishment felt in the presence of this holy yet terrifying 'creature', overpowered all other urges. With his duty of serving a large quantity of sweetened milk to the mystical guest done, the wise priest decided to leave.

'I shall take your leave now, my lord,' said Purohit, with a gentle bow of his head.

The gleaming guest nodded, his face still down into his palms. But just as Purohit ji was about to leave, the frightening visitor raised his head. While his long hair still covered his face, his eyes shot up and looked straight at the priest of Dev-Raakshasa matth, who nearly fainted with horror.

They were not human eyes. They ripped through the darkness and glowered like sinister Suns in a black sky.

They were the yellow and black eyes of an immortal, primordial serpent.

HARAPPA, 1700 BCE

'THE GODS... HAVE ABANDONED US!'

They watched him from the walls of the city's perimeter. He rode in towards the heavily guarded gates like a fearless lion.

For all those who had seen him before, he appeared magnificently different. Even in the darkness of the stormy night and the wildly flickering torches, something appeared to have changed about the son of the great Surya of Harappa.

None of them knew what had changed. None of them were aware how it had changed. And that was because not one of them knew in whose deific company Manu had spent the last few days.

Manu looked as dazzling as his great father, if not more. The mere sight of him made hundreds of Harappans break into tears of regret and remorse. They seemed to believe that none of this mayhem would have happened if the Surya were alive.

That the imminent catastrophe could be prevented if Vivasvan Pujari was alive.

Maybe they were right.

·‖ॐ‖·

He had his beloved partner Tara to his right. She rode by his side like a true warrior-princess, her sword dangling from her waist. Her favorite battle-axe was clasped firmly in her hand, as she looked prepared to clash with an entire garrison singlehandedly. Pundit Somdutt was to Manu's left. His widely respected presence added to the gravitas and trustfulness of the moment.

Apart from the warriors from his own household and Somdutt's troops, what lent an air of military superiority to Manu was the mighty force of the fish-folk riding under his flag. The Harappan people and soldiers had never seen such a formidable looking army. Just as they had stunned Manu with their synchronized galloping and choreographed movements, warriors of the fish-tribe took the Harappan populace also by surprise. They looked fierce, invincible.

As he reached about a hundred paces from the gates, Manu raised his right fist. This was a command to his troops to halt. In a few short moments, the noise of hooves and the clanking of armors went quiet. Harappan citizens were in a hushed silence, peeping from the parapets of the city's walls. They did not know what to anticipate from the son of Vivasvan Pujari. Was Manu going to sack the city? Was he here to avenge the horrible end of his wronged parents?

All that could be heard now was the whistling of the sharp winds and the frequent thunder, as the skies lit up.

Manu dismounted and was handed a torch by one of his comrades. He looked towards Somdutt, who nodded gently in supportive agreement. Manu walked slowly but firmly up to the city's walls from where he knew the trembling Harappans could hear him. As he reached closer to them, Manu unstrapped his sheathed sword, raised it for everyone to see, and then dropped it to the ground with a loud, metallic clang. It was his way of reassuring the people who once loved his great father that he was not here to harm them.

Little did they know then that Manu was there to rescue not just them, but all of mankind. The men, the women and the children. The old and the young. The rich and the destitute. The sinner and the saint. All of them.

He was there to save them from certain extinction.

He was going to protect them from Pralay!

·‖ॐ‖·

'Hear me, O dwellers of Harappa!' Manu shouted out to the thousands of people that were now crowded behind the high walls, stretching their necks to get a glimpse of the fabulous young man addressing them.

'A devastation beyond imagination befalls Harappa!' he continued. 'This blizzard that envelopes the lands like a hungry python; this incessant rain that soaks us to our souls; this thunder of Indra that roars and spews fire like a cosmic dragon – these are all nothing but omens of the colossal destruction that hurtles towards all of Aryavarta!'

The people of the great metropolis were stunned into silence. Given the unnatural, unnerving occurrences of the last few days, they were willing to believe anything. Amidst the commoners of Harappa, a not-so-common man stood wrapped in a shawl that covered him from head to toe. He was as eager to hear every word that Vivasvan Pujari's son spoke as anyone.

He was Pundit Chandradhar, the ephemeral, unfortunate king of Harappa.

·||ॐ||·

'A mountain of water races towards your city, O Harappans! A deluge so gigantic that it will swallow the entire settlement in less than a *prahar*. You must save your children. You must save yourselves. You have to trust me! We must evacuate the city...NOW!'

The deathly silence now gave way to frenzied murmurs on the parapets. Was this young boy to be believed? Had he seen this monstrous water mountain that he was talking about? And if he had, how could he outrace it?

'Why should we believe you, O son of Surya?' yelled out one voice. 'How are you so certain of this unspeakable fate?'

By now, Somdutt had walked up and joined Manu. Everyone recognized the erstwhile chief architect of Harappa and hundreds of folded hands went up in the air in deep reverence. What had added to the persona of Somdutt was that by now it was public knowledge that it was Somdutt and Somdutt alone who had stood with the Surya of Harappa in the latter's most trying hour. Today every single Harappan wanted to be Somdutt.

'The time for debate and discussion has passed, my friends! Every instant we lose draws us closer into the jaws of death and destruction,' said Somdutt, in a loud voice for everyone to hear. 'This young man is the son of the great Vivasvan Pujari - the man, the devta who saved this city and its people from the greatest of perils. You trusted him. I urge you today. Trust his worthy son!

Trust Satyavrata Manu!'

·||卐||·

Several men and women of the cursed city left for their homes in haste – to pick up their children and gather at least some of their precious belongings. The others remained on the city walls, anxiously debating the course of action.

Suddenly a shrill voice tore through the windy night.

'The Gods…have abandoned us!' shouted a very old woman.

In the darkness and in the commotion, her shaking, witch-like voice rendered horror into every heart.

'No, they have not!' Manu shouted back.

'At least One of them has not...' he whispered to himself a moment later.

Banaras, 2017

A CURSED ASURA EMPEROR, A DEFEATED KAURAVA PRINCE, A TREACHEROUS TAANTRIC

He looked like his entire body was engulfed in red flames.

The magnificent Vidyut was now making his way through the burning embers of Trijat Kapaalik's blazing ritual-pit. While he winced with pain with every step he took, the burning fire was no match for the inferno that was raging in the heart of the *devta*.

The Masaan-raja had gone too far when he had instructed his two brutal female companions to use their vile sickles on Dwarka Shastri, just the way they had deployed those to behead Bala. Intoxicated with their short-lived victory over the prophesied devta, what both Trijat and Brahmanand had failed to realize was that the great *matthadheesh* was Vidyut's only family left. His precious Baba!

And the last devta was not going to forgive them for this audacious sin.

·‖ॐ‖·

Brahmanand could not believe his evil, single eye as he saw Vidyut tear through the fiery pit, unmindful of the countless scalds inflicted on his skin by the burning coal. Vidyut appeared like a blurry, orange-hued primordial being emerging from the smoky depths of the Earth's molten underbelly. The two *daakinis* now had their attention drawn to the man they had just seen breaking rusty chains and shattering stone pillars with the raw strength of his lean, muscular frame.

But the most unexpected and baffling reaction came from none other than the Masaan-raja himself. Trijat stood frozen a few steps away from the pit, staring at Vidyut without batting his eyelids. As if in a trance, he kept repeating three words.

'It is he.

It is he.

It is he…'

For the first time since his followers had known him, they saw mortal fear on the face of the lord of the cremation grounds.

·‖卐‖·

Vidyut had no doubt in his mind. The two daakinis had to be punished severely. They had decapitated Bala mercilessly, that too when the fallen villain's hands were tied and he was defenseless. Even now, they had been more than willing to execute Vidyut's great grandfather at the behest of Trijat Kapaalik. They were not human. Not anymore. And they had to be neutralized.

Vidyut was determined to make sure they never harmed another soul.

She was faster than the devta had anticipated. As Vidyut leapt out of the pit and dashed towards the daakini closer to Dwarka Shastri, she moved with the slippery swiftness of a serpent. Before Vidyut knew it, she had cartwheeled behind him like an expert gymnast. In one practiced move, she viciously attacked the devta with her blunt, stained sickle. But the stoned killer had no idea who she was up against.

Vidyut did not as much but turn his head and, with the prowess of a skilled kick-boxer, swung around to strike the daakini across her face with his blistered, right foot. The kick hit her with the force of an express train. For all her martial ability, the ruthless assassin spat blood and crashed to the ground. It had taken Vidyut less than ten seconds to vanquish this depraved foe.

Ready for another bout, Vidyut turned to the other daakini. What he saw was very different from what he had expected.

The second murderess had dropped her weapon and was shivering with fear.

She slowly trudged backwards into a corner of the cave and crumpled down to her knees, tears rolling out of her blood-red eyes.

It was as if the petrified entrancing of Trijat himself and the punishing defeat of her twin had suddenly freed this unfortunate being from a dark spell.

·||ॐ||·

Vidyut was tired, wounded, burnt and gashed. But he was not broken.

He turned to look around at the *mahataantric's* henchmen who had wandered this hellhole, this *paataal,* under the stewardship of the wicked Masaan-raja for years. But none of them were to be seen in the glimmering red darkness of the underground cavern. The scoundrels had been summarily beaten and inflicted with extreme pain by the devta's initial assault. Having now seen this extraordinary man demolish stone walls and splinter steel chains, they had fled.

At the time when the Masaan-raja needed his followers most, he had none to stand with him by his side.

Whether it is a cursed *asura* emperor in ancient *Aryavarta*, a defeated *Kaurava* prince hiding in the depths of the *Dwaipaayana* lake or a treacherous taantric who has lost his path - every time, in every world of every universe...*this* is how evil ends.

Alone.

Harappa, 1700 BCE

CHANDRADHAR

The sight was both unbelievable and awe-inspiring.

Tens of thousands of Harappan men, women and children were now thronging the dark streets of the metropolis, that glowed blue every now and then under sky-ripping and deafening thunder-flash. They braved the screaming storm and the pounding, cold rain.

They all had reposed their faith in one man. Yet again. They had reposed their faith in Vivasvan Pujari. Even in his death. Now, they all had unshakeable belief that if Satyavrata Manu had imbibed even a speck of the character of his great father, he was their best bet towards survival.

Even after being swallowed by the merciless deluge of the

mighty Saraswati, the Surya of Harappa had not abandoned his people. He lived on in their hearts, in their remorse and in their hope.

·||卐||·

The more prosperous merchants and priests were mounted on their steeds, their families following them in covered horse-carriages. Thousands of others trudged along in bullock-carts, carrying hastily bundled provisions and precious belongings. But the vast majority lumbered along on foot, oblivious to the daunting, never-ending journey that lay ahead of them.

The Harappan army had all but disbanded itself and had joined the civilians in this great exodus. The intoxicants that were maliciously administered by the blind Mesopotamian wizards Ap-Sha-Gun had finally loosened their grip on the minds and nerves of the Harappan warriors. They were now distraught with guilt, tearfully reminiscing the days when the Surya of Harappa had held their hands and taught them to wield the sword. Thousands of them fondly remembered how the devta had demonstrated to them how to tame an *ashva*, the beast they were so proud of today.

These soldiers knew they were defeated and leaderless. The tale of Ranga's violent end had reached their ears days before this momentous night, and they could see the victor of that bloody duel humbly reaching out to offer them a helping hand. They had also heard about the Rain of Blood under which Vivasvan Pujari was rescued. Neither were they ignorant of the ghastly killing of another commander of their forces at the hands of the Surya.

What they could not do for the mighty devta Vivasvan Pujari, they would now do for his valiant son.

They had tacitly accepted the command of Satyavrata Manu.

·||卐||·

The wise, brave yet miserably unfortunate Pundit Chandradhar sat at the entrance of his personal residential chambers in his grand palace. He had performed a private *yajna*, to summon all his valor, all his skill and all his courage from the deepest recesses of every cosmos his spirit had ever lived in or visited. He had unsheathed his favorite long-sword that stood like a gleaming pillar in front of him. His hands rested on the mighty sword's handle while its tip scratched the shining floor below.

If his nephew Manu had come to avenge the humiliation, suffering and death of his parents Sanjna and Vivasvan, he was not wrong in doing so.

But you shall have to pass me, my boy.

Chandradhar was not worried for his own life. He had died from inside the day he had been a silent spectator to the lynching and public torture of his dearest friend, mentor and the protector of Aryavarta, Vivasvan Pujari. But despite the venomous conspiracy she had hatched, despite her insatiable lust for power, despite her hate that had brought Harappa to the brink of destruction and despite her cruelty, Priyamvada was his to protect. She was the love of his life.

She was his wife.

By now, Chandradhar was well aware that his blind love for Priyamvada was nothing more than a disease in his head. It made him forget reason. It made him sightless to reality and logic. It had made him a monster.

Even after all the bloodshed and betrayal, all the death and all the destruction around him, the first and last king of Harappa had not opened his eyes.

He never would.

And for this very reason, history would erase him from its pages forever.

Barrackpore (Bengal), 1856

THE GREAT ARYAN INVASION

It was way past midnight.

Even though he was used to turning in by 9 pm in the heat of the Indian summer, tonight the British officer was glued to the papers on his cluttered mahogany desk. He was reading in the dim light of an oil lantern, his room filled with thick smoke from the cigarettes he rolled frequently.

This is unbelievable.

Wayne Ashbrook was a young officer on the rolls of the formidable East India Company. Over less than a couple of centuries the Company had transformed from being a docile trading outfit that paid taxes and homage to the Mughal court, into a mammoth imperialistic beast that dominated all of India. With the defeat and killing of the seemingly invincible Tiger of Mysore, Tipu Sultan, on 4th May, 1799, the East India Company became unstoppable. And with this dominance came what was going to draw the violent history of the subcontinent over the next few decades – British arrogance.

The English officers, clerks and soldiers that boarded ships and arrived on the ports of Bombay and Calcutta during the earlier years of the Company, fell in love with *Hindustan*. From Indian clothing to Indian wives, these Englishmen embraced the country with open arms. But then things changed. The new wave of Company officers came in with the conceited air of rulers, brimming with disdain for everything native. Consequently, hate began to simmer in the ranks of the Indian sepoys. Silent nods and glances among them were a telling sign of an impending, brutal uprising.

An ancient prophecy condemning mankind to hatred and killing was once again going to come true.

The curse of the Blood River was going to come true.

·||卐||·

He cleaned his round reading glasses every now and then, as he sifted through the papers yellowed with age. Wayne Ashbrook was different from most British officers around him, and deeply admired India's rich culture and unmatched heritage.

Born in Manchester and raised in a family that struggled for years to make ends meet, Wayne had fought hard to complete his education and get enlisted in the reputed East India Company. As he grew up amidst bullies at school, who were spoilt brats of textile barons, he learnt to appreciate gentleness. As he made way through the complex maze of the nouveau riche Manchester society, he began to deeply admire simplicity.

And it was their gentleness and simplicity that made Indians win the heart of this young, honest officer.

To his own peril.

·‖ॐ‖·

'I...I need an audience with Colonel Sanders right away,' he said to the English-speaking Indian butler who opened the door of Colonel Mark Sanders' sprawling bungalow in the heart of the Barrackpore *chhaavni* or cantonment.

Wayne had gathered his papers and ridden out to meet his superior. He had received these rare and mysterious set of documents from an old Hindu priest at *Prayag* or Allahabad in the North Western Provinces of Agra and Oudh (modern-day Uttar Pradesh). The priest had amazed Wayne by saying that he had waited for Wayne for over forty years. When the Englishman had replied saying he was not even born forty years ago, the mysterious priest had stunned him by describing everything about Wayne – his birthplace, his parents and his life-events.

'This, Hindustan, is where all civilization really began, Wayne *saahab*. Take these scriptures and exhume the truth if you can,' the priest had said, handing over a bundle of rough paper with his wrinkled hands. But ever since that day what had kept Wayne awake during nights was what the priest had cautioned out as Wayne's palanquin had moved.

'They will not think twice before harming you, saahab. Beware the dark forces of evil.

Beware the Order…'

Wayne could not help but think.

If the priest could see everything of my past, he can also see the future. He knows what is going to happen to me.

But what Wayne unearthed from the scriptures was far more potent than his fear.

·||卐||·

'This is preposterous, Wayne!' snapped Colonel Sanders as he slammed a fist on the table in his study.

Taking a moment to calm himself down, he walked to the thick wooden cabinet in one corner of the vast, lantern-lit room. He opened a panel and picked out a shining flask of scotch whiskey. Without a word, he poured two double drinks into crystal glasses. He turned to Wayne and handed one glass to the sweating and anxious young officer. Sanders then settled down behind his desk. He took a sip of his fine whiskey and lit a pipe. He then gestured to Wayne with his smoking pipe, asking the officer to take a seat across the table.

'Look, Wayne, I handpicked you for this assignment. I am not saying that you are not a good anthropologist and historian. In fact, you are bloody good! But I also brought you directly under my command because of the sensitivity of this assignment. I always knew I could rely on you.'

'Yes, Sir…' replied Wayne as he took a gulp of the golden liquid in his glass. He needed to soothe his jangled nerves.

'So, when you say you have studied these copies of ancient hand-written scriptures, and that the Aryans never came from outside India, you pose a big threat to the larger scheme of things,' said Sanders, trying very hard to hide both his fear as well as his cruelty behind the veil of a glib smile.

'Colonel Sanders, Sir, if you allow me to explain – the ruins that were discovered in 1842 by Charles Masson are not some ordinary settlements. It is clear from these medieval papers that were prepared by creating careful replicas of ancient scriptures. They say the original manuscript was written by none other than a great sage-king called Satyavrata Manu!'

·‖ॐ‖·

Sanders' grip tightened on the revolver he always kept taped under his desk.

Then it loosened.

I cannot do it myself. Not here. Not in the heart of the garrison.

Wayne had absolutely no idea how close he had come to death. He continued his elucidation with the faith of a true scholar.

'I consulted several Hindu pundits over the last few days, Sir. They tell me that this Satyavrata Manu was not an ordinary man. He was the savior of all of creation during the great deluge or *Pralay* as the natives call it. Manu is to the Hindus what Noah is to us Christians, Colonel. In fact, some etymologists indicate that Noah is not the name of a person at all. It is a derivation from the native terms *Nauka* or *Naiyya* or *Naav*, which basically mean a boat!'

There was a cold silence in the room. In his quest to unfurl what he believed was a path-breaking reality for humankind at large, Wayne failed to notice the chilling distortion of Sanders' face.

'Sir, those remains are of the greatest civilization of ancient earth. The Saraswati civilization, Sir! India is the epicenter of mankind's progress. It is the land with a heritage richer than any country or region of the world! And we must bring this glorious truth to the fore, Sir.'

The old, wrinkled priest was right.

The Order was listening to Wayne.

·||ॐ||·

He thanked the Editor of the Calcutta Tribune and left the stuffy offices of the reputed daily.

As he walked past the noisy, crowded streets and stalls of street food towards the quieter alleys of bustling Calcutta,

Wayne was a worried man. He was deeply disturbed with the way Colonel Sanders had forfeited his papers at gunpoint. He had never imagined such conduct from a senior officer of the East India Company and was glad he had created copies of the medieval documents before riding out to meet Sanders.

He was lost in thought when a voice called out to him in the fading light of the evening.

'Captain Wayne Ashbrook…?'

'Yes…' said Wayne, as he turned to see who had called out for him.

·‖卐‖·

Wayne's mutilated body was found hanging on a tree outside the Writers' Building secretariat the next morning. The newspapers declared it an act of violence by two Indian sepoys. But the truth was something else. Something terrible.

The prophesied blood-thirst was about to raise its head again.

Banaras, 2017

RAAKSHASA-BALI

Vidyut picked up a thick blade left behind by one of the followers of Trijat and cut the ropes that tied the great matthadheesh's hands. He then freed Balvanta, before coming back to his Baba, lifting him up from the ground and wrapping him in a tight, long embrace.

'I'm sorry I took so long, Baba. I'm sorry I let myself be struck from behind…'

Dwarka Shastri was in a daze. A minute ago, he had been a razor's edge away from a ruthless, painful death. In the bat of an eyelid, he had witnessed the fall and phoenix-like rise of his marvelous great grandson. But most of all, he had counted every breath, every moment. The moments of the hour of his own end. And the hour had come and gone!

His *kundali* had clearly marked this specific time for Dwarka Shastri's demise and it was riddled with the highest degree of *Maarkesh* – the inescapable period of death.

But here he was, alive. The great Dwarka Shastri stood hale and hearty, when he should have departed for the realm of the spirit world.

Something had changed his destiny.

Something…or *someone*.

·‖ॐ‖·

Vidyut gestured to Sonu to take the psychopath Professor Tripathi or Brahmanand into captivity. He nodded at Balvanta to do the same with Trijat Kapaalik. He then turned all his attention back to his Baba.

What Vidyut had failed to notice was the barbaric rage convulsing in Balvanta's bloodshot eyes.

Dwarka Shastri could not hold his tears back and let them flow freely. Vidyut also wept, his head resting on his tall great grandfather's still powerful shoulders. They had been through a lot, physically, emotionally and spiritually. However, in a few moments, the devta realized that his Baba was now sobbing inconsolably. That was odd. Even after the trauma they had been through, it was not like the towering Dwarka Shastri to break down like this. Vidyut lifted his head and looked at the matthadheesh's face, his hands still clasping his Baba's arms.

'Kya hua, Baba…?' he asked gently. 'What happened, Baba?'

Dwarka Shastri looked up with his moist eyes and put both his palms on his great grandson's cheeks.

'Tum vaastav mein devta ho, Vidyut…!' responded the old man. 'You are indeed a devta, Vidyut!'

Vidyut gave a tired grin.

'Of course not, Baba. I know I have used the half-human, half-God phrase for myself twice in the last few days, but those were more like battle-cries of sorts. I cannot explain… but it made me feel stronger, more intense. Like I have said these words before…' said Vidyut, a little lost in trying to recollect where and when in the past he had uttered these haunting, perennial words.

He had spoken these words at a Great Bath turned into a bleeding, torture arena. Back in 1700 BCE. Back in the last days of the ancient metropolis, Harappa.

But not as Vidyut.

'Listen, you who are already dead. Listen, you congregation of corpses. Listen, you fools.

I am half-human, half-God!'

·||卐||·

'I have no such illusions, Baba. I am no devta, no half-God. I am just your Vidyut. Just a man.'

The matthadheesh shook his head, heaved a big sigh and spoke. Only this time, to Vidyut's shock, his trembling hands were folded in reverence towards his own great grandson.

'Only a true devta can overpower *Kaalchakra*, the incessant wheel of time. My death was written, Vidyut! Nothing in this universe could have changed it. My time had come. But that time has come and gone!'

Vidyut stood there listening, unable to really comprehend what his Baba was saying.

'Don't you see, Vidyut? It is *your* presence that has changed everything. It is your will that has altered space-time. When outside this evil priory you told me that you will come back for me – the cosmos was listening, Vidyut.

And obeying you!'

·‖ॐ‖·

Vidyut was in no frame of mind to believe such an audacious theory, even if it came from his beloved Baba.

'We need to leave now, Baba. We can have this discussion once we are back in…'

Even before Vidyut could complete his sentence, a loud scream tore through the underground cave.

'Vidyut dadaaaaa….!!!'

Vidyut turned to see Sonu yelling out to him. The young lad was petrified, pointing towards the Masaan-raja's ritual pit.

As his gaze darted to where Sonu was pointing, the devta broke into a cold sweat.

·||ॐ||·

'NO BALVANTA DADA…STOP!' screamed Vidyut, as he rushed to cover what felt like a thousand miles.

Balvanta, the war chief of the Dev-Raakshasa matth, had Trijat Kapaalik pinned against the boundary of the mahata-antric's own ritual pit, originally meant for the dreaded *Raktbeej Anushtthann*. Balvanta's mighty foot was on Trijat's chest, with the fallen aghori's head dangling just above the burning coal and flesh.

He was pleading for mercy.

·||ॐ||·

Vidyut knew he could not run faster than Balvanta's axe was going to fall.

'He has defiled our matth, Vidyut! He tried to kill you, our prophesied savior! And then he dared touch a blade to our matthadheesh's throat!' shouted Balvanta, as he said a fever-ish prayer to *Mahakaal*, the God of Death, and raised his gleaming axe.

Balvanta then stared straight into the wide eyes of the stu-pefied Masaan-raja, and screamed out words that were only a little different from what Trijat had himself announced some time back.

'Aaj issi anushtthann agni mein…raakshasa-bali chadhegi!'

'Today a demon shall be sacrificed in this very ritual fire!'

Harappa, 1700 BCE

'COME WITH ME TO LIVE ANOTHER DAY, O PRINCESS OF MOHENJO-DARO!'

'Where are you headed, Manu?' shouted Tara, as she saw Manu turn his neighing horse towards the citadel of the new king of Harappa.

'I have to save them, Tara. I have to save Pundit Chandradhar and Priyamvada. It doesn't matter anymore what they did to my family and to me. I have seen it in Matsya's eyes. As we defy this great deluge, every soul deserves to be resurrected. Eventually, pralay will cleanse everyone in the manner it chooses!'

'But the flood rises, Satyavrata! You may not have the time to return before the giant surfs swallow the city!' screamed Tara, in a vain attempt to hold Manu back.

The son of Surya turned once again, his horse circling like a whirlwind. Even in this turbulent night, Manu had a wickedly romantic smile on his face.

'Don't know why, but I love it when you call me Satyavrata!'

Tara blushed.

That was all he said, as he gave her a long, loving look and rode off into the stormy night.

Tara was dumbfounded. Just a few days ago Manu had sworn vengeance. And here he was, galloping into the doomed city to protect the very two people who had together destroyed his world.

What has brought about this profound change?

She found her answer in an instant. She smiled.

Matsya.

·||ॐ||·

She could sense it was the last night for Harappa.

In the eeriness of this ominous night, she saw his lone horse galloping towards her palace, her home. She braced herself for death. While she knew her husband Chandradhar was an accomplished warrior himself, but the all-consuming choler of revenge would have made Manu twice the fighter he was.

That blood would spill in her very own abode seemed certain now. Whether it was going to be the blood of Vivasvan Pujari's son or that of her own husband, was yet to be seen.

Manu rode his horse straight into the central atrium of the king's palace, the hooves of the sweating beast pounding on the shining stone floor, echoing and roaring through the citadel palace's lofty halls. When he found the ground level to be empty, Manu spurred his horse on and climbed up the massive staircase that led to the higher floor of the building. It was not to show aggression or disrespect that Manu chose to ride into the king's luxurious residence. It was urgency.

The flood was coming.

·‖卐‖·

The menacing tip of Chandradhar's heavy sword scratched the polished floor creating sparks, as the wise king of Harappa dragged it along as he walked to face Manu.

He knew it was going to be the greatest battle of his life.

He was wrong.

As Manu saw his once beloved uncle standing in the hallway of the higher floor, he dismounted. The massive room was lit with flickering torches and the fine, translucent curtains on the large windows fluttered violently, as squealing wind swept through the entire building.

Manu folded his hands in a greeting to his uncle. Despite all his noble intentions, his young heart was on fire. For one moment, he felt the urge to draw his scimitar and avenge his parents that very instant. Scenes of his dying mother and his tortured father were haunting him. But then somehow the smiling face of Matsya kept dancing in his eyes, slowly chiseling him into the splendid man he was destined to become.

'*Vijayi-bhava*, Manu,' responded Chandradhar. 'May you be victorious, Manu.'

Only a man as magnanimous as Pundit Chandradhar could bless even his adversary with victory. He had not forgotten his beloved sister Sanjna. His remorse was deeper than the darkest crevice of the mighty Himalayas. His soul wept for his late friend. If he were alone, he would have given up his mortal body long ago. But he was not alone. He had Priyamvada.

·||ॐ||·

As the two men stood face to face, the stunning Priyamvada appeared from nowhere and walked quietly into the hallway. She was barefoot. Her long white dress flowed like a cloud behind her on the floor. Her beautiful hair was open and the kohl of her eyes had smeared onto her fair cheeks, mixed with her tears. She had a haunted look about her. And yet she looked striking.

Manu clenched his fists and ground his teeth to swallow his rage as he saw this woman. He knew Pundit Chandradhar was merely a pawn, an emotionally manipulated husband. The real evil that had destroyed not just his own family but all of Aryavarta – lay curled like a venomous snake in the heart of this wretched lady.

But he once again reminded himself of why he was here, and looked at Priyamvada as he spoke firmly and loudly.

'Come with me to live another day, O Princess of Mohenjo-daro!'

Alibaug, Off the Coast of Mumbai, 2017

EMPIRE OF CRIME
& BLOOD

Aslam Biker was sweating.

He awaited the arrival of the man whose voice was all that he had heard over the years - the unimaginably powerful and dangerous man who made Aslam's blood curdle with just his hissing, monarchical speech from the other end of the phone line.

And it was not every day that Aslam Biker's blood curdled.

Given that he was one of Mumbai's most daring and feared underworld dons.

·‖卐‖·

His real name was Aslam Razi. But now everyone from the street urchins of Colaba to the Chief Minister of Maharashtra knew of him by the name Aslam Biker.

When he started his career in petty crime, there were two Aslams in his *jhopar patti* or slum colony. Aslam Razi's father was an honest textile mill worker, who had saved money and bought a sparkling new 100 cc motorcycle. What the old man did not know was that his swift motorcycle was rolled out nearly every night by his criminal son, and used as an escape vehicle after the *supari* or contract killings that he executed.

As time passed and Aslam's legend spread, it was his motorcycle that became the identity by which he was differentiated from the other, more docile Aslam in the colony.

In a matter of a few years, his surname Razi was forgotten. From the dance bar circles to police records, he was known by only one name.

Aslam Biker.

·‖卐‖·

The super luxury Sikorsky S-76C helicopter, more commonly known as the Black Hawk, slowly kissed the greens of the massive beach house that Aslam owned. The primary passenger of the chopper was the one who had kept Aslam alive in the midst of brutal Mumbai gang wars over the years. He was the one who had opened doors of the banks in Zurich for Aslam Biker. He supplied the latest automatic weapons used by Aslam's 'punters'. It was his phone calls that had kept the claws of the justice system away from Aslam.

As the door of the shining silver helicopter flung open, Aslam and his men noticed that while this metallic bird looked like a luxurious flying machine, it was nearly military grade. The owner of this fleet of choppers took his own security very seriously.

When the glossy wood and beige leather interiors of the Black Hawk were visible, they saw him. Surrounded by a posse of men who could have easily been mistaken for the US President's security detail, he sat. Just as Aslam swallowed a nervous lump, the blonde, handsome man turned slowly to look at the Mumbai don. Aslam was no more than a foot soldier in the blonde man's mammoth global empire of crime and blood.

·‖卐‖·

As he walked down the steel and mahogany step-ladder of the Sikorsky S-76C, he looked like a force of nature. Features so handsome that he appeared almost feminine, were matched by the athletic built of this undisputed kingpin of international organized crime.

His hair was neatly pulled back from over his forehead and a pair of Maybach The Diplomat 1 sunglasses accentuated his extraordinarily flamboyant, boyish appearance. It was a separate matter that all his boyish charm vanished into thin air when the ivory handle of his custom Colt Python revolver could be seen staring nonchalantly from under his belt.

His black jacket fluttered in the sea breeze as he stepped on to the turf tarmac. It was now that Aslam Biker decided to gather the courage and greet his Italian overlord. As he moved forward, one of the blonde don's men stretched out his left arm, gesturing the Mumbai gangster to stand back. The man held a ready semi-automatic MAC-10 machine gun in his right hand.

The powerful guest relented. He nodded to his human Rottweiler to make way.

As Aslam Biker stepped forward, his heart froze. The don had slowly taken off his Maybach glasses. His deep green eyes tore deep into Aslam's soul, reminding him what the meaning of real fear was.

He could only mumble out a couple of words...

'Welcome to Mumbai...Maschera.'

Harappa, 1700 BCE

KARMIC DEBT

'Draw your sword, my son,' said Chandradhar. 'You are en-titled to quench your grueling thirst for vengeance. And I am duty-bound to protect the only woman I have ever truly loved. We are both only doing what we ought to do as honorable men.'

Priyamvada stood like a statue, listening to the two brilliant men. Her breathing was heavy, labored…as if her breaths carried the enormous weight of her burdened conscience.

'I am not here for revenge, Pundit Chandradhar. As you might have noticed, we face certain doomsday. The city is going to fall. You need to come with me…now!'

There was a moment of silence in the sprawling hall, as the

vicious breeze blew Priyamvada's hair over her pretty face and thunder turned the room white for a few seconds. Chandradhar could not believe what he had just heard. He stood frozen for a while before turning to look at his distraught wife. The relief on his face was palpable.

·‖ॐ‖·

'But why, Manu? I heard everything from the city walls when you spoke. The people follow you! The army follows you! And they do nothing wrong. But why us? Why are you here to save the two of us…the two of us who have snatched everything away from you?' exclaimed a shattered Chandradhar, his eyes welling up and his voice breaking.

There were a million things Manu wanted to say. A million things he wanted to ask. But this was not the hour. He simply responded with what his heart was brimming over with. With what he felt was his true identity.

'I do this because I am the son of the great Vivasvan Pujari…the glorious Surya of Harappa.'

Manu paused to get a grip on his choking voice, before completing what he wanted to say.

'I know he would have done the same.'

·‖ॐ‖·

Pundit Chandradhar wept disconsolately as he crumbled to his knees.

He wanted Manu to attack him. He wanted this young man to extract his vengeance. He had been preparing himself for a final battle. But nothing could have prepared him for this act of nobility from this strapping young lad. For Pundit Chandradhar, Manu's forgiveness and generosity were infinitely more painful than the tip of his arrow would have been.

In a moment of insanity, the last king of Harappa picked up his sword, rushed to Manu and pointed it at him in an offence stance.

'Pick up your sword and fight me, you young scoundrel!' he yelled at Manu. 'I know this is what you are here for! Draw your scimitar and show me what you are made of! You think Pundit Chandradhar is some Ranga who you will defeat with ease? No one can beat me, lad! The only man or devta who could…is not in Harappa anymore. So, fight me!'

Manu did not flinch. For the first time, he felt pity for the poor man in front of him.

And then he noticed Priyamvada. Her expression had changed, softened. She was weeping, with nothing but love and repentance written all over her face.

What a sight it was! There was no need for retribution anymore. Chandradhar and his unfortunate wife Priyamvada were already burning in the furnace of pain, suffering in far more agony than what a sword, spear or an arrow would have inflicted.

It was now that Manu learnt how the ceaseless cycles of karmic debt worked. The cosmos had already triggered the destined punishment for the sins committed by Priyamvada and her husband. It did not involve blood and gore. No human intervention was required. No personal vendetta was needed.

The universe was going to settle all debts. In its own way.

·‖卐‖·

'This is where our journey ends, Manu...' said Priyamvada, keeping her soft, shivering hand on Manu's cheek.

The distant rumble of the approaching deluge was now nerve-wracking. Manu knew that if they did not ride out this very instant, all three of them would be engulfed by the water-mountains that galloped towards this ill-fated metropolis.

'Why don't you understand, we must leave now, O wise Pundit Chandradhar!' said Manu, nearly screaming. The urgency of the moment was beyond all niceties.

'Leave us here and go, Manu. Let this golden city, that today faces devastation as a result of our depravities, be our final resting ground. You are now beyond doubt a true reflection of your great father. And this could mean only one thing – that the Creator has chosen you for a very big task. You must ride out now, Satyavrata, and go fulfil your divine destiny.'

Manu ignored what Chandradhar said, turned towards Priyamvada and stretched out his hand.

'Climb on to my horse, my lady. This beast is strong enough to carry all three of us away from this cursed city...'

Priyamvada's eyes were unable to hold back her tears, which she kept wiping from the fine cotton sleeve over her wrist. She now looked at Manu with deepest admiration and kindness.

'I have no divinity in me, O valiant Satyavrata. Perhaps no trace of humanity left either. But if I have a heart that still beats, eyes that still weep and hands that can still rise to bless, my spiritual bond with the universe is not all lost.'

Manu was listening intently to this beautiful witch of a woman, who in her present avatar could have enchanted the entire world with her charm and goodness.

'I bless you, Manu…' the princess of Mohenjo-daro continued, with a beatific, tender smile. 'May you succeed in whatever sacred mandate the cosmos has entrusted you with. May you find the kindle of inner peace and the gift of everlasting love.'

She stepped forward and kissed Manu on the forehead, before pronouncing the final part of her benedictions for the young man who was about to wage war against nature's most destructive primal fury.

What she blessed him with was to come true…in its entirety.

'May your name become eternal, immortal, O Satyavrata Manu!'

Banaras, 2017

THE KILLING OF A HUMAN BEING

It had been sixteen hours.

'Nothing, Baba…' said Sonu, as he returned with an untouched plate of food in his hands.

Immediately upon their arrival at the Dev-Raakshasa matth, Vidyut had stormed into his room and locked himself up. He had not responded to anyone for sixteen hours since. He had not eaten anything.

The devta's soul was scarred.

Beyond redemption.

·||ॐ||·

In his own moment of barbaric insanity, and in his savage zeal to avenge the humiliation of his matthadheesh, Balvanta had hacked Trijat Kapaalik's head off with his heavy axe. It all happened in a few split seconds, before Vidyut could reach him and stop him.

All Vidyut could do was to helplessly witness the horrific sight of the Masaan-raja's head plummet into his own ritual pit, his long hair crackling in the fire that soon engulfed the mahataantric's skull.

And this was the last straw on the camel's back. When he had packed lightly in his Gurgaon penthouse for what he thought was going to be a two-day trip to Banaras, Vidyut had no inkling of the bloodshed, the conspiracies, the black-magic and the deceit that awaited him. And yet he had braved everything with extraordinary grit – he had fought mercenaries, locked horns with a supreme assassin, endured the worst of betrayals, witnessed the beheading of Bala and come to terms with ancient curses and prophecies. But the taking of a human life by one of his own clansmen was not something he was going to be a part of.

Life, regardless of whether it resided in a good heart or evil, was sacrosanct. Vidyut could not identify with any individual or institution that believed or acted otherwise. There could be no justification for the killing of a fellow human being.

Balvanta's heinous, mindless act had done greater damage than the war-chief of the matth could have ever imagined.

It had shaken Vidyut's faith in the Dev-Raakshasa matth.

And in the very purpose of its existence.

·‖ॐ‖·

It was in the wee hours of the morning that Purohit ji offered his first prayers of the day. As he was circumambulating one of the gigantic Shiva statues in the central gardens of the *Dev-khannd*, he noticed something he did not expect to see.

Vidyut sat at the stairs of the great Dwarka Shastri's cottage. He was fully dressed and Purohit ji's heart sank when he saw Vidyut's small backpack by his side. It was clear to the old priest.

Vidyut was leaving.

Purohit ji walked up to the last devta, who greeted him with a weak but polite smile.

The wise priest pointed at the vacant space next to Vidyut and asked in a voice as soothing as the early morning breeze that caressed them, 'May I?'

'Of course, Purohit ji,' replied Vidyut, as he moved his backpack to make room. Despite all of Vidyut's civility, the old priest could sense a deep gash, a festering wound in the devta's heart.

·‖ॐ‖·

'So, you are leaving?'

'Yes, Purohit ji…'

There was silence for a minute as both men looked out into the bluish orange sky. With every passing moment, the ancient city of Kashi seemed to be waking from its holy slumber. Birds had begun to chirp and the cows were mooing, being lovingly fed by several families around the matth. Temple bells, both near and far, blended with the sacred sound of morning *aarti*.

'Tell me, Vidyut…why are there so many stories in our *puraanas* that narrate the victory of good over evil?' asked Purohit ji, without turning to Vidyut.

Vidyut understood where this discussion was being steered to. He was in no mood to debate something he considered to be the most unspeakable of sins.

'Look Purohit ji, you know how much I love and respect you. But I beg you to leave me alone for now. Nothing that you say can change the fact that I saw a man butchered in front of my eyes yesterday, and I could do nothing.'

'That is not the answer to my question, Vidyut,' replied Purohit ji calmly. 'No one can stop you if you have made up your mind to leave. But no matter how upset you are, it would be most unfair to not allow the matth to even defend itself.'

'Defend itself? Did you say defend itself?? God, I cannot believe this!' exclaimed an exasperated Vidyut.

He shook his head in disgust, picked his bag and started walking away.

Purohit ji hesitated for a moment. But then realized it was now or never.

He shouted out to Vidyut.

'If you think we are the ones who started this violence, you are wrong, my devta.

Do you not want to know how your father, the great Kartikeya Shastri, was killed, Vidyut?'

Harappa, 1700 BCE

HARAPPA – CURSE OF THE BLOOD RIVER

'Go faster…faster, my trusted friend!'

Manu was talking into the ears of his powerful horse, spurring him on to outpace the giant mountains of water that were now visible at the dark, crimson-sky horizon. The deluge was more mammoth, more monstrous than human imagination could envisage. Despite his rare valiance and extraordinary resilience, even the son of Surya broke into a cold sweat as he saw the distant waves that all but scraped the sky.

Only the Gods could foretell the destruction this mother of all floods was going to unleash. Nothing could be heard except for the earth-shattering din of the approaching messengers of human extinction. The wind seemed to be moving faster than arrows as a result of the all-consuming torrents that seemed to surround the glorious city of Harappa from all sides.

It was only now that Manu fully understood what Matsya had been warning them about over the last few eventful days. *Pralay* — the great deluge — had descended upon the planet to potentially destroy every life form on it. From the first glimpse that Manu saw as he galloped like lightning, he was convinced.

Pralay was indeed the end of the world.

·‖卐‖·

They now stood atop a steep hill that overlooked the great metropolis of Harappa from a far distance of a *yojana* (a *yojana* is considered equivalent to 14 kilometers) - Tara, Somdutt, Satyavrata Manu and the platoon of the fish-folk. Behind them was an enormous caravan of fleeing Harappan men, women, children and livestock. In the few hours that Manu, Somdutt and their fellowship had been able to buy for hundreds of thousands of inhabitants of Harappa, they had succeeded in evacuating the city of all its citizens.

All but two.

Pundit Chandradhar and his beloved wife Priyamvada had chosen to stay on in the city as it fell prey to the annihilating deluge, Harappa being the first among numerous such settlements that were to be devoured by the great flood in the days to come. As the last king of Harappa and the princess of Mohenjo-daro forced Manu to ride away from the city gates just in time, the young lad could not help but turn every now and then. The last glimpse he caught of was of the fading silhouettes of the unfortunate couple appear on the citadel's terrace.

They had decided to welcome the great flood by offering themselves as the cursed city's last sacrifice to the Gods.

·||卐||·

As he had galloped away to the temporary safety of higher ground, Manu's mind was still with the dying husband and wife.

Is there a misfortune greater than a heart filled with unbridled ambition? What throne can be so bejeweled that its glimmer numbs the spirit to the pain and suffering of human souls? And how does it all end?

With his heart full of love and forgiveness, Satyavrata Manu mumbled his final sendoff to the royal couple.

'Goodbye, O wise Pundit Chandradhar. Farewell, O beautiful princess of Mohenjo-daro.'

The first cleansing that Pralay had successfully engineered — was of Manu's hate.

·||卐||·

It was a sight that none of them had thought was possible. None of them had imagined that a river, as mighty as it may be, could dwarf even the mighty oceans. But here it was. The Blood River!

Manu, Tara and Somdutt, all broke into tears as they saw the first lashing waves shatter the perimeter walls of this once-splendid city. And this was the assault of just the first foot-waves of the real monster that was coming to engulf Harappa. As a devastating blanket of water curled above Harappa like the hood of a colossal serpent, moments before swallowing the entire city in one single sweep, Manu whispered a silent prayer. In an instant that seemed to last forever, the great deluge consumed the entire city of Harappa in merciless mayhem.

The tens of thousands of Harappans broke into wails and moans as they beheld their beloved city perish. They saw every building, every temple and every orchard get destroyed. The proud citadels fell like anthills against a sledgehammer. The giant granaries were swept away like mounds of sand. The Great Bath was submerged so deep like it would never see the light of the day again. Brick by brick, lane by lane, home by home…Harappa was lost forever.

It was the cosmos that had once given humankind the will, the enterprise and the grit to build a city as magnificent as Harappa. And it was the very same power of Creation that was reclaiming its own bounties.

The curse of the Blood River had only just begun to unleash its wrath.

Banaras, 2017

KARTIKEYA

Vidyut's steps froze as he heard the chilling words spoken by Purohit ji.

'Do you not want to know how your father, the great Kartikeya Shastri, was killed, Vidyut?'

What Vidyut had been told since he was a child was that his father, Kartikeya Shastri, had died in a car accident in San Francisco during a rainy night of that ill-fated November of 1991.

Is there anything about my life that is real? What is this place? Who are these people?

Vidyut dropped his backpack wearily, trembling with both anger as well as a burning desire for the truth. He turned to the old priest who still sat on the staircase.

Purohit ji could sense Vidyut's raging impatience and growing distrust. He knew he had to bring the anguished devta back into the fold of the last real defense for humankind – the Dev-Raakshasa matth!

He spoke quickly, clearly.

'The man who Balvanta killed yesterday was a part of the same lethal, gigantic organization that killed our beloved Kartikeya, Vidyut.

Trijat Kapaalik was one of the many powerful members of the New World Order.'

·‖ॐ‖·

They were now walking along the lawns of the Dev-khannd. For all the hate and hurt that Vidyut nursed in his heart, his affection for Purohit ji outweighed everything. He had agreed to spend time with the wise old priest, till the great Dwarka Shastri rose for the day.

'What I am about to tell you will be hard to grasp, Vidyut. And even harder to believe. The scale and imperishability of this unimaginable conspiracy will take anyone by shock. But everything I tell you now, or your great grandfather shares with you later – is all true. Every word of it.'

Vidyut nodded. But the reality was that he was not interested in anything else for now. He just wanted to know who took his beloved, doting father away from him when he was all of eight years of age. He had seen his mother, the beautiful and caring Pooja, suffer quietly for years. He had spent his entire childhood fatherless, in near-hiding, prohibited from visiting Banaras for reasons unexplained till date.

Purohit ji continued.

'The Order that Constantine the Great commissioned right after the Council of Nicaea, did not take much time to morph into a dangerous and unstoppable cartel of some of the world's most powerful and intellectually gifted men. The rise and fall of the Knights Templar was just one among the many early games of power, deceit and global control that this Order had begun to play. Slowly but surely, their design and their ambition turned more and more nefarious.'

Vidyut was getting impatient. For now, he had no interest in the sequence of events. He did not care for any New World Order. All he needed to know was who the killers of his father were.

'With all due respect, Purohit ji, I am in no frame of mind to assimilate this long and intriguing history of this Order you and Baba speak about. Will you please be kind and tell me who murdered my great father, your beloved Kartikeya??'

Purohit ji fully empathized with Vidyut's unenviable situation. He stopped and turned to his devta.

'Just keep one thing in mind, my dear Vidyut. While no one else's loss can be compared to yours, we all loved Kartikeya as much as we love you. Perhaps a little more.'

With tears in his eyes, the old priest raised both his hands and stared at them. He then looked up at Vidyut.

'I raised Kartikeya with these very hands, O devta. He was like my first-born son.'

Mohenjo-Daro, 1700 BCE

THE MOUND OF THE DEAD

'You will be foolish to attempt this, O Satyavrata.'

It was the seven young sages, the divine Saptarishi, speaking to Manu. The son of Surya was pacing up and down the vast, torch-lit cave in which they had taken refuge for the night.

'The great sages are right, Manu. Mohenjo-daro is nearly thirty yojanas from here. Even the fastest and strongest ashvas cannot reach the city in time,' added a tense Tara or

Satrupa, worried deeply that Manu was on the verge of embarking upon a suicidal mission yet again.

But she understood his painful predicament. Mohenjo-daro was the second most populous city of Aryavarta. If this metropolis was devoured by the great deluge, it would mean certain death for countless inhabitants of the glorious city.

'But how can we sit back and do nothing...??' said Manu irritably. Deep inside, he knew the odds were insurmountable. 'Have all of you forgotten how many souls reside in that magnificent city? Tens of thousands! Perhaps over a hundred thousand! How can we leave them to their certain annihilation?'

There was a cold silence in the high cave, as the dim torches gave it a solemn, dull orange hue.

The gloom of the cave appeared to embody the hopelessness that was slowly creeping into the hearts of those who had taken shelter in it.

·||卐||·

'I will go!' a voice rang out.

Everyone turned to a dark corner of the cave, where Dhruv sat sharpening his arrows on a stone sill. This remarkable young man with beautiful brown hair flowing well below his muscular shoulders, was Manu's childhood friend and ablest warrior.

'What do you mean, Dhruv?' asked Tara.

Dhruv stood up, picked up his bow and his quiver stuffed with arrows, and walked up to the comparatively brighter center of the cave. He faced Manu, Tara, Somdutt and the Saptarishi. The seven serene ascetics sat in a partially meditative state.

'Permit me to ride out to Mohenjo-daro, Manu. I will go alone and will gallop day and night. If my horse does not survive this grueling journey, I will walk to Mohenjo-daro!'

'Don't be ridiculous, Dhruv!'

This time it was Pundit Somdutt who spoke.

'I admire your courage and your willingness to sacrifice yourself for the sake of others. I really do. But trying to reach Mohenjo-daro now is nothing short of madness. The way our observers are reporting in, the flood would reach the walls and rip the city apart in a matter of hours, not days...' said Somdutt.

'But we can't let them all die!' screamed Manu, his eyes wide with horror and helplessness. A high-pitched statement from Manu was enough to quieten any gathering he stood in.

Dhruv walked up to his friend and kept a hand on Manu's shoulder.

'One of us has to go, Manu. If we abandon that city today, both you and I know we will not be able to live with this burden on our conscience. And we cannot risk you, my friend. You are too important for the Ark, and for whatever is left of the human race. Permit me to go, my king.'

Manu did not say a word. He picked up his sword and walked

up to Tara. He kissed her on the forehead, looked into her eyes and whispered, 'You know I have to do this, Tara. I am Vivasvan Pujari's son. And the great Vivasvan Pujari would never leave people behind.'

Without waiting for Tara to say anything, Manu turned to Dhruv.

'We both ride to Mohenjo-daro this very moment, brother.'

·||ॐ||·

'It is too late…O son of Surya.'

Before Manu and Dhruv could step out of the cave, one of the magnificent sages spoke aloud, still in a state of trance.

The tonsured and clean-shaven sage looked nothing more than nineteen. All seven of the Saptarishi were young boys, but radiated a brilliant halo. They seemed to glow with su-pernatural life-energy. To Manu it seemed as if Matsya had left a small part of him behind with the holy Saptarishi. Or so Manu hoped.

The young sage opened his eyes, as if they were looking into some far away horizon.

'It is too late, Satyavrata. The devastating waves have struck the city… moments ago.'

With this the first sage closed his eyes. Before a horrified Manu could ask anything, the second sage opened his eyes, ready to speak.

'The deluge has struck the gates, the walls and the citadels. Mohen-jo-daro has fallen O great king, never to rise again.'

Thereafter, reverberating through the grief-stricken silence of the cave, the remaining five sages made their terrifying pronouncements one after the other.

'The deafening cries of the drowning masses make the entire universe weep. The great cleansing has begun…'

'Forever shall this city be remembered, shrouded in mystery. Forever shall its name remind us of the great deluge…'

'Muaa', as the Sindhu inhabitants of the city today call their dead, and 'Muaan' in multitudes, shall stick to the name of this cursed metropolis and its unfortunate inhabitants till the end of time…'

'It shall forever be called Muaan-jo-daro.'

'It shall forever be called - The Mound of the Dead.'

Banaras, 2017

THE MURDEROUS CODE

Vidyut sat with his eyes fixed at a spot on the floor.

They were now in the great matthadheesh's room. Both Purohit ji and Dwarka Shastri could see the distress and dis-illusionment on Vidyut's face. They knew they had to do something quickly. The last devta could not be permitted to drift away. Not now.

Not with the *Rohini Nakshatra* being just three days away.

·||ॐ||·

'This battle has been raging for hundreds of years, my son,' said Dwarka Shastri. 'Is it really possible to fight an enemy who is hell bent on genocide and subversion of billions of human beings with non-violence?'

Vidyut did not respond. Dwarka Shastri continued.

'I agree what Balvanta did was deplorable, Vidyut. And it could have been avoided. It ought to have been avoided! But what other alternative did we have? If Balvanta had left Trijat alive, the mahataantric would have come back at us with twice the venom. Yes, we could have taken him captive. But we took Bala captive too. We all know what happened there.'

There was silence in the room for a minute, before the matthadheesh spoke again.

'We cannot be at war with a ruthless monster, that treats human lives with absolute contempt, that sheds the blood of innocents with reckless brutality - and try to remain unblemished ourselves, Vidyut. You have to understand this very clearly, my son – we are at war! It may not appear to be so at the face of things, but that is the reality.'

Vidyut was listening. Deep at the core of the storm his mind was going through, the one thing he was certain of was the impeccable moral character and unquestioned humanity of his great grandfather.

'There is no doubt we are at war, Baba. First Romi Pereira and the highly-trained mercenaries. Then Bala's cold-blooded murder. Followed by the mahataantric and Professor Tripathi. I understand we are battling someone exceptionally powerful and relentless,' said Vidyut.

Both Dwarka Shastri and Purohit ji were relieved to see the

devta break his silence at last.

·||卐||·

'Despite everything we are faced with, Baba, I cannot accept the taking of a human life. I could have killed Romi if I wanted. I could have killed each one of the mercenaries. But I did not. And that is what my father and mother taught me. That is what Purohit ji taught me. That is what *you* taught me, Baba.'

Dwarka Shastri nodded.

'Which is why Purohit asked you about the battle between good and evil as depicted in our puraanas, Vidyut.'

Vidyut looked up suddenly, his eyes wide with disbelief.

How could Baba know about this? He was not even there when Purohit ji said it!

The last devta could not hide his amazement and looked at Purohit ji, who simply smiled. Vidyut shook his head and smiled himself. Both these men knew that the great matthadheesh was *trikaal-darshi*, or the observer of all three realms of space-time.

'Hinduism or *Sanatana Dharma* propounds nothing but universal peace. It champions *sarva-dharma-samabhaava* or affectionate coexistence of all religions and faiths. It teaches the path of detachment and the search for *Brahmma*, or the ultimate truth. Why, it even encourages the whole world to be one large, unified family when it pronounces *Vasudhaiva*

Kutumbakam.'

Dwarka Shastri waited for a few seconds before continuing. He wanted his great grandson to absorb every word he spoke.

'And yet *Maa Durga* beheads *Mahishasur.* Lord Krishna kills the demon *Narakasur. Maa Kaali* exterminates thousands of demons that emerge from the blood of *Raktbeej.* Lord Rama kills *Ravana* and Shiva destroys the *Tripur* demon. Indra vanquishes *Vritrasur* and the *Narsimha* avatar of Vishnu tears open the belly of the raakshasa tyrant *Hiranyakashipu.* This is all just to send one critical message to us humans, Vidyut.

That evil needs to be fought. That tyranny needs to be defeated. And if violence with an oppressor is needed to prevent mass violence against millions of innocents, then that is the path to be taken by the virtuous.'

⠿

'But Baba, the Masaan-raja was unarmed. He was defeated. What code of war permits the killing of someone in that state?'

It was now that Purohit ji erupted. He stood up from his chair, red-faced. He walked a couple of steps towards Vidyut before shouting in a voice brimming with angst and long-subdued anger.

'The same code that permitted the killing of the great warrior-priest Advait Shastri when he was unarmed! The same code that allowed your ancestor Markandeya Shastri to be hacked to pieces when he was alone in worship. The same murderous code that found Captain Wayne Ashbrook hanging from a tree!'

Vidyut was stunned at Purohit ji's words. But the indignant priest was not finished. He screamed out his last line with tears rolling down from his eyes.

'The same code that permitted your father, Kartikeya Shastri, to be hunted, surrounded and killed thousands of miles away!'

The Dark Forests of Aryavarta, 1699 BCE

DAITYA

He was panting heavily, his lungs all but out of breath. But there was no way he could stop.

He had to reach his prized alchemists before *they* reached them.

He was tearing his way through the dense forest, his feet slipping frequently on the slushy ground. His strong wrist clasped the handle of his heavy sword, ready to plunge into the gut of any enemy that was unfortunate enough to come in its way.

His appearance had changed drastically over the last few months of death, devastation, battle, hate, dejection and hope. His once tonsured head was now covered with long locks of hair that bounced off his lean, strong shoulders. His clean-shaven, boyish face was now battle-hardened, with a sharp stubble over his strong jawline. His face and body were covered with scars from blades and arrows of all kinds. But there was one feature that had not changed one bit despite all the odds that had come in his way over the last few months.

His deep, righteous, almond colored eyes.

The penetrating honesty of Satyavrata Manu's eyes had remained unchanged.

·||ॐ||·

Everything had been an uphill task for Manu ever since the momentous night of Harappa's destruction had unfolded in front of his eyes. The next few days and nights had been spent in a frantic effort to evacuate the great cities of Kalibangan and Dholavira, besides other smaller townships and settlements. They had succeeded in pulling out vast numbers and saving innumerable lives, before the great flood had struck ruthlessly, mercilessly…systematically.

As weeks and months had progressed, the deluge had engulfed hundreds of yojanas of land into its bottomless belly. Lands that once lay barren, infested with nothing but cacti and lizards, were now covered under what appeared to be the deepest of oceans. Hills and mountains that once stood like enormous titans against the skies, now lay submerged under stormy waves that kissed the thunderbolts ever so frequently.

The great cleansing had also unearthed what lay buried deep inside human hearts and souls. It had brought out the vilest poison of human depravity, just as it uncovered astounding generosity and goodness that were thus far unknown to man. On one end the destruction and mayhem made some men and women risk everything to protect one another. Yet on the other, it transformed human beings into monsters that, even in the face of imminent extinction, left no opportunity to exploit the weak and the helpless.

In a matter of months Satyavrata Manu's world-view had undergone a sea change. He no longer believed that the human soul was filled with goodness unless compelled otherwise by circumstances. He had seen enough decadence of this dominant species of the planet to know one thing for sure.

Man was an expression of God on Earth.

Man was an imp of the devil.

·‖ॐ‖·

They hunted in packs like the hyena.

They prowled the dark forests day and night. Their eyes watched everything that moved in the dense jungles. They hunted, cooked and devoured a pride of lions with the same relish as when they bit into raw fish from the streams in the wilds. Each one of these vicious forest dwellers was known as a *daitya* across Aryavarta, and was feared by one and all.

Quite like the animals they lived amongst, only brute strength and combat prowess decided the leadership of the daityas.

Consequently, every chief of this vicious tribe had to challenge and publicly murder the previous leader in an unarmed fight unto death. It was little wonder that the current warlord who ruled the dark forests like its uncrowned king, was a beast of a man. Rumored to be over seven arms in height, he was believed to have torn open the gut of his predecessor with his bare hands, and tied the writhing man's intestines as his prized waist-band.

He was known across all of the forest lands and entire Aryavarta as *Nara-Munda*.

Banaras, 2017

KASHI VISHWANATH

He stood in a corner of the narrow alley leading to the temple, watching all the proceedings with great interest. The *Kashi Vishwanath Mandir* was by far more spiritually charged than any other place of worship he had visited before. The temple alone congregated more pilgrims annually that the Vatican and Mecca combined.

They were right. There is something strangely powerful about this place, about this ancient city.

No wonder the devta is here.

He could not enter the main temple premises, as foreigners were not permitted. But from outside the temple gates he could catch a glimpse of the *Annakoot* or the 'Mound of Nourishment', which served free meals to thousands of poor and destitute. He looked up from a distance at the temple's central dome, which was once made of solid gold. He could see the silver coinages embedded in the temple floor.

He was being stared at by passers-by. While foreigners were not a novelty in *Vishwanath Gallee* or the street leading to the shrine, the striking presence he carried about himself was not something they saw very frequently.

And justifiably so.

No one like him had visited the ancient city of Kashi before.

·||ॐ||·

He was both mesmerized and worried when he witnessed the *Gyaan-Vaapi* well, and the devotees around it. Known to be the source of infinite wisdom, the Gyaan-Vaapi well had several legends associated with it. One of those was that when a pillaging sultan's armies broke into Banaras and eventually into the Kashi Vishwanath temple's sanctum sanctorum, the chief priest of the temple lifted and embraced the *Shiva Linga*, before jumping summarily into the holy well – sacrificing his own life in order to prevent the divine Linga to be desecrated by the invaders.

He watched each one of them closely, every single devotee that came to pray at the sacred well. He looked at the evidently penniless young couples. He observed the shriveled old ladies, the half-naked senile men, the weeping babies, the crippled and the diseased. What was making him anxious was the depth of unquestioned devoutness that he saw in their eyes. They couldn't care less about their poverty. They did not let their handicap come in the way of their single-minded devotion.

Who can overcome a people with such intense and collective spiritual force?

Worse still, who can defeat someone who comes with this entire life-energy compressed into his supernatural being?

The devta must be stopped before it is too late.

·||ॐ||·

Fearless as he was, he had insisted on visiting the sacred temple and the holy well alone. He now walked out of the bustling street, pacing swiftly as he always did. As soon as he came to a wider road, he was surrounded by his security drill and was lost in the midst of trained fighters.

Vidyut, Dwarka Shastri, Damini, Purohit ji, Naina, Sonu, Balvanta and the entire Dev-Raakshasa matth had reason to worry. The whole of mankind had reason to worry.

A very chilling reason.

The Maschera Bianca was in Kashi.

In a final bid to stop what was going to change the fate of mankind forever.

The Dark Forests of Aryavarta, 1699 BCE

ONSLAUGHT OF CREATION

Manu and his confidante, Dhruv, had their weapons drawn. As they escorted the four master alchemists through the dark forests, their eyes were peeled and their ears strained to catch the sound of any twig cracking as an indicator of someone approaching.

Despite the dangers lurking at every step of this God forsaken forestland, the alchemists had to be brought here. The divine Saptarishi, who were now Satyavrata Manu's spiritual guides and partners in combatting the onslaught of pralay, had listed down essential medicinal herbs and roots that had to be collected from the depths of the dark forest in order to be preserved and carried on the Ark.

·||ॐ||·

Manu had spent several weeks coming to terms with the fact that his beloved brother, teacher, friend and philosopher, the mighty Matsya, whom Manu believed to be an avatar of Lord Vishnu Himself, had left without even saying a final goodbye.

Matsya had left a note for Manu, urging him to call for help when all was lost. And he had left a crooked looking blow-horn for Manu. The strange horn was made of the remains of some mysterious sea-creature, and was to be used only when Manu felt that all hope had vanished for humankind, and never otherwise.

Even though months had passed and the monumental task of constructing the universe's most gigantic boat was under-way against all forces and furies of nature, Manu felt bitterly alone without Matsya by his side. When he had accepted Matsya's commandment of leading the building of the mas-sive Ark, he had done so believing that the magnificent blue-man would always be there to hold his hand. But that was not to be.

Satyavrata Manu was left alone. Alone with the gargantuan task of saving Creation against the onslaught of Creation itself!

·||ॐ||·

Manu and Dhruv had a small band of half a dozen fighters with them.

People had become the most precious resource for the builders of the Ark. Over the last few months, as the great deluge had raged on and plundered all of Aryavarta, they had succeeded in saving several hundreds of thousands of men, women and children. By now they had successfully evacuated the city of Kalibangan and sent riders to even the distant ones like Lothal.

Today each city contributed to the workforce and armies of Manu's Ark. All the able-bodied men were enlisted under the infantry or cavalry, just as a significant section of them was used for the main construction labor force. A well-equipped militia was needed to defend the very last civilized human colony, albeit temporary, from raids by large gangs of bandits and invading marauders of the warlords from the savage-lands.

The women were no less and contributed equally to the armed units as well as to the architectural workforce. They also formed and led essential teams that looked after the wounded and the sick, that built and managed massive kitchens, that protected samples of animals, plants, insects, metals, fabrics, books, herbs, seeds, firestones and maps. They forged weapons and kept detailed inventory for the construction of the greatest vessel ever known to man.

They all battled together to stay alive to see the other side of pralay.

The undertaking was nothing less than constructing a whole new world – that too under the punishing cold cloudbursts and heart-wrenching thunderstorms. Each high-ground they selected as their basecamp had to be abandoned in a few weeks as the deluge spread, threatening to engulf the entire planet.

It was.

Leaving aside a lone sacred city.

·||ॐ||·

The strapping young Dhruv raised his index finger, signaling to his small band to come to an immediate and complete standstill. He then raised all five fingers, indicating that everyone should be weapons-ready. His expert soldier's ears had caught the faint crackle of a dry leaf.

Manu, Dhruv and their six combatants now formed a circle around the four aged alchemists, scimitars, spears and bows ready to counterstrike in the event of an ambush.

One of the learned alchemists, who hailed from the far-off lands beyond the *Vindhya* ranges, was a bit confused. He could not help but ask.

'O mighty Satyavrata, we have been in the midst of adversaries several times before. Each more dangerous than the other. But never have I witnessed such alarm. Is there anything especially worrisome about the daityas?'

Manu did not respond. But his best friend Dhruv did.

'Yes, O wise one. The daityas are a bit more hazardous than any other foes we have confronted before.'

Manu looked at Dhruv and gave a look of disapproval. Dh-

ruv simply winked back at his friend and leader, and completed his statement.

'The daityas are *Nar-Bhakshi*, O learned one.

They are cannibals.'

Banaras, 2017

A TOTALITARIAN GOVERNMENT

Dwarka Shastri's heart wept along with his great grandson. But he knew this day had to come. And Vidyut had to confront it, one way or another.

After two and a half decades of believing that his father, Kartikeya Shastri, had died in an unfortunate car crash, the devta had discovered the reality.

Today he was face to face with the harshest, most unbearable truth of his life.

My father was mercilessly ambushed, outnumbered and…assassinated!

·‖卐‖·

'Tell me everything, Baba. No secrets, no filtered information, no waiting for the right time…I need to know everything, Baba.'

The grand old man knew the time had come.

'Everything, Baba…' said Vidyut, emphasizing on the *everything* very purposefully.

'Tell me about this New World Order. Tell me about the Rohini Nakshatra. What happened after the fall of the Knights Templar? Why was my father killed? Who killed him? Who is sending monsters like Romi Pereira and Trijat Kapaalik?'

Vidyut's eyes were shifting from those of his great grandfather to Purohit ji. He needed answers. Today.

'And Baba…what is the secret of the Black Temple?'

·‖卐‖·

'Like I was telling you, Vidyut…the planned and vicious manipulation of the 12th century Knights Templar represented one of the early successes of the New World Order. The Templars' meteoric rise to riches and unbridled power, and then their equally dramatic fall emboldened the Overlords of the Order like never before. They had succeeded in systematically establishing a military force. They seamlessly merged banking with politics. They concocted religion with conquest. They got the priest to partner with the king. They spawned a formidable military outfit when they chose to. They decimated the same at will.'

The matthadheesh paused for a moment, before speaking again.

'It is said that not all the Templars were executed on that fateful day of Friday the 13th, 1307 AD. Some of them escaped. Among them were those who were eventually handpicked by the Order. They were permitted to flee, so they could reach various parts of Europe and the Middle East, and establish new strongholds for the secret brotherhood. The Overlords were now supremely confident. If they could puppeteer the geo-politics of France and Cyprus, what stopped them from taking control of more regions, nations and continents?'

Vidyut was listening intently. Something seemed to slowly but surely convince him that this was all somehow connected to the matth, to his late father, to Romi and Trijat, and to himself.

And to Harappa.

·‖卐‖·

While he was getting a hang of how the Order had manipulated the Templars, Vidyut still did not understand what was it that they wanted to ultimately achieve.

'Baba, what does this Order want, really? Their attempt to control politics, nations and religion is understandable, but to what end?'

Dwarka Shastri took a deep breath and launched himself into the long-due explanation.

'As you know, it had all started in Nicaea, with the mighty emperor Constantine's desire to establish a one-world government. A new order of governance and of control, of the society and of the individual – a totalitarian government that transcended divisive forces of religious fanaticism, economic protectionism, caste, color, creed, language…why even patriotism! His rationale, however bizarre it sounds today, was theoretically correct and well-intended.

But it was set-up for failure right from day one. Diversity is what makes humankind the supreme species of this planet. It is diversity that is the progenitor of culture, of ambition, of art and literature, of scientific progress, of economic aspirations and so much more. Without this rich assortment of different peoples, we would be nothing more than a vast herd of sheep. If the world today has a Sistine Chapel alongside the ghaats of Banaras, if we have a global fashion ecosystem flourishing alongside a burgeoning sports industry, if there are healthy debates on euthanasia and abortions – it is all because we humans are dissimilar.

So, in other words, Constantine's plan was fundamentally against the primary reality of nature – evolution. He was trying to roll back the human race into a herd. But more than that, his greatest blunder was that he overlooked one extremely powerful force.

Human ambition.'

·||ॐ||·

101

'Before I tell you more about the New World Order and their unbelievably nefarious design, there is one last thing I want you to grasp, Vidyut. Do you know what their most precious takeaway from the entire bloody chapter of the Templars was? It was something that was going to make them an unstoppable global force.'

'What was that takeaway, Baba?' enquired Vidyut.

'It was something that tossed humanity's destiny under the heels of the Order forever, and paved the way for wars, dictators, mass exterminations and inhuman atrocities,' replied Dwarka Shastri.

'They had learnt that wars could be engineered.

That wars could be fought by them from *both* sides.

And this horrible, merciless *modus operandus* was going to ravage the world...again and again and again.'

The Dark Forests of Aryavarta, 1699 BCE

DHRUV

The arrow struck the approaching daitya's forehead, right between his eyebrows. The force of the piercing projectile threw the attacking cannibal's body back a few paces.

Two more screaming daitya's fell from the branches of high trees as two menacing arrows shot through them simultaneously.

Dhruv was, beyond doubt, Aryavarta's greatest archer. His bow and quiver were like an extension of his own body.

·||卐||·

Manu kicked the chest of a daitya, which hit him like a falling

boulder. In the same momentum, the son of Surya behead-
ed another attacker that was dangerously close to one of the
alchemists. As the headless body of the assailant spouted
blood, it sprayed across Satyavrata's face, hair and shoulders,
giving him a ghastly appearance.

By now Manu was used to the gore. He simply wiped his
face with his leather wrist-guard and continued to battle.

As he turned to scan the battle scene, Manu spotted a daitya
bowman take aim at Dhruv. Without a moment's hesitation
and with stunning precision, Satyavrata Manu held his thick
sword's handle with both hands, drew it behind his back and
shot it like an arrow fired from a powerful bow. The mighty
sword tore through the chest of the cannibal archer, pinning
him against a thick tree-trunk.

Dhruv noticed this timely intervention and nodded at Manu
in a quick acknowledgement of the life-saving help he had
just received. The warrior-prince nodded back at his closest
friend.

Together the valiant duo of Manu and Dhruv could crush
an entire army.

·||ॐ||·

It did not take more than a few minutes for the bloody skir-
mish to end. As Manu and Dhruv surveyed the outcome of
the short clash, they were satisfied with the results. They had
lost no men, while a dozen daityas lay slaughtered around
them. The ground beneath them, and the trees and bushes

in the vicinity were now painted crimson with the shower of daitya blood.

'This was perhaps just the first wave, Dhruv. We need to get the alchemists out of here now!' said Manu, even as he kept an eye out for more aggressors prowling behind the dense foliage.

Dhruv nodded in agreement and readied an arrow on his bow, as he led the march out of the woods.

What Manu did not know was that this attack was just a suicide scout mission. The nar-bhakshi were not to be beaten so easily.

As Satyavrata Manu, Dhruv, their alchemists and fighters left the boundaries of the dark forests, they were not aware of the cruel black eyes that were watching them from a hidden *machaan* in the high trees.

He was watching them.

And now the mighty Nara-Munda knew their battle style, their strengths and their weaknesses very clearly.

He marked the son of Surya for himself.

And swore to eat Manu's beating heart…raw.

Banaras, 2017

KEDARNATH

'I am well, gurudev,' said Naina. 'Yes…he is fine. Our devta is fine.'

She was walking around on the terrace of one of the wings of the Dev-Raakshasa matth, speaking into her mobile phone. Before this simple instrument became her constant companion, she was accustomed to using an Iridium 9555 satellite phone. The remote mountains she was stationed at before Vidyut arrived in Banaras, no other device could have worked. And now the person on the other end of the line was using a similar, advanced sat-phone, because he was beyond the reach of all other forms of communication networks.

She was speaking to Mahant Bhavaanishankar, a mystical *sad-*

hu from the high mountains of Northern Himalayas, whose hermitage lay on the banks of the *Mandakini* river.

The old *Mahant* (chief priest) had been the guardian of what was supposed to be the last Black Temple.

He was the high-priest at the *Kedarnath Mandir* in Rudraprayag, Uttarakhand.

·||ॐ||·

The Kedarnath temple is one among the supremely revered twelve *Jyotirlinga* of Lord Shiva. These twelve sacred shrines represent the epitome of Shiva's divine light and have been worshipped as perhaps the holiest pilgrimages for Hindus over hundreds of years.

The temple at Kedarnath is believed to have been built originally by the *Pandavas*, the five valiant and righteous brothers from *Hastinapur*, in order to please Shiva and seek his forgiveness for the bloodshed of the great *Mahabharata* war. As hundreds of years passed, the sacred sanctuary became a hallowed attraction for millions of pilgrims.

When large swathes of the hill-state were engulfed under water, the shrine remained miraculously undamaged during the flash flood that hit Uttarakhand in the year 2013. Said to have been saved by a large boulder that diverted the onslaught of the swelling currents of the Mandakini, the temple stands at its original spot even today.

How did this miracle happen? How did the mandir remain largely intact when everything surrounding it collapsed under the assault of the flood?

No one can say for sure. Perhaps an unknown divine force was guarding this precious precinct. Perhaps something so invaluable lay concealed in the heart of the temple, that even the Mandakini had to conform, despite being in vicious spate.

After all, Kedarnath was the last Black Temple.

Or was it?

·‖ॐ‖·

'It is close to us, gurudev, hidden away and protected by Baba himself…and we all await the Rohini Nakshatra with bated breath. But I still do not understand how Vidyut is supposed to unfurl a secret that dates back three thousand years. Are we not expecting too much from him?'

Mahant Bhavaanishankar laughed merrily. Everything he had devoted his life to was about to bear fruit in a few days. And unlike Naina, he was certain of the prophecy.

'Look, my *bitiya*…look how everything has come together just like it was meant to. Vidyut is in Kashi, just when the planets are about to juxtapose themselves for the holy nakshatra. The forces of evil are getting increasingly restless and Lucifer himself has arrived to wage the final battle. The great Dwarka Shastri lives beyond his *maarkesh kaalam* (the hour of death) and the vile mahataantric lies as ashes in his own ritual-pit. Don't you see, Naina…it is ALL happening the way it had been prophesied!'

The white-bearded Mahant laughed again, keeping his phone aside and sprinkling the cold water of a mountain-stream on his face. His devout laughter echoed across the snow-capped mountains that surrounded him.

Naina also broke into a smile of relief. She knew the Mahant was right. Everything was unfolding in precisely the manner it was supposed to. She crossed her fingers and whispered a short prayer.

However, notwithstanding the hope and reprieve that she could feel lighting up within her, Naina had latched on to one word that the Mahant had said. One name she did not understand.

Lucifer.

·‖ॐ‖·

'Gurudev, I did not understand what you meant by saying Lucifer himself has arrived. Who is Lucifer, gurudev?'

It was for the first time during this call that Bhavaanishankar became serious.

'There is little time now for me to explain everything to you, Naina. Just remember that to stop the greatest force of good, the greatest power of evil shall unleash itself.'

Naina was listening, but could not gather what the Mahant was trying to say.

'Just be aware, Naina…and inform the great matthadheesh.

Tell him the Devil now walks in Kashi.'

Ark Basecamp, Marshes of Aryavarta, 1699 BCE

THE LAST HUMAN COLONY

It looked as if all of earth had been painted with a broad brush of grey. As Manu and Dhruv rode through the central lane of their gigantic basecamp, everything appeared to be ashen in color. The slushy ground, the makeshift tents, the tattered clothing of his people, the animals, the distant mountains, the sky…every speck seemed to be a sorrowful grey.

This was during what was left of daytime.

The nights were terrifying, with crimson and black skies screaming death in the language of thunder. Hundreds of thousands of men, women and children spent these nights shivering under the feeble protection of their camp. One hour of sleep became more precious than a thousand horses.

Manu looked around himself at the sprawling, miserable city of tents that spread for miles in all directions. All he could see was a sea of humans battling every moment to live another day. All he could hear was the incessant wailing of infants, the unbearable cries of the wounded and the diseased, the whining of nervous beasts – all muddled with the shrill whistle of the perpetually blowing wind.

It had not stopped raining for several months. Everything and everyone was drenched all the time. The world was wetter than these wretched survivors could have imagined even in their worst nightmare. Scores succumbed every day, their bodies unable to cope with this unending assault of nature's fury.

·||ॐ||·

Dhruv could see the despair on his friend and leader's face.

The one thing Manu's childhood comrade knew was that if there was *anyone* who could pierce through the devastating waves of the great deluge and lead them all to the other side of pralay, it was Satyavrata Manu. He was convinced that Manu was the only man standing between the great flood and certain extinction of humankind.

Dhruv had taken it upon himself to never let this last ray of hope dwindle. He fully understood the excruciating pressure that Manu withstood every hour of every day. He knew how insufferable the burden of being responsible for hundreds of thousands of lives could be, especially against the given hostile odds. He spent most days almost entirely with the son of Surya, and was privy to his fears and anxieties. He knew Manu was unsure of his own capability in the face of such destruction – especially without Matsya there to guide him.

And yet Dhruv had witnessed the most spectacular evacuation and rescue campaigns over the last few months, under the dazzling stewardship of Manu. The son of Surya had stood on the fort ramparts of city after city, village after village…drawing people out of their homes, more through the magic of his personal charisma than the doomsday warnings he was the forbearer of. He had seen Manu riding into the eye of the storm if it meant saving a dozen more people, risking his life several times over in the process. Every time Manu came back with survivors, his stature grew.

Dhruv had ridden into the storm by his leader's side. He had unquestioning faith in this magnificent man.

He could never let Manu give up.

·||ॐ||·

'What troubles you, Manu?'

Manu did not respond. He did not turn to Dhruv. He just trudged on, his horse turning aimlessly into one of the narrow lanes of the basecamp. Dhruv followed his leader.

After several minutes of riding through and inspecting the

vast settlement, Manu spoke.

'Do you think we will escape the great deluge, Dhruv? Take a look at these people. With every passing day, they become weaker. The hope in their eyes dwindles a little more. Their stomachs are empty, their skin crumpled and their bones drenched to pulp! How long will they be able to go on?'

'As long as they see *you*, Manu,' said Dhruv. 'You are the beacon of hope for these hundreds of thousands of people. Why, most of them would have perished when pralay struck their cities and towns. Today every single one of them lives, breathes and fights to herald a new dawn for humankind - only because of you! They all believe that you saved them once, and that you will protect them forever. They have faith in you, Manu. Just you.'

Manu halted his mount and turned to Dhruv. His face was wrought with irritation as well as with helplessness.

'I am not what they think I am, Dhruv! You know me since we were children. I am just another ordinary fellow, who happened to have caught Matsya's fancy. I don't even know if the Ark will get built in time. I do not know if something so gigantic and enormously weighty will indeed withstand the vicious flood. It may sink like a rock, taking all of these people with it! For all you know, Matsya was just a handsome conjurer who had a way with words! I am not what he said I was. I am a fake, Dhruv!'

Dhruv stared into his leader's eyes with disbelief. He knew it was time that he put aside the exalted status of King Manu, and spoke like a true friend.

'You don't believe any of what you have just said, Satyavrata Manu. From what I have heard you and Tara describe, Matsya is truly divine. You love him more than you can say and are cross with him for leaving your side. And you know you are not ordinary, Manu. How can Vivasvan Pujari's blood be ordinary? This last human colony stands today because of you! This ocean of men and women survives to this day because of you! They are not being chopped to pieces and eaten alive by the daityas because of you! And if there is anyone I could bet my life on, anyone who has the ability and the character to vanquish the great deluge – it is you, my friend! It is Satyavrata Manu!'

Dhruv was nearly shouting by this time, the veins on his neck about to burst with the intensity he had put into those words.

The words hit home.

Manu tried to maintain his serious face, before breaking into a tired but affectionate smile. He needed the strength, the belief and the energy Dhruv had just lent him. Satyavrata grinned at his cherished friend and spurred-on his horse to ride away towards his own small tent.

As he cantered away, Manu looked back and addressed Dhruv.

'Get some rest, O mighty archer. Tomorrow we ride to the Great Ark.'

'To Manu's Ark!' replied Dhruv laughing, even as Manu shook his head in embarrassment and galloped away.

A TOTALITARIAN GOVERNMENT – PART II

They sat around a small ritual fire, that had slowly doused out on its own after the *pooja* was completed. Dwarka Shastri had taken a break for his evening worship.

'Like I explained to you earlier, Vidyut, the dark Order changed its name and form several times. Do not confuse it to be one single organization. It is a complex matrix of secret societies, organized institutions and powerful personalities spread all over the globe. Their aim is not just political. The New World Order is a centuries old network that envisions the control of the world population in the hands of a very few individuals.

They do not operate based on a political agenda alone. They control the world economy, religions, military action, civil wars, social discourses, media and of course, politics. The complex maze of kings, priests, warriors, gold and geography they crafted with the Knights Templar, only grew exponentially in terms of sophistication, scale and reach. Before anyone knew it, the world was being run as a war-economy.'

'What do you mean when you say a war-economy, Baba?' enquired Vidyut.

'Have you noticed something, Vidyut…whether it was the American war for independence or the French revolution, the Bolshevik storming of the Russian Tsar or the World Wars, the Cold War or the Middle East, Kashmir or Chechnya…the world has not been free of war and bloodshed even for a day?'

The devta was in deep thought. The great matthadheesh was right. But it could not be all so simple.

'You are right, Baba. But don't you think that is so because we humans or our species *Homo Sapiens* has a spectacular talent for self-destruction? Isn't forming groups, tribes or states, and then fighting to protect these identities an essential element of human evolution?'

Before Dwarka Shastri could respond, Purohit ji spoke up.

'Can we really be sure of what is the cause and what is the effect, Vidyut? What you have said about us humans is based on your observation of the continuous violence we inflict upon ourselves. But do we fight because we are genetically, biologically predisposed to bloodshed? Or have we accepted ourselves to be violent because someone or something has never let us live in peace? For example, a majority of the people of both India and Pakistan want harmony between the two nations. Four wars have been fought and innumerable lives have been lost. Both countries that should be investing into healthcare, education and employment, are busy building nuclear warheads and buying fighter jets worth billions of dollars. When for decades the ordinary Indian or Pakistani wants peace, what do you think is stopping it?'

'The New World Order...' concluded Vidyut.

·||卐||·

'Okay, Baba, now I understand broadly what the New World Order's design is, and that it is run by some extraordinarily powerful people who thirst for more power. But I am still not clear about exactly what they want to achieve with so much intrigue, influence and control.'

'Their goals are as simple as they are audacious, and are perhaps beyond the comprehension capability of ordinary folk. Here is what they want to establish as the New World Order –

A one-world economy.

A one-world religion.

A one-world military.

A one-world society.

And a one-world government...'

'...concentrated completely in the hands of their own so-called brotherhood,' said Vidyut, completing his great grand-father's sentence.

Vidyut was amazed at what he was hearing. He could not believe that something so sinister, something of such con-volution and massive dimension was lurking around the entire planet like a black shadow, and yet close to seven billion people lived in absolute oblivion!

Dwarka Shastri continued.

'Like I mentioned to you before, the first time a world-leader openly declared the name 'New World Order' was in 1921, when US President Woodrow Wilson used it in public. He was referring to the newly formed League of Nations post the aftermath of the First World War, but that was when we, the guardians of the Black Temple, knew that the Order had achieved dangerous proportions and was ready to unveil its hideous face on the world-stage.

Thereafter several influential men began talking about a New World Order from various public platforms and media. The list of these men included Presidents and Prime Ministers of developed countries. It also included business barons and thought-leaders. Is it a coincidence that the exact same term, the New World Order, has been used again and again for nearly one hundred years, from 1921 to now? It was a seed being sown, Vidyut.

It was as if the need for a New World Order was being arti-ficially implanted into the minds of the populace.'

·||ॐ||·

'Baba, earlier you had mentioned that the most potent *modus operandus* of the Order was that it fought wars from both ends. What did you mean by that? Which wars did they fight or control from both sides of the border?'

'I am glad you asked this question, Vidyut, because the answer to this will untie numerous knots of mystery and terror that surround the history of the Order. And how the impact of this secret brotherhood is far greater than you can imagine in your wildest dreams. Once you discover the truth, the world will never look the same to you.'

After everything that Vidyut had heard and been through, he was certain that nothing could shock him anymore.

He was wrong.

'Tell me please, Baba. I am eager to know what kind of an impression a group of determined and cruel people can have on our past and present. After all, how much can one secret society influence the course of history?'

The matthadheesh smiled but it never reached his eyes, that were now cold as stone. He asked Vidyut questions that his great grandson never saw coming.

'Who do you think was behind the French Revolution, Vidyut? And the disintegration of the Soviet Union?

Or for that matter...9/11?'

The Marshes of Aryavarta, 1699 BCE

THE ARK

Raindrops struck their faces like whiplashes, as they rode towards the great plains. A vast high-ground in the heart of the plains had been chosen as the construction site for mankind's greatest undertaking ever.

Dhruv led the mounted caravan as it made way through shrieking wind and torrential cloudburst. Nothing could be seen for miles except barren marshlands and distant mountains. The continuous downpour did not permit anything to grow. All vegetation of Aryavarta, but for the dark forests, had been washed away months ago. This band looked like they were riding on another planet, that had never hosted life in any form.

Tara and twenty members from her combat outfit comprising young women followed Dhruv closely behind. Given his deep admiration for this fierce and effective force, Manu had christened the women's wing with the name *Damini Sena*, or the Thunderbolt Army.

The Damini Sena was no less formidable than the best warrior-squads that rode under Manu's sparkling Sun-banner.

Manu had no inkling then that his beloved, late mother Sanjna would be reborn and take the name of Damini three thousand and seven hundred years from that day.

·||ॐ||·

Manu himself rode behind the massive horse-carts that were laden with provisions meant for the workforce at the site. Two hundred carts. And this was a comparatively small convoy. The supply lines for the construction site were open round the clock. Thousands of toiling men and women had to be fed, clothed and provided with raw material.

The caravan stretched nearly half a yojana in length, and was progressing towards its destination under a guard of one thousand, armed cavalry. In the past weeks and months several supply convoys had been attacked and looted by the brigands of the mountain-warlords as well as the vicious daityas. Manu was riding close to what was, in current times, an irresistible bounty for the attackers. He knew they were being watched at every step. He also knew how critical it was for these rations and materials to reach his people at the construction site.

·‖卐‖·

They rode over a patch of rocky hills, over which a road had been built for the supply-carts to cross with ease. As they arrived on the other side, they saw it.

They were still very far from the high-ground, still at least a day's ride away…and yet they saw it rise from the horizon like a Colossus.

The Ark.

·‖卐‖·

Each time he set his eyes upon the mammoth Ark, Manu felt a strange mix of pride and hope. In a little over just eight months, they had succeeded in building the basic framework of this enormous boat that was larger than anything the human mind could fathom. From a distance, the Ark looked like a giant grey screen had descended from the heavens, splitting the earth and the skies in half.

As one rode closer to this marvel of ancient engineering, it blocked the horizon in totality. It was like riding towards a wall that stretched from and to infinity. Slowly, the skeletal details and the raw robustness of the vessel would become clearer. Hundreds of thousands of the mightiest oaks had been harnessed and bent using brute force to form the gigantic hull of the Ark. Nearly an equal number of the strongest tree trunks, vine-cables and enormous rocks had been deployed as stilts to hold the giant boat aloft.

Upon even closer approach, one could spot what appeared to be millions of tiny, moving figures. From a few miles away, it could be determined what these creatures were. They were people! So many in number that they looked like termite infesting a banyan tree trunk. Tens of thousands of men, women and children working incessantly under insufferable conditions to keep the hope for mankind alive.

It was a spectacle in every sense. Hundreds of thousands of people from different cities, provinces and languages came together to shoulder this heroic enterprise. Every copper nail that got hammered into soaking wood took humankind one step further away from definite extinction. They fought hunger, disease, wild animals, bereavement, mutilation and all imaginable forms of suffering every hour of every day. But soon this collective endeavor made something very clear to the entire universe. That one instinct buried deep inside the spirit of man was more powerful than the greatest forces of nature.

The instinct for survival.

·||ॐ||·

But the building of a monumental Ark came with its own price.

Every day several workers died in accidents. The unceasing thunderstorms and violent rain made movement and judgment blurry at all times. Some slipped and fell from the top rungs of the Ark to certain death. Others got crushed under dislodged beams that were as heavy as rocks. Yet others were struck by deadly lightning that now rained ominously, striking the great Ark at several places at the same time. On top of all of this, every day several men and women succumbed to construction related injuries or sheer exhaustion.

But the leading cause of the loss of human life was something else.

Dozens of sleeping men, women and children were dragged away in the horror of the screaming nights.

To be eaten alive.

New York, 2017

THE STONEFELLAR FAMILY

He excused himself from the board meeting he was presiding over and walked swiftly towards his own lavish office chamber that overlooked the imposing Manhattan skyline. He was 44, with blonde hair and wore the finest business suit money could buy. But what he wore with most ease was an expression of regality…of someone who was born into extraordinary wealth and power.

He swiped his iPhone to receive the incoming call. The heir of the Stonefellar family knew better than to miss a call from the Big Man.

They were partners. They both occupied seats at the highest

bench of the Order. They were both among the Overlords – the Supreme Masters of the world's most powerful and sinister secret brotherhood.

'Greetings, Holiness,' said Frank Stonefellar. He was sixth-generation rich and was a billionaire many times over. Neither he nor his Hollywood movie-star wife were fully cognizant of the spread of their financial interests. His family had its forceful tentacles into every global business that mattered – oil, pharmaceuticals, infotech, media, arms and most of all…international banking.

'Hello, Frank. How is business, my son?'

'All well, your Holiness,' replied Frank.

'And how are Beatrice and little Simon? He must be what, six now?'

'With your blessings, they are both doing good, father,' said Frank, getting irritated with the niceties. He knew the Big Man was not nice, and couldn't care less for Frank's wife Beatrice and his son Simon.

In fact, Frank was waiting for the right time and the right opportunity to get the conniving old scoundrel eliminated.

·||ॐ||·

'Hearing from you is always a delight, Father. How can I be of service?'

The Big Man knew that a poisonous serpent lurked behind the glib words of Frank Stonefellar. He was well aware of the tycoon's pedigree.

They are a family of deceivers. For generations. Once I am done with the devta and the Black Temple, it will be vital to end the Stonefellar bloodline for good.

Forgive me Lord, for Simon is a child. But what must be done, has to be done.

·‖卐‖·

'The pleasure is mine, Frank. You are an old friend I trust deeply and love from the bottom of my heart.'

'The feeling is mutual, your Holiness. In fact, Beatrice was asking when we will have the honor of hosting you again.'

The Big Man feigned a polite laugh. He decided to come to the point.

'Beatrice is as generous as she is beautiful. Now listen, Frank, you know what is going on in that dangerous Indian city on the banks of the Ganges, right?'

'Yes, father. I am counting the minutes to the prophesied hour now. Everything we have accomplished over millennia, all the sacrifices, all the cleansing, the corporations, the wars and the epidemics…all for this one final hour. We cannot fail now, father. We must not fail!'

'We will not, Frank,' responded the Big Man from Rome. 'The Maschera is our deadliest asset. He has never failed in the past. And you know what makes him different…what makes him invincible. You know what darkness prowls behind this mask.'

Both Frank Stonefellar and the Big Man knew what was at stake. They both knew that if Vidyut was not stopped, they would lose the final battle. The grand world order they envisioned would scorch to vapor in the heat of what was coming.

They knew if Vidyut succeeded in unfurling the secret of the Black Temple, a force mightier than any other in the universe would descend on planet earth. A force so devastatingly omnipotent, that even their all-powerful global brotherhood would not be able to stand in its way.

Just like the great Dwarka Shastri and Purohit ji, the Big Man and Frank Stonefellar were also convinced.

This battle between Vidyut and the White Mask was going to decide the fate of humanity till the end of time.

Rashtrakuta Kingdom, 762 Ad

PRITHVIVALLABHA

'The riders from Kashi have arrived, my lord.'

The mighty King Kannesvara, better known across the far lands and the seven seas as the indomitable Prithvivallabha, turned to face the general of his army - his *senapati*.

This is the moment I was born for.

Prithvivallabha was the most powerful king in the southern peninsula of the Indian subcontinent. The tales of his valor had travelled far. In a short span of a few years since ascending the throne of the Rashtrakuta dynasty, his armies had crushed numerous formidable opponents like King Sripurusha of Gangavadi and the Shilaharas of Konkan. He had also vanquished the Chalukya ruler Vishnuvardhana.

But it was not his conquests alone that made Prithvival-labha's glory reach dizzy heights both south and north of the Vindhyas. It was also something else.

Prithvivallabha was a great devotee of Lord Shiva. And he was a legendary builder of splendid rock-cut, cave temples.

However, even he did not know that his most profound work was yet to take shape. A monument that would make him battle both man and God, and immortalize his name forever.

'I shall welcome them myself,' said the king, as he wrapped a royal stole around his shoulders and prepared to step out of his residential chamber.

As he stepped into the vast courtyard of his beautiful palace along with his senapati, Prithvivallabha saw the entourage from Kashi enter from the front gate. His heart skipped a beat when he noticed the horse-cart that trudged in the middle of the convoy, surrounded by saffron and crimson-robed warrior-monks of Varanasi's mystical Dev-Raakshasa matth.

He closed his eyes for a moment and muttered a prayer to *Harihara*, a sacred form of the lord that combined the divinity of both Shiva and Vishnu. Prithvivallabha knew that if there was any day in a thousand years when the unity of Shiva and Vishnu was to be celebrated, it was today.

As the horsemen trotted closer and dismounted one after another, the king saw their leader. It was the current reigning matthadheesh of the Dev-Raakshasa clan, the widely revered taantric and saint, Durgadas Shastri. He rode right in front of the horse-cart that carried a massive, ancient trunk made from a strangely unrecognizable alloy.

The two great men looked at each other and smiled. Their mutual admiration and affection was evident to the Rashtrakuta senapati, who was busy welcoming the warrior-monks with scented water and traditional *chiroti* sweets.

'Welcome to my humble abode, O great Durgadas Shastri,' said the king, his hands folded in veneration.

The 8th century matthadheesh dismounted, walked up to Prithvivallabha and placed his hands on the mighty king's shoulders.

'It is a delight to see you again, my old friend. Last time we met, you were a young prince,' said Durgadas Shastri.

'And your hair was black…!' quipped the king, as both men shared a merry laugh.

With the pleasantries over between the two old friends, Durgadas politely refused a tray of refreshments. The matthadheesh drew the king's attention to the very precious cargo he had brought along.

'This is now yours to protect, O king,' he said, pointing to the long, alloy trunk.

Prithvivallabha looked at the trunk, mesmerized. Whatever lay inside the metallic box seemed to cast a spell over the king.

The Rashtrakuta emperor walked slowly towards the horse-cart and gently brushed his fingertips on the alloy trunk, completely overwhelmed. He then placed both his hands and rested his forehead on it.

And wept with tears of devotion.

·||ॐ||·

'But Shastri ji, the Kashi Vishwanath mandir has been described in the *Kashi Khanda* of the *Skanda Purana*...it is meant to be eternal. How can it be destroyed by any force on *Prithvi*?'

They were now in the king's majestic dining hall. Despite a fifty-six-course meal being offered by the emperor, Durga-das Shastri ate only a bowl of rice boiled with milk. Like all his predecessors, he was an ascetic - who had devoted his life to protect the secret of the Black Temple. He also knew, that true to the ancient curse of the Blood River, he was going to die a violent, brutal death.

'The temple is eternal and it shall remain timeless. But it will change its shape and form, Prithvivallabha. A few centuries from now, the shrine will fall. Only to rise again. And again. Eventually the secret of the Black Temple will return to Kashi, O king. It will return when the devta arrives. Until then, you are among the chosen guardians.'

The emperor was listening, hardly able to believe his good fortune. Being granted the opportunity to guard the world's most priceless treasure was something he was willing to die for.

'I will do as you command, O great sage. But I need your wise counsel. Which one, from among my humble shrines, do you deem suitable to be the next Black Temple?'

'None of them,' replied Durgadas plainly.

·||ॐ||·

The king looked bewildered as he saw the matthadheesh get up from his dining chair. If none of his grand temples was worthy of the responsibility he was being asked to shoulder, what was he to do?

He did not have to wait for long. Durgadas Shastri's eyes were sparkling with the excitement of a young alchemist. He looked straight at the brilliant Prithvivallabha and pronounced with a prophetic air.

'Build a temple that is indestructible, O mighty Prithvivallabha! Cut out a chariot for the lord from the hardest rock that you so expertly carve as if it were fresh butter. Sculpt it deep into the bosom of mother Prithvi, a temple so impregnable that the secret of the Black Temple remains protected for centuries to come. Even thousands of years from now men should marvel at your architectural triumph.

And call this spectacular temple by a name that becomes an immortal tribute to your deity, the God of Gods, Lord Shiva Himself.

Call it the *Kailasa* temple of Ellora.'

A TOTALITARIAN GOVERNMENT – PART III

'There is a scientific or you may say evolutionary basis on which the secret brotherhood has planned its ultimate vision spanning millennia. While Constantine was probably not aware of the socio-political alignment of his plan with what was anyway the progression of the human planet, the malicious successors of the Order are well in the know.

As described beautifully by Yuval Noah Harari in his book *Sapiens: A Brief History of Humankind*, the world and the society moving towards unification is a sort of universally accepted anthropological truth. In the year, say, 20,000 BCE the earth was divided into tens of thousands of human bands that lived like hunters and gatherers. By the year

2,000 BCE they were organized into large settlements, were comparatively civilized and had learnt agriculture. These included the Indus Valley region, Mesopotamia, the Egyptian civilization and more. Slowly, trade started to flourish between these settlements and the human race began to get even more unified through the principles, needs and benefits of economics.'

They had now spent over seven hours together. Vidyut was completely spellbound at the narration of the great conspiracy being unfolded page by page as Dwarka Shastri spoke continuously, tirelessly.

'Harappa had well-developed trade relations with the Mesopotamian people, who in turn had commerce links with Egypt. Thereafter, religion emerged as the next social medium for unification. Buddhism and Christianity started to spread rapidly across large parts of Asia and Europe. But despite the flourish and the reach of religion, it was still not the number one consolidating influence. The greatest cohesive force by far was – conquest!

Trade and religion were followed by the empire-building ambition of some of history's most unforgettable individuals and monarchies. Whether it was Alexander, Samudragupta and Genghis Khan or the Roman, Spanish, Portuguese and British empires, the world slowly but surely moved from being a sparsely populated planet with tens of thousands of tribes, to a global map that could be portrayed clearly under a few hundred nations and states. This unification continues even till the most contemporary history. Why, even the Indian sub-continent lay fragmented into 565 princely states till as recently as 1947. Today it is one country, one identity – India. So, you see, Vidyut, the Order believes that what it is doing is simply what nature and destiny expect it to! They think of themselves as modern-day conquerors, simply accelerating what is eventually inevitable!'

'But that is absurd, Baba! The socio-political and geographic evolution you have so deftly encapsulated, took thousands and thousands of years of natural progression to occur. The New World Order, in that comparison, is an infant! Moreover, the amalgamation of so many human societies and civilizations happened not as an outcome of a purposefully chalked-out game plan. It was a complex process involving innumerable factors that defined the journey and landscape of the human race in almost a Darwinian method of natural selection, so to speak. How can anyone in their right senses even dream of manipulating such a behemoth dynamic?'

Dwarka Shastri once again gave a tired, almost dejected smile.

'Those who have already manipulated it successfully several times over, Vidyut.'

·||卐||·

'While the Order routinely morphed into several forms and names, and spread its tentacles into various powerful offshoots including the *Freemasons*, the *Order of the Skull & Bones*, the *Priory of Sion* and the *Rosicrucians*, the most formidable among all were the dreaded *Illuminati*,' continued the great matthadheesh.

Vidyut was a bit concerned now. While he did not want this life-changing discourse to stop, and he was thirstier than ever to know more about the forces that assassinated his beloved father, he did notice that for hours his old Baba had not even taken a sip of water. He had refused all his ayurvedic medicines and was clearly exerting himself too much.

'Baba, we can continue later. You should get some rest now. You have been speaking for hours together,' suggested Vidyut politely.

Dwarka Shastri ignored his great grandson's advice. The matthadheesh's entire life, all his work, each one of the excruciating battles and the horrific sacrifices…everything now danced in front of his eyes. Everything that he lived and breathed for, now stood staring at him.

The prophesied hour was upon them. The terrifying yet much-awaited *guest* had arrived and waited patiently in the dark, sacred cellar below the raakshasa-khannd of the matth.

In a few hours, the planets would start juxtaposing themselves.

This millennia-awaited, this specific, historic Rohini Nakshatra was about to arrive.

·||ॐ||·

'Consider a few strange facts about history's greatest tectonic-shifts. Let's start with the Bolshevik movement or simply the Russian Revolution of 1917 that led to the fall of the Tsarist regime and established the Soviet Union. As we know, the Bolsheviks followed the ideology propounded by Karl Marx and stormed the Tsar's palace to wrest control of the country. But do you know, Vidyut, till just four years before the great revolution, the Bolsheviks were nothing more than a small political unit with no real influence? Then how did they suddenly emerge as such a formidable force that they toppled the all-powerful Tsar himself? What helped them achieve such meteoric rise? *Who* helped them?

Let us take an even older example. Let us delve a little into the French Revolution – a world-event that has inspired as much romantic literature and theatre as it has enthused revolutionaries of all times. But what did the French Revolution really achieve in the immediate term? It led to what is today known as the *Reign of Terror* and massive loss of human life. And yet, what if I tell you that in the year 1784, a full five years before the revolution actually broke out in France, a secret letter from Adam Weishaupt, the Founder of the Illuminati, to a man named Maximillien Robespierre, detailed out how the revolution needs to be systematically brought about? Vidyut – the French Revolution was not simply an uprising of the poor and the exploited against their rulers. It was a planned socio-political project engineered by the Illuminati!'

There was stunned silence in the room. Even Purohit ji did not know the intricate details of the Illuminati's work on profound world-events like the emergence of the Bolsheviks and the French Revolution. Finally, after a few seconds, Vidyut spoke.

'Who are the Illuminati, Baba? How are they connected to

the New World Order?'

Dwarka Shastri took a deep breath, and began the most mysterious chapter of the bloodcurdling tale that he was unwrapping layer by layer.

The Marshes of Aryavarta, 1699 BCE

THE ARRIVAL OF PRACHANDA

Satyavrata Manu stood leaning over the design charts spread out on a makeshift wooden table that was built by sawing a massive tree trunk in half. The charts were made on hardened cotton sheets and detailed out the structural plans for various sections of the Ark. They were gathered in a semi-built cabin of the giant-boat. This secluded area served as Manu's control bay for the gargantuan project.

Manu's long hair was tied behind his head in a braid, and large, circular *kundals* dangled from his ears. On Tara's insistence, he wore kohl in his eyes, which accentuated their burning intensity. Manu looked every bit the ancient priest-king that he was going to be remembered as till eternity.

'This does not appear to be right,' he said to Somdutt, who was standing across the upturned tree-trunk, studying another chart.

'What, Manu...?' enquired Somdutt.

Over the last few grueling months, Manu had learnt the art and science of shipbuilding at a furious pace. He spent several nights under a flickering burner, studying the texts recommended by Somdutt. He sat attentively in the sessions conducted by the chief architect with his team, and took notes. He spent hours understanding the nuances of Vedic mathematics and architecture from Somdutt and asked hundreds of questions. So much so that in a short span of a few months, even the chief architect had begun to value Manu's structural inputs for the construction of the great Ark. It was anyway something that was far beyond the imagination and intellectual capacity of any one human brain.

'There is too much cable being used in the stern rudder. So much bronze will increase the weight of the rudder radically, making it impossible to maneuver. Remember there is provision for only fifteen hundred men to pull from either side.'

'Hmm...I think you are right. What if we increase the number of masts and reduce dependence on...'

Before Somdutt could complete his sentence, a soldier of the fish-folk came in with a message Manu did not expect.

'*Pranaam*, Satyavrata,' said the messenger. 'A very large armed contingent is approaching the great Ark. And the riders from our outposts bring disturbing news.'

Manu's fist tightened around the handle of his sword.

'And what is that disturbing news?'

The soldier hesitated for a moment before breaking the news.

'It is the asuras.'

·||ॐ||·

'They don't seem to be attacking,' said Dhruv, as they stood atop the Ark and observed the incoming asura troops.

Dhruv was right. The asuras trudged towards the Ark at a slow pace. While all of them were armed, none were weapons-ready. And from what Tara, Dhruv and Manu could make out from a distance, the asuras seemed to be tired. Very tired.

'Ask our fighters to be ready. But not a single arrow should be unleashed unless the asuras attack first,' Tara instructed the commanders of the Ark's armed corps.

'And request the kitchens to prepare a lot of hot broth. Looks like our guests are going to need it,' added Manu, as the fight commanders prepared to leave.

·||ॐ||·

Prachanda looked impressive even in his fatigued state. He rode at the head of his huge platoon, and while he failed to appear as gloriously regal as his magnificent predecessor

Sura, he compensated for it by looking a lot less arrogant. A lot less cruel.

Manu stood a mile from the great Nauka now to receive the visitors who, it was clear by now, came in peace. He was accompanied by his inseparable friend Dhruv and his trusted counsellor Pundit Somdutt. Twenty choicest warriors of the fish-folk stood behind them, just as a contingency arrangement for any unexpected ambush.

The reputation of the asuras travelled far ahead of them.

And except Prachanda, no one at Manu's Ark knew anything about the last battle of Vivasvan Pujari.

·‖ॐ‖·

They now sat in one of the large halls of the Great Ark, on rough mats made of animal hide. Satyavrata Manu knew he needed as many allies as he could muster. By now the Ark was believed to be the ultimate savior by one and all, far and wide. It was the accepted last hope and the last boat for humanity. It was clear that pralay was going to inundate all of Aryavarta. And the proverbial pirates were watching. They wanted to snatch this boat.

Having the asuras on his side would mean a lot more defense muscle for Manu's Ark. He knew a great battle was looming. Therefore, welcoming the king of the asuras with open arms came naturally to the son of Surya. Slowly but surely, Satyavrata was also learning diplomacy.

·‖卐‖·

The dampness of the wooden walls and pillars was palpable. And just like every single corner of the behemoth, the ceiling dripped continuously from hundreds of places in the giant hall.

Prachanda was in a state of complete stupefaction. Beholding the Great Ark from both far as well as from close was a life-altering experience. That something so massive could exist was in itself a jolt on the senses. On top of that being asked to believe that it had been built by humans and not some celestial titans, was a nerve-wracking ordeal.

The new emperor of the mighty asuras looked up and down, stared into all directions, admiring the scale of what he was seeing. He was still in one of the very low rungs of the colossal boat. Already the small, round windows brought in shrieking winds that were freezing the wise asura and his commanders to their bones. He dreaded to imagine what it would be like at the highest deck of this great vessel, way above the clouds, amidst the screaming skies.

·‖卐‖·

'Please begin the humble meal, O Prachanda. While most of us are *shaakahaari*, the meat has been prepared especially for you and your men,' said Manu, as he invited the asura king to break bread with him.

Prachanda was amazed to notice the resemblance between father and son. Not just the same strong jawline and the identical sparkle of the eyes, Satyavrata Manu even spoke with the same authoritative humility as his magnificent father did.

The meal was simple, and yet quite a spread in the given wretched times. Prachanda and his men dug their fingers into the fresh rice cooked with chunks of goat meat and spices. After their harrowing journey through the cold crevices of the mighty mountains of the north-west, this hot meal came as a life-saver for the asura and his commanders.

Even as he was about to feed himself with the first morsel of meat and rice, Prachanda stopped.

'Is anything the matter, my friend? Why do you hold yourself back?' asked Manu.

Prachanda spoke without hesitation.

'What about my soldiers, Satyavrata? They are famished and weak after the long, grueling...'

Even before Prachanda could complete his sentence, Manu intervened.

'Do not worry about them, O king. As we speak, they are being served a hot broth of meat, vegetables and rice. Once they have eaten, the Ark's physicians will tend to the weak and the sick.'

Prachanda smiled and gratefully filled his mouth with the piping hot meat and rice.

'You are just as kind and as righteous as your great father was, O king Manu. You even speak in the same manner!'

At first Manu nodded in polite response, but in a moment, he stopped chewing and looked up. Something was not right here.

'Pardon me, O asura king…but how could you have met or spoken in person with my father? He succumbed to his wounds soon after he was tortured at the Great Bath…'

Prachanda appeared bewildered, as he looked around at the men seated over the meal, before exclaiming confidently -

'That is not true, Satyavrata. Vivasvan Pujari did not die at the Great Bath.

I was witness to his last, his greatest battle that changed the course of destiny.'

Banaras, 2017

9/11

'In 1776 the Bavarian philosopher Adam Weishaupt founded the Illuminati. While the earlier principles of the Illuminati were to reject the bondage and social hierarchies that came with the orthodox Roman catholic church, soon the mystical society started drawing members from the richest and most influential families of that time.

It is recorded in the secret chronicles of the society that are available only to a select few, that members of the Illuminati came from families that remain among the richest in the world till date, including even the powerful Medici of Florence and the Stonefellar family. As the Illuminati grew, it became clear that their goal was to establish a totalitarian world-government by any means available. In 1972, the

American economics professor Antony Sutton wrote in his work *The Best Enemy Money Can Buy* that the Illuminati controlled and manipulated every single war and civil unrest of the 21st century, including the rise of the Soviet Union as well as that of Adolf Hitler. He claimed that every conflict from Kosovo to the Arab Spring, was funded and maneuvered by the powerful secret society using its fronts on Wall Street. And that it was the Illuminati banking dynasties of the US that actually supplied ninety percent of the Soviet Union's military technology to the Communist state, thereby unleashing what was going to convert the world into a war-economy for the next three decades – *the Cold War.*'

The great matthadheesh now indicated that he needed a glass of water. Vidyut quickly got up, filled his Baba's glass from the mud *suraahi* and handed it over to the grand old man.

'Their *modus operandus* was complex but effective – create social unrests in countries, make them weaponized, build distrust and tension between governments and the people, fund opposing factions with money and arms, cause civil wars, send in the so-called peacekeeping troops, ensure that peace never returns to the regions and eventually - coffers of bankers, pharma companies, oil barons and manufacturers of arms and ammunition keep brimming over by hundreds of billions of dollars. And together this rapidly prospering brotherhood goes on tightening its grip on the world!'

·‖卐‖·

'What about 9/11, Baba? You mentioned something about the heinous act of terrorism that shook up not only New

York city or the United States, but the entire world. It is hard for me to believe that the Illuminati had anything to do with it.'

Dwarka Shastri nodded. He was in deep thought. He knew the gravity of the topic and its implications.

After a few moments of pause, he began cautiously.

'The American people are highly educated and well exposed to the modern world, as compared to perhaps some of the lesser developed countries. And despite their deep belief in democracy, they are strangely susceptible to being brainwashed and manipulated. For centuries, they have debunked the Illuminati and the New World Order as nothing more than conspiracy theories. But they forget that in the year 1798 it was one of their own Founding Fathers, George Washington himself, who wrote a letter to his successors warning them of the growing influence of the Illuminati. Would someone as accomplished and responsible as George Washington, believe baseless theories unless he had hard evidence?'

'He would not,' responded Purohit ji, who was himself finding several revelations around the Order for the first time today. Dwarka Shastri had saved the most intricate details of the global conspiracy for the prophesied devta who was supposed to end it all.

Or was he?

·||卐||·

'There are several conspiracy theories about the reality behind 9/11, and I see no merit in talking about all those. So, I will simply ask you a few questions, Vidyut, and you must answer those to the best of your ability.'

'Of course, Baba,' replied the devta.

'Which is the richest institution in the whole world, Vidyut?'

Vidyut did not expect this question, but responded nevertheless.

'Cannot really say for sure, Baba...maybe the company Google? Or Microsoft? Or perhaps Walmart or Amazon?'

'No. It is the government of the United States.'

'Oh...of course...' said Vidyut, scratching his head.

'What do you think is one of the greatest investments or expenses of the US government outside its own soil?' asked Dwarka Shastri.

'Err...funding its military presence in regions where it is at war, like when in Iraq or Afghanistan. Or maybe in sponsoring its global military infrastructure under organizations like NATO?'

'In short...for waging war, correct?'

'Yes, Baba.'

'Who approves these war-spends?'

'The US senate, I should think...'

'Excellent. Now tell me, my son...where does all this money

go? I mean, do you know how much the battle-gear of a single US soldier costs? Let me tell you. It costs about 17,000 US dollars to equip one infantryman of the US military. Close to 2 million US soldiers fought in the Iraq and Afghanistan wars. Do the mathematics, my son. Can you imagine the purchase size of such equipment when the US goes all out into war? Do you know that the American tax-payer spent around 4.5 billion dollars in just the air-conditioning of the US army barracks in Iraq? So, we are speaking about not billions, but trillions of dollars being spent on war.'

Vidyut nodded thoughtfully. He was wondering how his great grandfather knew details of US military expenditure, sitting here in the Dev-Raakshasa matth!

'You did not answer my question, Vidyut. Where does all this money go?'

'Well, it probably all goes to the manufacturers and distributors of arms and ammunition, besides suppliers of other military equipment.'

'Yes. Billions of dollars go into the bank accounts of the arms lobby. Billions to private security companies like Black Sky. Billions and billions more to manufacturers of everything from fighter jets to night-vision glasses to mosquito nets!

Now tell me this, Vidyut - who elects the US senate?'

This one was easy.

'The voters of America,' replied Vidyut with a confident shrug.

Dwarka Shastri was happy at the speed with which this discussion was progressing.

'Therefore, you would agree that the US senate would be answerable to the people of America about state spending, would you not?'

'Yes, Baba...like the government of any democracy should be.'

'Absolutely right. But have you ever thought about what cause can be so drastic, so heart-wrenching...that it gives an elected government the moral right and public support for unbridled drain of the state's money into the treasure-chests of private defense contractors?'

Vidyut could not fully understand what the matthadheesh was asking.

Dwarka Shastri continued. His excitement as well as his fury were palpable.

'The crumbling of the World Trade Center sent ripples into the American psyche. It carved a deep, permanent scar...of fear, of hate and of retribution. In one stroke, it rallied the entire country behind backing an indescribably expensive war against an enemy that no one really knew.'

The grand old man was relieved to see an expression of sudden clarity on Vidyut's face.

'Why did I not see this before, Baba...? 9/11 was the greatest and most inhuman blood-sacrifice made by the Illuminati - to facilitate history's greatest financial heist!'

The Marshes of Aryavarta, 1699 BCE

THE NIGHT OF THE BLUE FIRE

They waited for their king.

A king who had felt the arrow of betrayal pierce through him.

Deceived not by a scheming courtier. Let down not by an ambitious second-in-line to the throne.

He felt horribly betrayed by not one, not two...but three of the people he trusted the most in this world.

His late father's virtuous friend Pundit Somdutt.

His very own Tara. His beloved Tara.

And Matsya.

Matsya lied to me!

·||ॐ||·

Leaving behind his recent guests, Prachanda and the asuras, leaving behind all his friends and counsels, Manu had held Tara by her arm and had walked away towards a relatively vacant section of the Ark. They had much to talk about.

Tara sat on a stone stool, her face buried in her palms, and she wept.

Manu stood at a distance, looking aimlessly into the horizon from a high deck of the Great Ark.

'I lied because I wanted to save you from becoming a monster, Manu!' screamed Tara, her voice still breaking in sobs.

Manu did not flinch. As if he had forgotten about her presence altogether. He was in a miserable state. Tears rolled down his cheeks as he pictured his wounded, heartbroken father combatting Sura and his elite troops – all alone. His heart wept when he imagined the *Rakt-Dhara*, the Blood River devouring his beloved Baba. He wondered how he would face his mother Sanjna in the afterlife.

There was more. The emotional wringing that Manu felt stabbing into his soul was being further tormented by the other horrifying details that Prachanda had shared. The new asura king had informed Manu about the dark prophecies of the great sages, as well as the haunting curses of the Saraswati, of *Sara Maa*.

·‖卐‖·

Manu could now almost hear the dark curses one after the other. He could imagine his father, broken, alone and crest-fallen on that fateful night of the Blue Fire.

First, the curses of the Blood River rang menacingly in his mind –

"The Saptarishi loved you like one of their own. I loved you like a son. The Gods bestowed you with divinity and you bore it with grace and worthiness - until your hate became your undoing, O devta! And with your corruption comes the great culling! The Asuras have sinned beyond measure. The Harappans have sinned as a collective. Kings have sinned and priests have sinned. Demons have sinned and devtas have sinned. Humankind compels the universe to unleash the cosmic cleansing! I shall forever forsake this land of immeasurable immorality and return to the holy womb of Mother Prithvi. The Saraswati, the River of the Wise, will fade into legend. But not before She unleashes her final punishment on those who have wronged her.

Bewaaaaare...PRALAY...ESHHYATI...!

THE GREAT DELUGE...IS COMING...!"

Satyavrata Manu could not help but recreate the next curse in his imagination. He remembered what Prachanda had told him in great detail by now. He remembered how the rakt-dhaara was not done with just one curse. Her powerful, echoing voice continued to lacerate Manu -

"Humanity holds in the heart of every individual the potential to become a God. Yet, instead of seeking spiritual salvation within and without, human kind uses its gifts to betray, murder, plunder and avenge. This is the fate your species has chosen! So be it! The Gods will never release you from your hateful destiny. The serpents of violence and bloodshed will never loosen their stranglehold on mankind, which shall kill and destroy each other in the name of the very Gods it has betrayed today! Never shall carnage and butchery leave your side. This is my curse, O fallen devta! Humankind shall hear the shrieks of boundless suffering till the end of time!

I CURSE YOU! I CURSE YOU ALL!"

Tara was now staring at Manu with red, teary eyes. She knew he was not just enraged. He never went quiet like this. Not with her. Not even on the rare occasions when he let anger cloud over him.

By now, Satyavrata Manu was almost transported to the night of the Blue Fire, to the scene of the raging battle between his great father and the forces of the demon-king Sura. He could almost see that horrible night unfolding in front of his eyes...

Just like the five sons of the Saraswati, the cindering sixth sage now spoke, from the heart of the blue embers.

"You make a feeble attempt to stop these butchers with mere words, O devta! And that when you are the possessor of the mighty cosmic weapon granted to you by the Gods! That when you bear the great Rat-na-Maru! So be it.

Just the manner in which you have watched the divine Sages burn one after the other on this fateful night, fate will watch your lineage perish violently, son after son, generation after generation. I curse you and your entire bloodline, O fallen devta...

Every single son of your descent will die a death as violent and as horrible as the spectacle today!

I CURSE YOU! AND YOUR ENTIRE BLOOD-LINE!

THIS CURSE SHALL LAST TILL THE END OF TIME!"

Before the sixth Saptarishi softly erupted into ashes, his voice spoke for the last time...and this time with more pity than fury.

"You have turned truly blind, Vivasvan. A supreme human that could once gaze deep into the souls of men and into the sands of time, is today oblivious to his own child.

Your son lives, O tarnished Surya! And it shall be he, who will see the first rays of morning after the Great Deluge subsides.

Manu Pujari...will be the protector of all Creation!

AND SHALL BE KNOWN AND IMMORTALISED AS SATYAVRATA MANU...THE GUARDIAN OF ETERNAL TRUTH!

We pity you, you unfortunate father, you corrupted half-God!"

·‖ॐ‖·

Manu felt he heard Tara's voice from afar, only to realize she was standing right next to him, her fingers clasped around his arm, begging him to forgive her. He had gone into a trance. A trance of guilt, of sorrow and of fear. The curses were all coming true, one after another. Aryavarta had burnt in the fire of bloodshed ever since. If these haunting prophesies had come true to the last word, the ones to follow would also not fail. His own bloodline, and the rest of humanity – were condemned to the merciless claws of the Blood River's curse.

As he slowly came back to the present and felt the chill of the cold, moist wind on his face, he felt Tara kissing him gently, repeatedly. She pecked him softly on his jaw and neck. She was whispering into his ears with love that could melt the cold heart of even the pitiless Gods that had unleashed pralay on mankind.

'You are mine, Manu...forever! I could not have let you go. The furnace of vengeance would have burnt you and all of us to ashes. Matsya knew this to be true. What he did, what I did...was only to keep hope alive for all these hundreds of thousands who depend on you for everything, Manu.

Please forgive me for saying this, O mighty Satyavrata...but I saw what the great Surya had become. I was there in the Rain of Blood. I could not let you walk on the same path.

I could not let you become a demon.'

Banaras, 2017

THE COLD EYES OF DEATH

Aslam Biker watched from a distance, through one of the large glass windows. It was nearly mid-night.

The entire gymnasium of the sparkling Banaras hotel had been reserved for the Maschera Bianca.

The entrance of the hotel health-club had been sealed and was guarded by the heavily armed fighters of the European crime lord.

The White Mask liked to work on his icy mind, his indestructible body and his dark soul in complete solitude.

·||ॐ||·

It was only at this late hour that Vidyut found the time to catch up on his much-needed workout. After a long day with his Baba and Purohit ji, and an onslaught of nerve-wracking information, the devta sought refuge in the endorphins his body would release and relax him.

He worked out alone on the terrace of his living quarters, being assisted only by Sonu once in a while. His devoted follower helped him with everything – right from bringing water bottles to helping his devta lift heavy weights in the absence of any support equipment.

Vidyut's magnificent body gleamed under a film of its own sweat against the silver moonlight.

·||ॐ||·

That one man could lift so much iron was an unbelievable sight for Aslam. While he was a regular at the gym himself given the demanding needs of his violent career, never had he seen such a sight.

The Maschera lay on the sophisticated bench, wearing nothing but a black, Israeli Krav Maga lower. His torso looked like it was made of pale white steel. Grasping the chrome rod right above his chest he pumped weights that would otherwise need a heavy crane to lift. His veins appeared ready to burst as blood gathered in his head due to the inhuman strain. But the White Mask went on.

For some reason Aslam Biker felt he would vomit. It was a strangely grotesque sight. This was all abnormal, all very repulsive. What started as an impressive workout schedule, was turning into a display of superhuman, unnatural physical might.

·‖❀‖·

Every new day brought with it something unique that dazzled Sonu about his devta.

Sonu was no stranger to physical endurance and exertion. He was a fit young man himself who practiced hours in the matth *vyayaam-shaala* every morning. He was also a regular at the Banaras *akhadaas* where he observed *pahalvaan* or wrestlers that were strong as bulls.

But something was different about his Vidyut dada. Something magnetic, something almost divine.

And Sonu was not the only one watching the muscular grace of Vidyut. Someone else was too.

From her own terrace a few paces away, Naina could not take her eyes away from this golden man. She remembered his masculine fragrance. She nearly felt his soft lips on hers once again.

At that hour of the night, at that very moment - she needed him. She needed her man, her Vidyut!

While fear was watching the White Mask, it was love that blanketed the last devta.

·||卐||·

It was as if Aslam Biker's feet had been nailed to where he stood. He could not move. Despite the madness going on behind the window he stood staring at, something urged him to stay. To watch what unfolds.

The Maschera was now pounding on a massive punching bag that hung in one corner of the gym area. His hands were taped and he began striking the heavy bag in a slow but practiced rhythm. By now he was drenched in sweat and his beautiful blonde hair was thrown back.

And then he increased the pace. What followed was almost like a machine-gun fire of punches on the heavy, red-leather bag. The young, green-eyed, screw-driver murderer from Milan had grown up to become, among other things, an extraordinarily skilled fighter. He was firing his fists at a pace that made Aslam dizzy.

In a matter of a couple of minutes, the gangster from Mumbai noticed another bizarre sight. Even through the thick plaster taped around the fists of the Maschera, his knuckles had turned pink with blood. As moments passed, the hands of the White Mask were red with his own bleeding, but he kept striking the leather bag – as if he felt no pain.

As if he were not human at all.

·||卐||·

Vidyut was now in the second segment of his drill.

What Naina, who was a little far away, and Sonu, who stood right there, could not believe was the prowess Vidyut had over *Ashtaannga Yoga*. After his rigorous freehand and weight training, the devta had now begun the softer yet equally demanding end of his regimen.

But that was not all. Ashtaannga yoga, which is a system of yoga recorded by the Vamana Rishi in the ancient manuscript of the *Yoga Korunta*, was not the only form of healing and training that Vidyut was practicing. He was beautifully combining, as Naina could tell, Ashtaannga yoga with *Qigong* (chee-gong) – the Chinese science of mental and physical nurturing.

Moving his hands in slow circles, it was as if Vidyut was performing a choreographed stage-show, his brute physical strength matched equally by the grace of his yogic movements.

After a while, Vidyut sat down to meditate. His initial post-workout panting slowly transformed into peaceful, rhythmic breathing. The cool Kashi breeze emanating from the nearby Ganga, caused Vidyut's long, beautiful hair to flutter.

His expression slowly began to resemble that of an accomplished, young sage. He had almost an unnoticeable, a beautiful smile on his meditating face.

To those who loved him, he looked every bit like a God.

·||ॐ||·

The Maschera Bianca now sat in the center of the massive, brightly-lit, luxurious gymnasium of the palace hotel.

He sat on the floor, doing what seemed like some form of penance. Some evil, deranged form. Unlike what Aslam Biker would have expected from a man who was meditating, the Maschera had a terrifying scowl on his face. This form of concentration reminded Biker vaguely of Japanese Samurai meditation. But it was not as pious as what the Samurai practiced. It was something different. *Ninja, maybe?* - thought the Mumbai don. By now he could only see one side of the Maschera's expression.

Even as the White Mask mumbled some chants that Aslam could not hear from where he stood, the Mumbai *bhai* decided to leave. He had had enough. He was grateful that the Maschera had not seen him peeping into what was supposed to be his personal time.

As he prepared to leave, Aslam's heart froze. From the side angle that he could see, the White Mask had suddenly opened his eyes.

Even before Aslam could move a muscle, the Mask turned to look at him.

From what he saw, Aslam could swear they were not human eyes.

The Mask's green eyes had completely vanished. The open eyes that stared at Aslam through the window – were as white as a grave shroud.

They were the cold eyes of death.

The White Mask looked every bit like the devil.

The Marshes of Aryavarta, 1699 BCE

THE PUJARI BLOODLINE

'I have a message for you from your father, Satyavrata,' said Prachanda.

Upon the asura king's request, Manu was now giving a guided tour of the great Ark to Prachanda.

He had forgiven Tara. He understood why she did what she had done. He loved her too much to be angry with her for long anyway. He had also pardoned Somdutt for hiding the truth about his father from him. He was much too indebted to Somdutt. He could find a glimpse of his great father in the chief architect's face.

But he had not forgiven Matsya. He knew Tara and Somdutt were, after all, ordinary mortals. They could not have disobeyed the word of Matsya. They could not have outdebated him. But Matsya was God. He could have done things differently.

If he wanted, he could have let me meet my father one last time. He could have let us say goodbye.

Satyavrata Manu's bitterness towards Matsya was nothing but an outcome of his boundless love for the magnificent fish-man. It was just the kind of irritable yearning a child feels for a merchant-father who is away at sea for months.

Only in this case, Matsya *was* the sea.

·||ॐ||·

'What message, O mighty Prachanda...what did my father say?' asked Manu eagerly. Any word from his beloved father was a precious gift for this young priest-king.

Prachanda stopped and turned to Manu.

'The only solace your great father had in his last moments, was that he knew you will live to see the other side of pralay. The last Saptarishi had assured him. He had also pronounced that you will be the savior of mankind in this final hour.'

Manu sighed and shook his head. He did not know what to say, what to believe. For now, pralay seemed undefeatable.

'We will see what happens, O king of asuras. Please do share my father's message,' urged Manu.

'The Surya was confident that besides taking tens of thousands of fellow humans on the Ark, you will also save several species of plants and animals. He had no doubt that you will carry the essential herbs, the yarns, the seeds and the alloys. But he specifically asked me to convey to you that your greatest duty is to carry the wisdom, the knowledge of our world to the new dawn of humanity.'

Satyavrata Manu was not very clear what his father meant. But he was determined to go to any length to fulfil his late father's last wish. His final commandment.

'I am very aware of the critical role our ancient and present knowledge will play in the coming era, O king of asuras. Which is why our cargo includes the most essential of books, maps and scriptures. We are also taking with us the most learned among scholars, alchemists, physicians and architects. The Saptarishi are with us and so are the...'

'This is not what your father meant, Manu,' interrupted Prachanda, his hand up in the air, indicating that Manu should stop talking.

After a moment's pause, he continued.

'Will the current scriptures that you carry, narrate the saga of the Great Flood, of pralay, to future generations?'

'No, they would not,' replied Manu thoughtfully.

'Will they elucidate the story of Matsya?'

'No...'

'Let alone the others. Will the books you carry even have the story of Satyavrata Manu, of Satrupa and of the Great Ark?'

Manu was silent.

Prachanda now spelled out what Vivasvan Pujari had asked him to convey to his son Manu...word by word.

'You must write the scriptures anew, O Satyavrata.
Write about the ancients.
Write about the present.
Write what is good and what is bad.
Pen down what is righteous and what is depraved.
Write the stories of the Gods and the tales of the demons.
Write about Vishnu and write about Pashupati.
Write about the Surya and write about the Saraswati.

What you write today shall remain immortal, O Satyavrata.
What you write will be the sacred Shastras...
...to be studied and worshipped by mankind till the end of time!'

Manu's eyes were brimming with tears. He could almost hear his father say these words. With folded hands, he bowed to Prachanda, who for now seemed to embody his beloved father.

'If you think I am capable of such an arduous undertaking, if you believe I can document the holy *Shastras*, then I shall do as you command, father...' he said.

'I shall write the Shastras. *Yoga-shastra, Nyaya-shastra, Dharma-shastra, Vastu-shastra, Moksha-shastra, Rasayana-shastra, Kavya-shastra* and numerous others. My descendants will add on to these scriptures, generation after generation.

And so that none of us ever forget this sacred promise

I make to you, from today we shall be known not by the bloodline name of Pujari, but by the title of Shastri!

My children and their children will forever be known as the authors of the Shastras.

They shall forever be called Shastri.'

Banaras, 2017

NAINA & VIDYUT

It was nearly 2 am.

Vidyut was physically and mentally exhausted.

Yet, sleep was hard to come by.

He had discovered a lot during that day about the Illuminati, about the New World Order and their ghastly grip on the planet and its people.

But he still did not know exactly *who* killed his father. *Why* they killed his father.

·||ॐ||·

After a long shower and a light meal that had followed his workout, Vidyut had retired for the day.

He was tossing and turning in his bed when he heard a faint knock on his door.

Vidyut got up and opened the old, loud, iron latch.

It was Naina.

Despite all that stood between them, despite all the right and all the wrong, Vidyut and Naina could not pull away from each other's heart and mind. Naina knew Vidyut was spoken for. But her beating heart overpowered her logic, numbing all her senses. Vidyut knew he belonged to Damini. But something about Naina made him forget all reason, all propriety...even all divinity.

And yet, barring a moment or two of human weakness, it never made him forget Damini.

Naina wore a loose black shirt, that was buttoned down more than usual. Her eyes sparkled and her skin glowed like pearls. She was delighted to find Vidyut without his vest. She stepped forward and pressed her lips on his chest, keeping them there for a while. She then started kissing him repeatedly all over his shoulders, chest and neck.

Vidyut was on the verge of picking her up in his arms and taking her to bed. She was simply irresistible. A woman of her beauty, deeply in love and burning with passion – it would have taken a devta to refuse her.

Vidyut was a devta.

After a few brief moments of giving in, Vidyut gently pulled away.

Naina did not seem to notice. She stepped forward, shut the door behind her and flung her arms around her devta.

'Make love to me, Vidyut...' she whispered into his ear, as she bit into his earlobe softly.

Vidyut slowly held her wrists and broke her grip around him. Even before she could react, he looked into her eyes and pulled her into a warm embrace.

That was the most the devta could give Naina this night. She needed a lot more. So did he.

But Vidyut had made a promise to Damini, 3,700 years ago.

Vivasvan had made a promise to Sanjna.

They were going to crossover to the other side – together.

·||ॐ||·

Naina was not an ordinary woman.

She knew how to handle adversity. She could combat villains head-on. She had known loss when her parents had left her forever. She knew how to tackle hate and fight demons.

But she did not know how to handle rejection.

Not from Vidyut.

She sat huddled into a chair, embarrassed and broken at being turned down by the only man she had ever really wanted.

'I should go!' she exclaimed and got up, wiping the tears flowing on to her cheeks with her beautiful fingers.

'Don't go, Naina…' said Vidyut, as he held her by the hand. 'We need to speak, don't we?'

Naina nodded. She knew there was too much that bound them together. Too much that could not be left unsaid, unheard.

·‖ॐ‖·

'You do know if Damini was not the love of my life, nothing could have kept me away from you, Naina? You do know that, right?'

'What do you want from me, Vidyut?' retorted Naina. She was not prepared to rank second. This was not some contest for her.

Vidyut sat at Naina's feet, caressing her hand lovingly.

'I want you to be my best friend forever, Naina. With Bala gone, I am left alone. I need a friend I can trust. I need a friend I can love…'

Naina smiled, tears still rolling down her stunning face.

'You know what, Vidyut…Damini is really lucky. Not everyone finds someone who loves them so passionately, so uncompromisingly…'

She was looking straight into his eyes, pain brimming over

with every teardrop that fell.

Vidyut bent forward and kissed her on her cheek.

'No, I am really lucky. Not everyone has someone as gorgeous as you falling for them!'

Naina shut her eyes, clearly in more longing, more emotional suffering than she could bear.

She then opened her eyes, got her usual naughty tinge back into them, and spoke with an air of disdain.

'Falling for you? Whatever made you believe that Mr. Half-human, half...'

She could not complete her sentence. Naina fell into Vidyut's arms and cried till her tears went dry.

The Marshes of Aryavarta, 1699 BCE

GUPTACHAR

Prachanda and his prime commanders were in a daze.

They had been walking for seven hours now, and had still not covered even a small fraction of the Ark's expanse. The giant vessel looked clumsy, creaky and ready to disintegrate at the assault of even a minor wave of the great deluge.

And yet somehow it looked majestic, impregnable and the only boat that could withstand the doomsday flood that was engulfing all of known prithvi.

'The bottom most section or the bilge is where we store all the heavy material that would normally sustain comparatively less damage because of the dankness and the humidity. This underwater section holds ballast cargo such as copper weapons and the big serpents and reptiles! Our largest reservoirs for fish and ocean-creatures are also placed in this lower section.'

Manu was describing various parts of the Ark in a matter-of-fact manner. For the listeners who were absolutely new to this wonder of engineering, it was all like a fantasy story! Copper weapons with reptiles! Ocean-creatures on a boat?

Satyavrata had been speaking for hours. He now gestured to his friend Dhruv to take over the guided tour.

'The hinged rudder in the front of the Great Ark is made from ten thousand oaks. Each rudder of the boat has inset handles and rope levers for one thousand and five hundred men to pull on either side. We have not been able to test this, but all mathematics suggests that the weight of the rudders below water would get lowered significantly - enough to be maneuvered by this unit of men.'

Dhruv was visibly proud of what they had built.

॥ ॐ ॥

Even someone as brave as Prachanda was afraid.

The rope ladders that Tara, Somdutt and scores of their soldiers were so simply using to climb up and down the steep hull of the Ark, seemed nothing less than death-traps to the asura-king and his men. One slip meant not just death. It meant falling freely for so long that every thought around the resulting impact could be contemplated with ease. The dark clouds and incessant rain made the ascent and descent even trickier. It was like climbing down into a smoky, freezing hell.

And then Prachanda saw Manu and Dhruv. They were simply using ropes to glide up and down the immeasurably steep hull. Both of them grabbed two separate ropes. Using their legs, they pushed themselves into the air and, like skilled mountaineers, slid down in long, expert moves. In a matter of moments, they had vanished far below into the mist.

Prachanda and his men had no choice but to begin climbing down the rope ladder that, when compared to Manu and Dhruv's mode of transportation, now looked like a luxury.

As they reached one of the lower decks, relieved at not having lost any man to the ordeal, the asuras continued their wide-eyed discovery of this architectural marvel.

'The seventeen levels below the main deck are all meant to accommodate the living quarters of our people. There are twelve hundred cabins on each level. Four people to one cabin gives enough room for everyone to stretch their legs and get sleep. Women and children will be rotated in two shifts. The able-bodied men will be scheduled into three shifts, so each man gets at least eight hours of rest in a day. In this manner, we hope to be able to accommodate close to two hundred thousand souls. Just that the cabins will be nothing more than a box of sorts with one small window. The trouble is, we do not know how long it is going to take for the great flood to subside. It could be months...years...,' Dhruv continued.

Prachanda was listening carefully. He was wondering if kings were going to be offered independent cabins. He quickly rubbished the thought. Every cabin meant four lives. Four human lives!

·||ॐ||·

Prachanda poured himself a generous helping of the wine he had brought with him. He offered a glass to Manu, who politely declined. Dhruv decided to give the asura king company and happily accepted the goblet. And then several of them.

But the conversation was not going to be as merry as Dhruv had expected.

'There is a reason I have travelled all the way across the mountains with so many of my men, Satyavrata. As you know, the *guptachar* or spy network of the asuras is very strong. We have penetrated every tribe and every village across the badlands where the bandit warlords rule with their savage militia. They have always been cruel brigands who attack, loot and murder whoever they find. I have heard they have made several attempts to overpower even your supply caravans. But recently, a far more worrying phenomenon has been reported by my spies.'

'And what is that, O mighty king?' asked Somdutt, who was also present on the table.

'In the last few months the spies have been seeing something they had never witnessed before. The villages and encampments of the bandit warlords are being visited by unexpected emissaries,' said Prachanda, as he gulped down his glass of wine.

'Whose emissaries, king Prachanda?'

This time it was Manu who asked the question. He was dreading the answer. In a moment, he realized that his fear was not misplaced.

'Emissaries of the daityas, Manu. The barbarian Nara-Munda is sending messengers to all the bandit tribes. This is extremely disturbing because this has never happened before. The daityas and the bandits have always been at loggerheads. But now things are changing…'

'What purpose can this solve? What does that beast Nara-Munda want from the bandits?' asked Dhruv, unable to comprehend what both Manu and Prachanda had well understood.

Manu turned to his friend.

'They are burying their hatchets just to fight against us. Nara-Munda wants to unite all bandit tribes under his banner, Dhruv.'

'But why?' scowled Dhruv, still not getting the danger that was looming.

Manu responded simply, but his cold tone betrayed the deep disquiet his heart was going through.

'They want to steal the Ark.'

Banaras, 2017

GODS & DEMONS

Vidyut cherished every opportunity to have a meal with his Baba. It was around 9 am in the morning. They were sitting on straw mats that had been laid out on the floor of the verandah of the great Dwarka Shastri's cottage.

Some young students from the matth were serving breakfast to their revered matthadheesh, to their favorite Purohit ji and to their beloved Vidyut dada.

While Dwarka Shastri and Purohit ji ate a simple breakfast of *chuda-matar*, they had insisted that Vidyut be served some delicious, piping hot *kachori* and *jalebi* from the most famous *halwai* of Banaras. For all his divinity and his valiance, they still treated Vidyut like a little boy.

Once breakfast was done with and they were served some hot herbal tea, Dwarka Shastri resumed the grave discussion that was incomplete even now.

'We are descendants of Satyavrata Manu, Vidyut. Do you know that name?'

Vidyut went blank for a moment. Anyone who had a good idea of Hindu mythology had heard of Satyavrata Manu – the great sage, the great savior. He did not know how to react. Never in his life had one statement made his heart leap with both awe and pride in such an instant.

'Whaaat?' was all Vidyut could blurt out.

'Yes, Vidyut. You remember I told you about Vivasvan Pujari, the devta who walked this earth 3,700 years ago. The very same devta who now resides in you, reborn to fulfil his divine destiny. You would recollect that as I narrated the haunting story of Harappa's last days, I also mentioned the Surya's son, Manu.'

'Yes…yes you did, Baba…'

'That son of Vivasvan Pujari was none other than the immortal Satyavrata Manu – the builder of the Great Ark, the one chosen by Matsya, the writer of the Shastras…we are his descendants, Vidyut.

We are the bloodline of the magnificent priest-king who saved humanity from *Pralay* – The Great Deluge.'

·||ॐ||·

'The most mystical and frightening aspect of the secret brotherhood of the New World Order is their deep and intense understanding of the spiritual realm. Like I mentioned before, they consist of some of the most intelligent men in the world. Geniuses, you might say. Yet, unlike the common perception of geniuses who most people think would be logical atheists, the members of the brotherhood are deeply entrenched into the otherworldly forces, both good and evil, that impact our planet.'

'That is quite a revelation, Baba. Who would expect these genocidal scoundrels to be believers in God?'

The matthadheesh shook his head in disagreement.

'I did not say they believe in God, Vidyut. I said they believe in the *existence* of God, just as they actively seek ethereal assistance from the Devil himself. Since the beginning of time, both good and evil have played a role in the balance of the cosmos. The continuity of life and love on the planet are indicators that the forces of virtuosity are more potent than those that want to transform the world into a dark realm. But this battle is eternal, Vidyut. And the order thinks they can turn the tide in their favor.'

Vidyut was trying to grasp what Dwarka Shastri was explaining. But an everlasting struggle between good and evil, between Gods and demons...this was too much to accept just like that.

Before Vidyut could ask for a more detailed explanation, something startled everyone in the verandah, right from Purohit ji to the youngsters serving their teachers. Something seemed to rumble underneath the floor. It was like a muffled roar emanating from the heart of the earth. Everyone froze as they heard and felt the inexplicable quake that lasted only a second or two. It seemed as if something gigantic just moved right below the matth's precinct. They looked at each other, baffled and nervous. Vidyut noticed that his Baba was unfazed.

Dwarka Shastri could see the curious anxiety on his great grandson's face. He also looked at Purohit ji, who was nearly pale with fear.

'Keep calm, both of you…all of you,' snapped the matthadheesh, as if he wanted to hush up what had just happened.

'When a great *Dev-Raakshasa yuddha* or a war between Gods and demons is about to unleash itself, the forces of both darkness and of light step in to take their places in the womb of *prithvi.*'

·‖ॐ‖·

'When the Great Ark finally survived pralay, a celestial fishman called Matsya passed on an ancient secret to Satyavrata Manu. A prophesy, a world-event related to our times or *Kaliyuga* as we call it. Vivasvan Pujari was one of the guardians of this secret, which Matsya then passed on to Satyavrata Manu and his bloodline – us.'

'Wow! Did you say Matsya again, Baba? Are you talking about the Matsya *avatar* of Lord Vishnu? Are you saying the mythological story of Manu and Matsya is actually true??'

Dwarka Shastri chuckled.

'Is the story of Jesus Christ true, Vidyut? And of Prophet Mohammad? Of Siddhartha Gautama or the Buddha? If we believe in all of them, why is it so hard for us to believe in the existence of Lord Rama, Krishna or Matsya?'

Vidyut nodded, almost apologetically at having asked the silly question, that too to someone who had devoted his entire life in protecting the prophecy of Matsya.

The matthadheesh could see through Vidyut. He knew his great grandson had not asked the question out of doubt or skepticism. It was pure curiosity to confirm the truth. He smiled and spoke again, this time to ease Vidyut.

'Who can say if Matsya was an avatar or a man? Even when the Lord descends on earth, He comes in the form of a man, whether it was Rama or Krishna or Buddha. When He comes as a holy messenger, He comes as a prophet in the form of a man. When He comes as the son of God, He is still a human being, who loves, bleeds and feels pain. The Gods and men are not as different as we think they are, Vidyut.

And this is precisely what the New World Order wants to exploit.'

The Marshes of Aryavarta, 1699 BCE

DEADLIEST WEAPON ACROSS ALL OF THE KNOWN WORLD

'It has to be someplace secluded, where no one can see us.'

Prachanda had passed on detailed information to Manu and Dhruv about the ongoing conspiracy the daityas and scores of bandit tribes were hatching against the Great Ark. He also made it abundantly clear to Manu that if Nara-Munda succeeded in his design, he would amass such a mammoth army of savage, bloodthirsty fighters that it would become more or less impossible to stop them.

Apart from offering his own asura contingent to join in the defense of the Ark in exchange for a seat for each of his men and their families, Prachanda took Manu to the side and spoke with evident discretion.

'If the daityas and the bandit warlords combine forces and attack the Ark, it will perhaps be your life's greatest battle, O son of Surya. Even after the Harappan army behind you along with the mighty fish-folk, even after my own warriors fighting under your banner – we will still be outnumbered five to one.'

Satyavrata was listening pensively. For all their depravity, the daityas and the wild bandits were fearsome warriors. Given the odds that Prachanda was describing, saving the Ark from falling in the vile hands of the barbarians would be extremely hard. And if the Great Ark was lost, there was little doubt in Manu's mind that all the residents of the giant vessel would be either butchered or enslaved by the savages.

'What do you advise, O great king Prachanda? How can this battle be won? For it must be won!'

Prachanda smiled.

'Not all is lost, Satyavrata. There is a reason why I asked to speak with you in private. You see, it was not just a message that I carried from your father.

I also bring with me the deadliest weapon across all of the known world.'

·||࿕||·

There were twelve people who stood around the heavy, bejeweled copper trunk. Manu had specially invited the holy Saptarishi. Besides them there was Satarupa, Somdutt, Dhruv, Prachanda and the priest-king Satyavrata Manu himself.

The trunk was beautifully designed, embedded with the most precious and ornate gems available across Aryavarta. From its sparkling condition, it was clear that the asuras had taken great care in delivering this precious cargo. Prachanda had spared no effort in offering the respect this divine consignment commanded.

'The terrifying scene is still fresh in my mind, and it will forever remain etched on my soul. The fierce night when Vivasvan Pujari singlehandedly fought a whole battery of elite asura soldiers. The monstrous skies, the gruesome killing of the Saptarishi, the curse of the Blood River, the prophecy of the dying sages, the celestial blue light and the final battle... it was all too ghastly, too haunting...'

The asura king suddenly appeared to be in deep duress. Manu could see him break into a cold sweat as the erstwhile lieutenant of the great Sura attempted to recall and narrate that horror of a night. Clearly, the night of the blue fire had left a permanent scar on Prachanda's mind and spirit.

Manu stepped forward and put a reassuring hand on Prachanda's shoulder.

'It's alright, O mighty Prachanda. It is all in the past. We are here now and we have a daunting journey ahead of us. We need your experience, your wisdom and your valor, O great king.'

Prachanda gave a hint of a nod to Manu, acknowledging the

support. He continued to unravel the tale behind the power-ful weapon he was about to demonstrate.

·‖ॐ‖·

'Vivasvan Pujari was undoubtedly the greatest warrior of all time. We had fought him before, only to be summarily vanquished. I then witnessed him dive into the heart of the Harappan encampment at the mountains of brick and bronze. It was the most daring offensive one can imagine. The precision with which he shot multiple arrows at the same instant is something unthinkable for anyone who was not there to witness it in person,' said Prachanda.

'I am his disciple, O Prachanda. No one has seen the Surya's skill with the bow closer than I have,' said Dhruv, beaming with pride.

By now it was hard for Manu to hold back his tears. He yearned for his father's love, for his blessings. Hearing about his valor and dexterity filled Manu with pride. He was hon-ored, blessed to be the great Vivasvan Pujari's son.

Prachanda continued.

'But on the night of the blue fire, the Surya was wounded and broken. And not just physically. He was going through insufferable guilt and unbearable agony. In this condition when he was starkly outnumbered and surrounded by fifty of the finest asura warriors, I was convinced that he would be overpowered and killed.

And then something happened.'

Prachanda looked like he was transported back in time. From the large window in the chamber they had assembled in, his eyes were looking far into the stormy horizon.

Banaras, 2017

THE FINAL SOLUTION

'The prophecy that Matsya shared with Manu had been protected for millennia, buried deep in the underbellies of a series of Black Temples that were built and guarded with the sole objective of keeping the secret safe. It is something that the universe had foretold, and yet something that needed to be protected against the dark forces of evil,' said Dwarka Shastri.

Vidyut could sense he was finally coming closer to the secret of the Black Temple. He could see the anxiety on his Baba's face grow with every minute.

'Keeping the secret safe turned out to be a lot harder than anyone could have imagined. It led to centuries of nightmarish intrigue, bloodshed, wars and assassinations. The secret brotherhood discovered the divine purpose and the unstoppable power of the Black Temple soon after the demise of Constantine the Great. As I told you, the brotherhood has deep insight into the spiritual realm. Their black magicians, exorcists and demon-worshippers were soon alarmed with what was coming. They knew if the New World Order was to ever become a reality, they had to seek and destroy what lay buried in the heart of the Black Temple.

And then began the deadly war between the New World Order and the bloodline of Vivasvan Pujari and Satyavrata Manu. It was during these centuries of lethal intrigue and violence that our forefather, Pundit Bhairava Shastri, laid the foundation of the Dev-Raakshasa matth in the year 1253 AD – in order to establish a sacred stronghold for the guardians of the Black Temple.'

Dwarka Shastri continued to connect the dots for Vidyut, who was now desperately thirsty for the truth...the whole truth.

It was now that Purohit ji leaned forward and spoke with utmost respect, 'Gurudev, it is time we initiated Vidyut into the secret of the Black Temple, don't you think? He is the chosen One, gurudev.'

Vidyut's heartbeat stopped as he turned to look at his Baba's reaction at this suggestion. Something he had waited for, for so many days of unbearable delay, was now about to unmask itself.

Dwarka Shastri nodded and said just one word.

'Tomorrow.'

·||ॐ||·

'It was an unbelievable turn of events when Harappa – where the entire saga started – was revisited by the East India Company in the early 19th century. One of the most influential companies of the world with a standing army even larger than that of the British crown, the East India Company was infiltrated by the secret brotherhood. Their objective was dual. First, they went in, blew up portions of the ancient ruins in their attempt to locate what they thought was the very first Black Temple. It was only later that they discovered that the Black Temple was not any one shrine even at the time of Harappa, but a whole series of them. And it was then that they understood why we had been building a new Black Temple every couple of centuries. It was in order to keep the forces of darkness at bay.

Second, by this time the East India Company had decided to annex the entire Indian sub-continent. Masters of the craft of managing mass human psyche, the Overlords of the brotherhood decided to first annex the minds of the Indian natives. And revelation of Harappa's superiority over the West at its time was going to be a major impediment in their way to subjugate the entire populace. The rest is history. Creation of the fake Aryan invasion theory, propagating it via schooling systems that the British themselves established and finally recruiting so-called historians to write and rewrite the Aryan invasion theory so many times that it began looking like the truth. A truth that had no witnesses, no record and no evidence.

Recruiting both Western and Indian historians, archaeologists and anthropologists was not their only method of brainwashing the entire planet about the supremacy of some European 'Aryans' who came riding in like conquerors into India. Their methods also involved eliminating those who had unearthed the truth and refused to budge. Captain Wayne Ashbrook was one such blood-sacrifice made by the New World Order.'

'Who was Captain Ashbrook, Baba?'

'A righteous Englishman who wanted to bring the truth of Harappa to the fore. He was an honest officer, and the guardians of the Black Temple tracked him for a long time. Eventually we handed him original scriptures hand-written by indigenous *rishis* of the early-Vedic period, well before the propounded timing of the supposed Aryan invasion. He researched deeper and was going to publicly debunk the Aryans-were-outsiders theory. That was, of course, something the Order could not allow. Captain Ashbrook was brutally murdered on the streets of Calcutta.'

·‖卐‖·

'Baba, just for my clarity, may I please highlight the chain of events so far? Please correct me if I am wrong. It is important I get the chronology right.'

'Yes, of course, Vidyut,' replied the grandmaster. 'Let's hear you outline the violent journey of the brotherhood and the Black Temple.'

Vidyut took a deep breath and smiled at his Baba.

'Okay, here goes. It all started back in Harappa, when our great ancestor Vivasvan Pujari was betrayed and framed by his friend and brother-in-law Pundit Chandradhar and his wife Priyamvada.

As Vivasvan Pujari escaped from captivity in the Rain of Blood and joined forces with the demon-king Sura to wrest his vengeance, his mortally wounded son Manu escaped from the battlefield with the help of Pundit Somdutt.

On one end the Surya of Harappa crushed the forces of the metropolis at the mountains of brick and bronze, and on the other his son Manu met the magnificent fish-man, Matsya, for the first time.

As Vivasvan Pujari discovered that his son was alive and witnessed the inhuman murdering of the Saptarishi, he fought the asuras and killed their cruel king Sura in the process. During this time, the burning sages and the Blood River cursed not just our bloodline, but the entire human race with endless violence and suffering. The sages instructed Vivasvan Pujari to send the Ratna-Maru to Manu.

In the meantime, Matsya took Manu to the Black Temple in the mountains. There he informed Manu about the impending deluge, about pralay. He also told Manu that his father, the Surya of Harappa, was a guardian of the Black Temple. And that Manu would take on the mantle thereafter.

Vivasvan Pujari perished in the great deluge and Manu was commanded by Matsya to construct a mammoth boat to protect mankind from the cataclysmic cleansing. Ever since then our bloodline has been the guardian of the Black Temple's secret.

Then in the year 325 AD, the Roman emperor Constantine envisioned and commissioned a New World Order, where he wanted to establish a one-world government, a one-world religion and a world without infighting and strife amongst humans. Our great ancestor Advait Shastri counselled him against it.

The New World Order quickly morphed into a tyrannical and merciless brotherhood that distorted Constantine's vision and began working towards a world and society they controlled in an absolute sense. The Knights Templar were the first successful experiment of the Order, where they propped up a formidable force when they wanted and struck it down pitilessly as they pleased.

Slowly but surely the Order spread its tentacles across the globe and its members were some of the world's most accomplished men and women. They are the hidden force behind some of mankind's most transformational events – the French Revolution, formation of the Soviet Union, the Great Depression, the Third Reich, the Cold War, the Arab Spring and even 9/11. They control the world through their phenomenal influence over banking institutions, defense manufacturers, politics, pharmaceuticals, oil, media, terrorism, technology and more.

The supreme Overlords of the Order are not only men of great talent and genius. They are sophisticated mystics who understand the otherworldly forces of good and evil very deeply. Something that lies at the heart of the Black Temple has been the secret society's greatest quest, as they believe the secret of the Black Temple carries with it an undefeatable force that can lay waste to the Order's nefarious vision. For this very reason, this brotherhood has been waging war with the Dev-Raakshasa matth for centuries.

It was the secret brotherhood that infiltrated the East India Company and went hunting for what they believed to be the first Black Temple in the ruins of Harappa. They well knew the glorious past of the civilization and that it was entirely indigenous. But they invented the Aryan Invasion theory because it allowed them to first psychologically dominate the sub-continent, and later create fault-lines between Indians based on this divisive hypothesis.

They assassinated anyone that stood in the way of their global design and calculation. Captain Wayne Ashbrook was one among many such eliminations. Romi Pereira, Bala, Trijat Kapaalik, Brahmanand...they were all members of that secret society. On one end, they want to keep me alive because I am the prophesied devta who can lead them to the Black Temple's secret, but on the other they are determined to kill me as soon as they lay their hands on it.'

Dwarka Shastri nodded slowly, expressing his satisfaction with Vidyut's encapsulation of the convoluted past.

'Can we please continue in the evening, Vidyut? I need to go and meet a very important visitor,' he said.

'Yes, of course, Baba,' replied Vidyut politely, although he could not help but wonder who this visitor could be that was pulling away Dwarka Shastri from this very important discussion – that too in its final chapters.

'Come to me at 6 pm this evening, beta. We do not have much time left. The planets are going to start aligning soon.

I have to tell you more about the Black Temple, about your ancestors, Markandeya Shastri, Advait Shastri, Durgadas Shastri…and of course, about my beloved Kartikeya.'

Dwarka Shastri sighed at the name of Kartikeya. His intense love for Vidyut's late father was evident.

'I also need to tell you about the Goa Inquisition, about Prithvivallabha and most of all – about the Order's *final solution*.'

'Ji, Baba…' said Vidyut as he got up to leave.

Just as he was about to step out of Dwarka Shastri's cottage, Vidyut could not shake off the term *final solution* that his Baba had used. It had a strangely sinister connotation to it. Something made him turn around and face his Baba again.

'Just one question, please Baba. Even if you answer it in brief. What is the *final solution* they have in mind, Baba? Solution to what exactly? It is somehow disturbing me more than anything else.'

Dwarka Shastri was silent for a moment, as he looked straight into Vidyut's eyes. He was not surprised to see an intense sense of intuition in Vidyut. He spoke matter-of-factly.

'They want to optimize the world's population from nearly seven billion to less than a tenth of that, Vidyut.

If the New World Order does indeed succeed in usurping global control under their totalitarian government, they will unleash the greatest human-culling since the beginning of time.

They will slaughter six billion human beings.'

The Marshes of Aryavarta, 1699 BCE

RATNA-MARU

Upon Manu's request, the Saptarishi stepped forward.

Prachanda had described how the blue flame had leapt towards the sky and in a loud, booming voice the seventh Saptarishi had instructed Vivasvan to burnish his sword in the raging blue inferno. He also then recounted how the battle thereafter was one-sided.

From that moment on, the Ratna-Maru had become a cosmic weapon – making its bearer invincible. The only precondition was that the sword selected its wielder and not the other way around.

The Ratna-Maru was fated to ultimately reach the hands of an extraordinary warrior.

A warrior who was destined to wage mankind's final, decisive war.

In Kaliyuga.

·||ॐ||·

It was dark in the chamber they had gathered in. In these last days and months leading to the full onslaught of pralay, it was always dark. The opulent copper box gleamed under the light from the flickering torches.

For Manu, the box did not just contain a divine sword. It housed the last object that his father had held in his hands. That made the Ratna-Maru a priceless gift for him.

The Saptarishi now stood surrounding the copper trunk, their hands folded. More than Prachanda and Manu it was the divine seven who knew the real purpose of this godly armament. They knew *who* it was meant for. They knew that Manu was only a conduit for the sword to fulfil its definitive cosmic destiny.

The Saptarishi now, in that very instant, composed and chanted a mantra in unison, invoking Lord Vishnu. The mantra they had just created would be intoned by billions of people for millennia to come, each time anyone wanted Vishnu to bless the beginning of something sacrosanct –

|| *'Mangalam Bhagvaan Vishnu;*

Mangalam Garuda Dhvajah:

Mangalam Pundari Kaakshaah;

Mangalaaya Tano Harih.' ||

The seven young sages then stepped closer to the box and all of them placed their palms on its shining surface.

What followed took everyone's breath away.

The eyes of the Saptarishi lit up with a bright blue glow. They seemed to be forging a connection with a greater, supernatural power. For a few moments, they stayed glued to the copper trunk, the blue incandescence emanating from their eyes getting brighter.

Manu, Tara, Somdutt, Dhruv and Prachanda stood frozen in their places, entranced by what they were witnessing.

Soon after the seven sages lifted their hands, the blue radiance slowly subsided. The Saptarishi looked at each other and exchanged pleasant grins. They then turned to Manu and one of them spoke.

'Step forward and unveil the splendid Ratna-Maru, Satyavrata.'

·||ॐ||·

Manu lifted the heavy lid of the gleaming trunk.

The magnificent long-sword lay cased in soft, dark brown leather.

Satyavrata knew this brilliant sword all too well. It had adorned his great father's waist-belt for decades. He folded his hands, shut his eyes in reverence to and in the memory of his father, and bowed to the mighty weapon that had won innumerable battles for Harappa.

And yet something was different about the Ratna-Maru. Its bejeweled handle glimmered with a bright shine. The ominous blade engraved with terrifying verses from the *Garuda Puraana,* that prescribes the punishments of hell, dazzled with a glint of blue.

Manu smiled.

The color of Matsya. The color of Vishnu.

'Go on, pick it up, Satyavrata,' urged Prachanda, who was deeply satisfied at having fulfilled his promise to Vivasvan Pujari by uniting the Ratna-Maru with the Surya's son.

·||卐||·

The Saptarishi and Pundit Somdutt raised their hands in blessing as Manu bowed to them. He then turned to Tara, who smiled and blinked at him with deepest love. His gaze then switched to Dhruv, who winked at him and gestured with his head towards the great sword.

Manu stretched his right hand, gripped the handle of the Ratna-Maru firmly, and whispered a prayer to Mahakaal, the God of death, asking for salvation for the souls of those who were fated to die by this divine blade.

He then lifted the heavy sword in one practiced swoop and raised it high up for everyone to behold.

At the very same instant the skies erupted in an unusually deafening thunder-flash. The universe was rejoicing!

As the Saptarishi, Somdutt, Prachanda, Tara and Dhruv

looked on with awe at the brilliant warrior and his glistening heavenly blade, the screaming sky illuminated the chamber once again.

Satyavrata Manu looked like a force of nature. A strong gust of wind blew his long hair as he appeared white against the blinding light of thunder, his eyes studying the menacing weapon.

The Ratna-Maru glimmered in a stunning blue.

Banaras, 2017

ADVAIT, DURGADAS & MARKANDEYA

Vidyut knocked at the great matthadheesh's door at exactly 6 pm.

As he entered the cottage he was first surprised and then ecstatic to see a beautiful visitor he had not expected to find there.

'Damini!' exclaimed Vidyut, as Damini ran up to him and held him in a tight embrace.

'Oh, Vidyut…' was all she could say.

Vidyut went red, shyly hugging the love of his life back. He knew such display of affection was not something the great matthadheesh was used to. Or would appreciate.

In a few seconds Damini realized the same and pulled away, not looking at the matthadheesh.

The devta turned to his Baba with shining, enquiring eyes.

'Baba…Damini…how?' he asked, smiling from ear to ear with happiness.

Dwarka Shastri was delighted to see the beautiful couple together. They were meant to be.

'Damini's presence is essential, Vidyut. What you are going to face, as well as what is going to emerge from the Black Temple, will both need every ounce of your spirit to withstand. You are incomplete without Damini, O devta. Shiva is only half without Shakti. Vivasvan is inadequate without Sanjna. She has waited 3,700 years…just to accompany you in the fiery quest that awaits you. Her life-energy, her unquestioned love, her golden soul…will all stand by you when you face *him*, Vidyut.

When you face Lucifer!'

·||ॐ||·

It was a large gathering now. Dwarka Shastri had called in everyone. What he was about to narrate was not fully known to anyone – not even Purohit ji or Naina.

Naina had felt a lump in her throat as she saw Vidyut and Damini sitting next to each other, fingers intertwined, deeply in love. Vidyut had pulled away his hand as he saw Naina enter the room. He could not bear to hurt her. But it was with good reason that Naina had made such an impact on Vidyut. She was truly extraordinary. She simply blinked at Vidyut, gave a warm hug to Damini and sat down close to Dwarka Shastri's feet – her usual place of comfort and love around her Baba.

Her heart wept. Her face glowed with a beaming smile.

'The killing of Wayne Ashbrook was a much later episode. The spilling of blood was going on for centuries. One of our greatest ancestors, the hooded warrior-priest, Advait Shastri, who was a close confidante of Constantine the Great and had even tried to dissuade him from unleashing his grand design, was the first to be surrounded by seventy knights of the Order. These knights represented the most primitive form of the Templars much before they officially arrived on the scene several hundred years later. Advait Shastri was assassinated ruthlessly. Of course, not before he had slaughtered twenty-seven of them, even though he was alone and unarmed. They say the battle raged on for hours and the field was sprayed red for hundreds of yards. Also, that the hooded monk was drenched from head to toe in the blood of the seventy knights. After it was all over, the surviving knights of the Order bowed to his mutilated body, stunned by his astonishing skill and valor. Advait Shastri found a legendary mention in secret Templar chronicles for hundreds of years. His battle technique was recorded and used to train the finest Templar knights who later led the Crusades.

This was in the 4th century. Constantine was privy to the secret of the Black Temple. By attempting to unify the world he was convinced that he was serving the cosmic order. But his devotion faded with his death, only to be replaced by the cruel Overlords of the brotherhood.'

There was a hushed silence in the room. Vidyut, Damini, Purohit ji, Naina, Sonu and Balvanta sat in a daze as they heard the matthadheesh turn the bloodstained pages of the Shastri clan's history.

·||ॐ||·

'We kept building temples every couple of hundred years – sometimes with the help of devout kings. On other occasions, we used the significant resources of the Dev-Raakshasa matth,' continued Dwarka Shastri.

'But why only temples, Baba? Why could the secret not be hidden somewhere else? In say a palace or under a grave for that matter? Why only Black Temples?' asked Vidyut.

'Good question, Vidyut. Tomorrow you will discover the answer for yourself. The indescribable radiance and celestial intensity of what lies buried in the Black Temple needs an equally powerful sanctum. Each Black Temple takes years of consecration by not just the chanting of mantras by hundreds of accomplished sages, but also by intricately engraving the most potent of those mantras in figurative forms into the walls, pillars and ceilings of each shrine. Any lesser structure would get burnt to ashes by the heat of the ancient secret.'

Vidyut nodded to express his understanding. Brave and

self-confident as he was, there was no lying to himself that he was nervous. Nervous about what lay in the Black Temple. More so about the name that was cropping up again and again.

Someone he was supposed to take on.

Lucifer.

·‖卐‖·

'The Black Temple kept changing its form, its manifestation and its location. Sacred temples like Badrinath, Somnath, Vishwanath, Kedarnath…were all built and served as holy Black Temples at different points. But the one temple that kept the secret secure the longest, for several hundred years, was the magnificent Kailasa Temple at Ellora,' elucidated Dwarka Shastri.

Damini and Vidyut exchanged glances. They had discussed visiting the mystical rock-cut temples of Ajanta and Ellora several times, but could never really make it. And now here they were, listening to the tale of the Kailasa Temple as a part of their own story.

'Our brilliant forefather, Durgadas Shastri, was the one who encouraged the great King Kannesvara, who was better known as Prithvivallabha, to undertake the building of the Kailasa Temple in the 8th century. How the temple was built, how it could harness technology that was not even available to mankind at that time, is a very different, very intriguing story altogether. For now, it will suffice to know that the safety of Ellora did not last forever.

Then came the Goa Inquisition, and our ancestor Markandeya Shastri, who fought the Portuguese plunderers in the 16th century.

After the Kailasa Temple at Ellora no longer remained a safe haven for the secret of the Black Temple, the location was changed numerous times. Finally, in the year 1572 AD, our ancestor Markandeya Shastri decided to take the precious, divine secret with him to the very peaceful Konkan region of our country, and conceal it in a Black Temple built at the coastal province of Goa.

For all his precautions and attempts to take the secret away from the reach of the Order, they caught up. What followed was among the bloodiest and most tyrannical ethnic-cleansing in the history of the sub-continent – the Goa Inquisition.'

Vidyut was well informed about the Goa Inquisition. He looked at Damini and added to what his Baba was saying -

'The Goa Inquisition that was established by the Roman Catholic clergy is strangely underplayed and understudied in our country, Damini. It was religious persecution in its ugliest form. Thousands of Hindus and Muslims burnt alive at the stake, starved to death in prisons and tortured by being skinned from head to toe – all for reciting a verse of their original faith or for using Konkani for worship or for writing.'

Damini found the description very disturbing.

'I had heard about the violence of the missionaries and the Portuguese soldiers in Goa, Vidyut, but I did not know it was so horrifying,' she said.

'Oh, it was worse,' said Vidyut, deciding to spare Damini more gory details of torture and persecution.

The matthadheesh continued his account of the Black Temple.

'However, the real purpose of the Inquisition was to find the Black Temple. The armies of the Portuguese king plundered Goa. Temples were destroyed at a merciless frenzy. Making sure that they missed nothing, even the mosques were not spared.'

Dwarka Shastri stopped for a breather. Damini used the opportunity to soak in all the information.

·||ॐ||·

'The final battle of Markandeya Shastri is a magnificent, mysterious saga of sacrifice and lionheartedness. But we don't have time for it today,' said Dwarka Shastri.

'We understand, Baba. But we do want to hear the story of the Kailasa Temple as well as that of Pundit Markandeya Shastri,' insisted Damini softly.

'Yes, of course, *bitiya*. When all this is over, I will tell you about it in detail. You both must know the tales of those marvelous men and their stunning pursuits. At this time, just know that whether it was Pundit Advait, Markandeya or Durgadas, all died fighting, protecting the secret of the Black Temple. And true to the ancient curse – they all died violently, painfully.'

'And so did my father, Kartikeya Shastri…' muttered Vidyut.

'Yes, my son,' replied Dwarka Shastri. 'But with Kartikeya it was a little different.

Kartikeya tried to, once and for all, burn down the entire Illuminati.'

The Dark Forests of Aryavarta, 1698 BCE

NARA-MUNDA

Even the ruthless bandit chieftains from the badlands were nauseated.

They had travelled from far lands at the invitation of the dreaded Nara-Munda. While they were all well aware that the daityas were cannibals, they could not believe the horrifying spectacle of the daitya stronghold that lay deep in the heart of the dark forests.

The stench of cindering human flesh was unbearable. Several fighters of the warlords threw up or passed out at the sight of human limbs and organs being roasted on open fires. Daitya children kicked around freshly chopped heads as playthings and the women wore jewelry made of bones from their own kind.

As a goodwill gesture, Nara-Munda had permitted each warlord to come with a posse of a hundred guards. But only minutes into the vast daitya camp it became clear to the bandit chieftains that they were now at the mercy of the feared daitya-king. It was for the first time that any of them was seeing the daityas in full strength. Their camp spread over miles and their mammoth numbers totally unnerved the unsuspecting visitors.

There were over a hundred thousand of them! All ready to die for Nara-Munda. All thirsty for human blood.

·||ॐ||·

They were now seated around a large fire, right outside the tent of the emperor of the dark forests.

All of them had heard about Nara-Munda. Heard a lot, in fact. About the sheer size of his gigantic frame, about his mindless cruelty and his fiery temper. By now each one of them was regretting having come to this rotting hell of a place. It was only the certainty of death at the cold, unstoppable hands of the great flood that had compelled these savages to visit savages even greater than themselves.

They knew that without the Ark they were doomed. And Nara-Munda was the only one who could create a real chance of getting it.

·||ॐ||·

What emerged from the tent was not a man. It was a monster.

Nara-Munda was nearly eight arms in height and towered terrifyingly above all else around him. With a girth as thick as an oaken tree-trunk, he looked like a mythical creature straight from the dark depths of *paataal*.

His biceps were fuller than the waists of most men. His legs looked like the limbs of a rhino. Every step he took seemed to shake the earth. His shaven bald head was smeared in red, which most observers could tell was stale human blood. The only clothing he wore was a tightly knit, knee-length lower made of elephant hide. His massive, muscular torso was tattooed with frightening faces of demons from daitya mythology, that looked like speaking, scowling faces in the orange light of the bonfire.

But the scariest element of Nara-Munda was his facial features. If pain had an expression, it would look like this giant cannibal's face. His massive head, his bulging eyeballs, his leathery lips, his sunken cheeks, his perpetual frown and those icy, permanently intoxicated eyes…made him look like the messenger of suffering and death.

He was one.

·||ॐ||·

'Welcome to our home, my friends!' shouted Nara-Munda, his arms outstretched, his voice throaty like that of an abominable giant.

The warlords had no choice but to offer bleak smiles and

nods in response. Each one of them was a feared militia chieftain in their own regions. But today, face to face with the colossal and cruel Nara-Munda, they appeared to be nothing more than helpless, wet puppies.

The beast continued.

'Today we gather here to forge the mightiest military alliance in history. Together we shall not only attack and capture the great Nauka, but also rule the planet once the deluge subsides. Our armies together will march like an ocean of arms and armor, and will sow fear in the hearts of the builders of the titanic boat.

I thank you all very warmly for submitting allegiance to my banner. From now on you will live and fight under my protection.'

There was stunned silence. None of the chieftains had offered any allegiance. This was supposed to be an alliance among equals. But Nara-Munda seemed to have a very different plan.

'And as an initiation ceremony into my sovereignty, please accept this humble offering from the daityas,' said the monster, as he gestured to his men to do the needful.

Plates were passed around to the warlords.

Roasted man-flesh!

·|| ꣍ ||·

Even as the chiefs of the wildernesses gaped at each other,

stunned at Nara-Munda's unbelievable audacity, one of the younger warlords decided to protest. He was sitting right next to where the daitya beast stood. He was quite a strong man himself.

'This was not what was communicated to us by your emissaries, O king of the dark forests. There is no question of your sovereignty. And what is this nonsense about serving us human meat? Once the battle is over, we will all decide who shall be the master and commander of the great Ark. You will have your say just as any of...'

Even before the young warlord could complete his statement, Nara-Munda's giant right fist moved with the speed of an arrow and struck the man across his face. The impact of the blow was more lethal than a stone mace. The young chieftain spat oodles of blood, his teeth flew out from his mouth and one of his eyeballs got dislocated from its socket and plunged out hanging from his cheek.

He crumbled to the ground, squirming with pain.

Nara-Munda leisurely walked up to the writhing man, looked at him struggling and slowly put his gigantic foot on the man's head.

The man was already half-dead with the blow, but he was alive enough to thrash around, in the agony of unbearable pain. He slapped his hands frantically at Nara-Munda's foot, pleading with him to let go. The daitya was slowly fracturing his skull.

The demon did not stop, did not show mercy. He did not know what mercy or compassion meant anyway. He kept pressing down his brawny pillar of a limb on the wretched man's cranium, which soon cracked, crushed and popped open from the top, spilling his gooey, bloody brain matter out on the ground.

The warlords could not believe the barbarianism of this beast of a man. Their hearts had stopped and their blood had frozen in their veins. It was way better to drown in the waters of the great flood than to serve this fiend. But it was too late. They were already trapped in the claws of the daitya emperor.

Nara-Munda looked around with bloodshot eyes, pausing his deathly glare at each of the warlords for a chilling moment.

He then growled like a fuming dragon.

'Anyone else wants to be the master and commander of the Ark?'

Banaras, 2017

THE BLACK DEATH

His phone alarm beeped heavily in the dark room.

Vidyut woke up at 4.30 am, as was instructed by his Baba.

Today was the day. The big day that the Shastri bloodline had been waging war for, over several centuries. The day against which Romi Pereira had cautioned Vidyut, moments before biting into cyanide. The moment that Bala had betrayed him for. The prophesied hour that Trijat Kapaalik had promised to keep Vidyut alive till, and the one-eyed monster Brahmanand had laughed.

The Rohini Nakshatra.

It was tonight, close to midnight, that the prophesied Rohini

Nakshatra was going to erupt in the night sky - creating a holy-hour that was second to none. A constellation in which the greatest avatars and the most magnificent prophets were born. A divine arrangement of the Sun, the Moon, the planets and the galaxies that, for a few minutes, made Kashi a perfect spiritual cocoon.

·||ॐ||·

Vidyut sat across the *yajna-kunda*, facing his Baba. It was still early in the morning and the matthadheesh had organized a *havana*, with a view to strengthen Vidyut for what lay ahead over the next seventy-two hours. The havana was arranged in a beautiful yet intimidating temple of *Kaal-Bhairava* that lay deep in the heart of the matth's raakshasa-khannd. Vidyut had never seen it before.

The temple walls were made of dark stone and had the figurines of Lord Shiva's various *gana* or disciples carved into them. There was a statue of Shiva-gana *Kannappa*. Also, one of *Poosal*. But the most dominating among those was the black bust of Bhairava that lay inset in the core sanctum of the temple. The people of Kashi say that Bhairava must be worshipped with great reverence, as he is the *dwaarpaal* or gatekeeper of Lord Shiva.

As several accomplished *pujaris* or priests of the Dev-Raakshasa matth busied themselves in the detailed preparations for the holy fire-pit, Dwarka Shastri began from where he had left off.

'Stopping the New World Order is not just about stopping

a sinister organization from taking over global control. It is much more than that. The secret brotherhood has its own plans for how they want to solve the problems of this world – terrorism, climate change, water-shortage…everything is on their agenda. But the solution they wish to implement is more brutal than anything history has witnessed before. As they see it, population explosion will be the fundamental undoing of the human race. So, in their view, by culling down ninety percent of the world population, they will be doing mankind a great service and offer it protection against certain extinction.'

This was getting more and more macabre. More insane than Vidyut could ever imagine.

'But this crazy, Baba! Are these people deranged or are they some lunatic doomsday predictors? Yes, the planet has issues. Yes, something significant needs to be done before we are over the tipping point, whether it is global warming or religious fanaticism. But how can the challenges of humankind be addressed by wiping out humankind itself?!'

Dwarka Shastri raised his hand in blessing the priests that were arriving into the Bhairava-mandir and bowing to him.

'What do you know about Black Death or the Black Plague, Vidyut?'

The devta was taken aback by this sudden mention of a medieval tragedy.

'A little bit, Baba. I know that it was a devastating outbreak. Black Death or the Black Plague or the bubonic plague spread like an epidemic of epic proportions during the 14th and the 17th centuries, especially across Central Asia and Europe.'

'And that major cities like London, Paris and even Moscow felt the blow of the plague,' added Damini. She had been called by Purohit ji to attend the havana by the devta's side, and she was as well-read as Vidyut was.

The matthadheesh was listening. Once Vidyut and Damini paused, Dwarka Shastri spoke again.

'You are right. Yet I say you both know nothing about the Black Death. No one does!' snapped Dwarka Shastri as he spoke the last three words.

The matthadheesh's eyes were burning with rage.

·||ॐ||·

'Millions of lives were lost. Or please allow me to correct myself - *tens of millions* of people died across Europe and Asia after being infected by the plague. It is well documented and accepted as the deadliest pandemic to have struck our species in its recorded history. It is hard for people to believe the figures today, but the Black Plague is estimated to have wiped out thirty to sixty percent of Europe's entire population!'

Vidyut was listening intently. While he had heard of the Black Plague and how it had ravaged the world for centuries, he was not aware of the extent of loss of human life.

Dwarka Shastri continued.

'The death toll was horrifying and it is hard for us to even imagine what the world would have gone through during the bubonic plague. It is estimated that world population came down from 450 million to under 350 million in the 14th century. You see, Vidyut, anywhere between 75 million to 200 million human beings succumbed to the plague. This one disease reduced world population by a whopping twenty-five percent! The Black Death killed half of Paris' population. It wiped out forty percent of Egypt. Half of Florence. Sixty percent of London. A third of Moscow. The list is endless. While these sound like statistics today, can you even begin to fathom the unspeakable pain and suffering the human race must have endured? Millions of children dying in the arms of their helpless parents. Streets of cities strewn with rotting bodies. Infants left crying in cradles, both parents lying dead. Riots, looting, murders…

It took the world over two hundred years to recover back to its original numbers.'

By now Vidyut's mouth had gone dry. He could figure why the bubonic plague had earned the morbid title of The Black Death.

But there was more to come.

·‖卐‖·

'For hundreds of years it was believed that the Black Plague was caused by the bacteria *Yersinia Pestis*, that spread across Asia and Europe along the Silk Route, carried by fleas and rats. But the guardians of the Black Temple knew that was not the whole truth. It was only as late as 1984 that the Zool-ogist Graham Twigg contested this theory. Without getting into the scientific facts and details of his argument, let me share with you his conclusion.'

The last devta was not even batting an eyelid. He was capti-vated by what his great grandfather was describing.

'Twigg concluded that the bubonic plague was caused not by Yersinia Pestis, but by a lethal form of anthrax.'

'Anthrax? Isn't that the feared bacterial spores that can be used for bio-terrorism?' asked Damini.

'Exactly, Damini. The Black Plague was the most merciless act of bio-terrorism in the history of man. Someone pur-posefully, with a preordained design of radically reducing the world's population, ruthlessly culled down a hundred million human beings.'

There was silence for a few moments, the only sound being the rustle of seating mats and *pooja* material being placed around them for the havana. The implication of what Dwar-ka Shastri had narrated was clear to Vidyut. But he needed to reconfirm it. Something like this was unthinkable, unpar-donable.

'Baba, are you saying that it was the Order that unleashed the deadly Black Plague on mankind?' asked Vidyut, his eyes red with horror.

'That is precisely what I am saying, Vidyut,' replied Dwarka Shastri simply. 'And they are going to do it again. This time, on an even larger scale.'

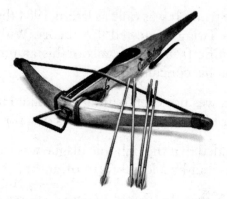

The Marshes of Aryavarta, 1698 BCE

MILLIONS OF ARROWS

Several weeks had passed since Prachanda had arrived at the Ark construction site with his men. The asuras had slowly but surely become an integral part of the great Ark's working and fighting force. The last basecamp and colony had been pulled out and all of Aryavarta's surviving souls were now aboard the giant boat.

Manu had found an invaluable ally in the asura-king. Prachanda had three decades of experience in managing and disciplining a vicious army. His proficiency was now extremely useful in organizing the varied troops of the Ark. There were the Harappan soldiers, tens of thousands of them. No less in number were the supremely skilled fish-folk, who Matsya had attached to his beloved Satyavrata. Prachanda's asuras added a few thousand more to this impressive military. Last but not the least were Dhruv and his handful of exceptional fighters – those who had been trained by the great Vivasvan Pujari himself.

The news of all the bandit warlords accepting the unfettered monarchy of Nara-Munda had reached Manu. He even knew the circumstances under which this forced coalition had been forged. It only added to Manu's worry. Nara-Munda was turning out to be more formidable than he had expected.

Now it was simply a matter of time. The decisive battle was looming. Whether the gigantic armies of the daityas would arrive on the horizon the next day or the next month was the only question left to be asked.

·||ॐ||·

'Our greatest advantage is that we have plain, barren marshes all around the Nauka for as far as the eye can see,' said Tara, as she circled an arrow around a drawing of the great Ark and its surrounding terrain.

Preparations for the inevitable war had been commissioned on full-scale by the defenders of the Ark. All the able-bodied men were now called-to-arms, leaving the final stages of the vessel's construction and maintenance to the elders, the women and the children. A large number of women also enrolled into the Damini Sena, boosting the numbers of Manu's forces quite significantly. Everyone contributed equally to this heroic, this historical contest between the spirit of man and the fury of nature. Daily meetings were convened to track progress and bolster defense measures in every manner possible.

'How is that an advantage, Tara? Barren marshes will only mean that enemy cavalry can gallop to the Ark without any natural hindrances. Their advance is going to be disturbingly swift,' questioned Prachanda.

'Yes, it will be. But not if we welcome them with a hail of arrows so dense that it covers every step of the surrounding marshes. We will inflict such heavy casualties on their troops that the approach grounds to the Ark will become a daitya and bandit graveyard!'

Manu was mesmerized as he saw his beautiful, romantic, loving Tara transform into a lioness. She was a born General.

'Okay, but how will so much firepower be garnered? We have archers alright, but not nearly enough to create such a storm of arrows,' interjected Dhruv. If anyone understood archers and arrows, it was he.

'I know. I have a plan,' replied Tara, confident as ever.

·‖卐‖·

'As of this hour, we have fifteen thousand warriors in the Damini Sena. Given the brutality and debauchery of our foe, I would much rather have them all on the Ark than on the ground, face to face with those barbarians. And this could mean a great tactical advantage. If we divide the entire Sena into three units, one unit fighting at any given point, we can have five thousand women archers atop the Ark, covering its perimeter in all directions. Given that we have another seven thousand bowmen in Dhruv's troops, we are talking about nearly ten thousand archers in action at every point in the war!'

Tara looked around the room, hoping to find some support for her proposition.

'Don't be absurd, Tara,' said Dhruv, getting up from his chair.

He could speak to Tara in this manner. They were childhood friends.

'You seem to forget that none of your Damini Sena are trained in using bow and arrow. The daitya and brigand riders are expert horsemen. They will be attacking with furious speed and will be moving targets. How do you expect novice archers to stop them?'

'I wish you used your brain a little more often, Dhruv,' retorted Tara, rolling up her eyes.

She could speak to Dhruv in this manner. They were childhood friends.

'We will divide the archers into two sections. The trained archers, your archers, will be positioned on the lower decks. On the other hand, the Damini Sena will take positions on the highest decks. All they have to do is to fire a volley of arrows high up in the sky, shooting their arrows like projectiles. That does not require much training, given the vast ground they have to cover. Anywhere their arrows land, they will find their mark. The enemy riders and foot soldiers who escape this barrage can be picked by your marksmen archers one by one as they come closer to the Ark. Don't you see, Dhruv, we will cut down enemy forces by half using just our archers! Our cavalry and infantry can then wreak havoc into the rest of them!' exclaimed Tara, her eyes wide and her arms outstretched.

Dhruv smiled, raised his eyebrows in evident appreciation and looked at Manu, who simply laughed and shrugged.

The ace archer then turned towards Tara and nodded melodramatically.

'Okay, my lady…let's do it!'

'Thank you, Dhruv,' said Tara. 'Now we have only one problem.'

Dhruv frowned. 'And what is that?'

'We will need to forge millions of arrows.'

Banaras, 2017

'KARTIKEYA TRIED TO BURN DOWN THE ILLUMINATI'

As the sacred havana reached its end, Vidyut touched his Baba's feet to obtain his benedictions. It was customary in *Sanatana* or simply, in Hindu families for the young to seek blessings of their elders in this manner.

For the next two days and nights, the devta was going to need all the blessings he could get.

'We will wait for everyone to leave, Vidyut,' muttered the grand old man. 'The time has come for you to stand face to face with your destiny.'

Damini did not want to leave, but she sensed that it was time she left the two Shastri men alone.

'Please allow me to take leave of you, Baba,' she said, getting up and folding her hands in a pranaam.

Dwarka Shastri smiled and bowed his head slightly, acknowledging Damini. Vidyut also turned and gave her an affectionate look as she walked out of the Bhairava temple.

'Baba…' said Vidyut, 'the pujaris are going to take some time in winding up the *poojan*. Why don't we sit in that corner and continue our conversation? I am still not aware exactly why my father Kartikeya Shastri was killed, although I can well imagine it now.'

·‖✸‖·

The Kaal-Bhairava temple was still filled with grey smoke from the ceremonial fire. Vidyut always found this delightful blend of yajna smoke, incense, marigold flowers and camphor, typical to temples, deeply moving. It gave him a profound sense of calm. It was the closest one could get to the fragrance of divinity.

'The war between the matth and the Order intensified after the Black Death. The plague had made it clear to us that the secret brotherhood was far more sinister than we had envisaged till that point. It was now that the Shastri clansmen decided to take the fight to the Order's doorstep. And then began the killings…' said the matthadheesh.

'What kind of killings, Baba?'

'Let that be, Vidyut. I know your view on violence. I saw it in your reaction when Trijat was executed. By the way, Balvanta also told me that you released that one-eyed demon Brahmanand. It was a huge mistake, Vidyut. You will regret it one day. Anyhow, let's not delve deeper into the assassinations. Just know that both sides were now hunting each other down. And your gallant father Kartikeya only did what he was expected to do. What he was ordained to do.

This was all prophesized anyway, Vidyut. Remember the curse of the Blood River. She had condemned mankind to eternal strife and violence. The New World Order is simply a manifestation of that curse.'

'Do share his tale, Baba. It is overwhelming to hear the magnificent achievements of our forefathers – Vivasvan Pujari, Satyavrata Manu, Advait Shastri, Durgadas Shastri, Markandeya Shastri…and finally Papa. It is all so mind-numbing, so gratifying.'

Dwarka Shastri smiled.

'You do know who is supposed to be the greatest of our bloodline, don't you, Vidyut? It is you, my son. You are the prophesied devta. The *last* devta! Greater than all of us combined!'

'Oh please, Baba…' said an embarrassed Vidyut. 'I don't know why you, Purohit ji and everyone else in the matth keeps saying that. I have achieved not even a fraction of what our great forefathers had. Why, I have not done anything that comes close to even your greatness, Baba.'

'You think combatting those deadly mercenaries singlehandedly was not great, Vidyut? Do you know anyone else who can do that? What about Romi Pereira, the killer behind some of the most high-profile assassinations of the last decade and a half? Do you know that the Masaan-raja was nearly invincible? You vanquished the most lethal taantric on earth. And don't forget Vidyut, I live and breathe today because it is your divine soul that protects me. Don't underestimate yourself, my son.'

Vidyut smiled and shook his head in polite disagreement.

'I could not have beaten Trijat Kapaalik without your help, Baba. The daakinis that emerged from the netherworld – I could not have fought them. The *Shiva-Kavach* command that you have, I just don't. So, it was not me alone, Baba. It was *us*.'

Dwarka Shastri laughed with delight. Something had just struck him.

'It bodes well that you believe even a devta needs help. By that logic, even God would require assistance, would he not, Vidyut? You know, my son...it is wonderful how you appreciate and talk about teamwork!' he said, still laughing.

Vidyut could not understand anything and gave a bemused look to his Baba, almost laughing himself just looking at the grand old man's glee.

'Vidyut...you are also in someone's team. That is what you have been sent for!'

·‖ॐ‖·

The devta had not understood what his Baba meant when he spoke about God requiring assistance or him being in someone's team. He decided to change the topic and steer it to what he longed to know most.

'Do tell me about my father now, Baba.'

'Yes, my son. I am sure you would have guessed by now as to who was behind the killing of Kartikeya. They were the same dark forces that slew Advait, Markandeya and Durgadas Shastri - the New World Order! But know this, Vidyut - blood was spilled from both sides. For every son that this family sacrificed in protecting the secret of the Black Temple, we eliminated several Overlords and accomplices of the Order. There were sensational political assassinations carried out by us when needed. On other occasions, the fight took the form of ethereal battles of occult and exorcism. Some of the others were just no-holds-barred street fights.

The scale finally started tilting in our favor when Kartikeya decided to take the offensive to their stronghold in the United States of America. It was in Kartikeya's time that the Order had to pay the heaviest price for every drop of Shastri blood they had ever drawn. But the Illuminati and the other secret societies that together form the New World Order, were too powerful even for Kartikeya. They finally caught up with their enemy number one, surrounded him and killed him on a rainy night in San Francisco. Even in his mutilated and half-dead state, my grandson and your father, the valiant Kartikeya Shastri, did not reveal the location of the last Black Temple.'

Vidyut sat there stunned. He wanted to burst out crying, but he could not. His veins were ready to explode with rage and vengeance.

'So, you see, beta,' Dwarka Shastri continued in a near-breaking voice, 'in every sense of the word, it has been a war. A war waging for hundreds of years. And we, the Shastri bloodline, lost everything we held dear during the course of this trying journey.

But I assure you, Vidyut, even then never *once* did we harm an innocent. Never once was our fight anything other than our holy duty towards protecting mankind. Not once, over hundreds of years, did our ancestors abandon propriety and *dharma.*'

·||卐||·

It was now that the real nature of this war sunk into Vidyut. From what he remembered of his loving father, Kartikeya Shastri was a soft-spoken, ever smiling, thorough gentleman, who read fairy tales to Vidyut at night. And here it was – the cold truth. Assassinations, occult, exorcism, killing of the Order's Overlords…this went deeper, farther than he had permitted his mind to wander. Every time Dwarka Shastri had spoken about this centuries' old blood-feud, somewhere deep down Vidyut knew what it meant. Just that it was hard for him to accept his father's, his grandfather's and all his forefathers' hands to be stained with blood, even if it were so in the righteous path of saving the meek from the monster.

Vidyut was faced with a choice. He could get up right now,

dissociate himself from everything like it was a terrible nightmare and turn his back on his great grandfather, on the matth and on this thousand-year saga of horror and viciousness...never to return again. He could go and live an affluent, metropolitan life in his glamorous penthouse with Damini, with all material comforts at his disposal.

Or he could inherit this war, embrace the violent legacy of his forefathers and fulfill the ancient prophecy.

In that very moment, Vidyut accepted his destiny. He looked at Dwarka Shastri with eyes that said everything to the grand old man. The devta clenched his teeth, shut his eyes and proudly embraced his bloodline for everything that it was. He bowed his head for a few moments, in silent salutation to his great ancestors who had sacrificed themselves one after the other at the altar of humankind's temple. When he opened his eyes, he was someone else.

He was the last protector of Kaliyuga's greatest secret.

The secret of the Black Temple.

The Marshes Surrounding the Great Ark, Aryavarta, 1698 BCE

THE MAN-EATING OGRE

The Ark looked like the darkest night had descended upon earth. Stretching for miles in length and taller than the tallest peak of the mighty Himalayas, from miles and miles away the entire Ark appeared to be a black, titanic block.

Not a single flicker of light was permitted. Not a single lamp could be lit. Manu, Dhruv, Tara and Prachanda had decided to use darkness as a battle tactic. Messages had been sent to the tens of thousands of inhabitants of the Ark – all days and nights here on were to be spent in complete darkness.

The reason was simple. The daitya attack, reinforced heavily by the brigands from the badlands, was now imminent.

Hundreds of daitya camps had mushroomed all around the Ark, at a distance of a few miles away. It was clear now that the cannibals and the bandits were surrounding the great boat from all ten directions.

The residents and fighters of the Ark were justifiably nervous, and visibly shaken - but they were not unprepared. In fact, the entire vessel was now a gargantuan garrison, ready for the terrible adversary they awaited.

·‖ॐ‖·

In the complete darkness, it was impossible for the attackers to spot where the thousands of archers atop the decks of the great Ark crouched, ready in their positions, fortifying the entire perimeter. Vast legions of the elite fish-folk infantry and cavalry had made their move in the blackest hours of the night, and were now waiting in enormous, secret chambers that the daityas could never foreknow even in their wildest imagination.

Sprawling, temporary kitchens had been set up deep inside the belly of the Nauka. So deep that the colossal cooking fires were not even remotely visible to any observer outside the Ark. This was done to ensure that a nourishing broth of hot vegetables and rice was supplied to the thousands of fighters on the frontlines at regular intervals. A thick soup of meat and rice was being cooked continuously in hundreds of oversized pots. This was to keep the asura soldiers fed during the grueling days and nights of battle that lay ahead of them.

Nearly every deck of the great vessel creaked under the bludgeoning weight of the latest cargo that had been added over the last few weeks. Arrows. And as Tara had planned – millions of them. Each Ark archer was now armed with more than a thousand arrows, ready to be replenished at a moment's notice.

But above all the other preparations and readiness for a full-scale war, what Manu was depending on most was the one weapon Matsya had bequeathed upon him before the magnificent blue-man had departed.

'Use it when you think all is lost, O Satyavrata,' Matsya had said. 'And *Agni*, the God of fire, will come to your aid.'

He had demonstrated it to Satyavrata and Dhruv in a secret location, after which he had supplied them with hundreds of barrels full of this alchemical wonder.

Gandhak.

·||ॐ||·

Somdutt looked unusually worried as he struggled through his rationed meal, taking minutes between each morsel. Manu sat beside him, eating his own rice broth in silence. By now their eyes were used to the perpetual dimness. Therefore, even in the pitch-dark cabin, Satyavrata could sense his trusted counsel's anxiety.

'Something seems to be bothering you, Somdutt ji...' enquired Manu.

He knew Somdutt was one of the people who would play a decisive role in the future of mankind. Without him the great Ark, this astonishing marvel of ship-construction, would not have been built. Working together over the last several months towards this daunting undertaking, the mutual affection and respect between both these iconic men had grown boundlessly. But most of all, Somdutt reminded Satyavrata Manu of his father, Vivasvan Pujari. Not for a moment could he forget that it was Somdutt alone who stood by the Surya when even the latter's own shadow had forsaken him. Manu had come to love the chief architect of Harappa as well as of the Ark like a father. Somdutt was the only parent Manu had left, since Vivasvan, Sanjna and Matsya had left him. In turn, the great architect loved the young priest-king like a son.

'Yes, I am worried, Manu. I am seeing all these battle preparations around me and it is all very heartening. With the combined forces of the Harappan army, the marvelous fish-folk warriors and the asura fighters, we do stand a small but real chance of repelling the colossal army of cannibals preparing to surround us. Between you, Dhruv, Tara and Prachanda we have excellent Generals to lead this *antim-yuddha* or last-battle of the human race, before pralay engulfs the entire planet.'

'It is reassuring for me to hear these words from you, Somdutt ji. But then what is it that is bothering you so much that you are unable to enjoy this frugal but delicious meal?'

Somdutt turned to look at Manu. Despite the all-pervasive darkness, Manu could see fear on the chief architect's face.

'Nara-Munda, Manu...we are not prepared for that demonic

fiend Nara-Munda!'

·‖ॐ‖·

'You all do not understand…he is *not* human!' yelled Somdutt to everyone sitting in the war-room of the Ark.

Immediately after he had expressed his concern to Manu over their brief meal, Manu had convened a meeting of the Generals. His closest and most trusted aides, Dhruv, Tara and Prachanda were now present. As were the Saptarishi.

'Nara-Munda is not born of natural procreation. I am not aware of how he has become what he has, but he is certainly a biological mutation of some kind.'

Everyone in the war-room was listening intently to Somdutt.

'Have you ever thought why even the great Vivasvan Pujari and the wise Pundit Chandradhar had kept the Harappan administration away from the dark forests of Aryavarta? Think about it. Even with the mighty army of Harappa riding under his banner, fully aware of his own divine valor, my friend Vivasvan Pujari never ventured towards the eerie forests,' continued Somdutt.

The reality was slowly sinking into everyone present. Clearly, the Surya of Harappa was trying to keep the metropolis safe from something. Something terrible that lurked in the dark forests. It was now that Somdutt had unveiled the truth.

'Even the Surya of Harappa, the slayer of the mighty demon-king Sura, the destroyer of armies, the invincible Vivasvan Pujari – even *he* did not want to lock horns with the man-eating ogre Nara-Munda!' concluded the wise architect.

This last, unsettling piece of information made Manu nervous.

Very nervous.

Banaras, 2017

ROHINI NAKSHATRA

'The holy Nakshatra is about to commence, gurudev!' announced a *sadhu*, an aged priest with a long white beard, as he entered the Bhairava mandir. The old man's eyes were filled with tears of joy as he looked at both Vidyut and Dwarka Shastri.

The matthadheesh closed his eyes, mumbled a prayer to Lord Vishnu and nodded at the old priest. 'Prepare for the prophesied hour, Mahant Yograj. The devta is ready!'

Vidyut was bewildered as he heard the exchange between the two men from the Dev-Raakshasa matth. Even before he could ask for an explanation, dozens of priests in crimson and saffron robes streamed into the Kaal-Bhairava shrine, collectively chanting mantras and throwing fistfuls of consecrated ash and flowers into every corner of the temple. Vidyut was amazed at the synchronization in the intonation of the mantras. The holy priests nearly half-sang the sacred prayers as if they were all in fact one person. The resulting effect was a booming, harmonious melody that seemed to make every pillar, every wall and every dust particle of the temple shudder in an overpowering, positive vibration.

'Walk with me, Vidyut. The time has come, my son. The moment this planet has been waiting for. The hour for which we have all bled over centuries. The prophesy of Matsya. The secret of the Black Temple awaits you, O devta!' pronounced Dwarka Shastri, shouting above the din of the chanting, gesturing towards Vidyut to follow him.

At the very same moment Damini walked in to the reverberating temple, looking around in a daze at the priests. Several hours had passed and she had been sent for by the matthadheesh. She was closely followed by all the others – Purohit ji, Naina, Govardhan, Balvanta, Sonu and other senior priests of the matth. By now several cymbals and tinker-bells used in yajnas and aartis had been taken out. They were being clanged and chimed at a high pitch, in rhythm with the sacred chanting.

Vidyut was an accomplished yogi and taantric himself. He now focused on the loud, mesmerizing intonations and immediately recognized them.

The priests were collectively chanting the ultimate prayer of Lord Shiva – the very blessed – *Rudra Path*!

The devta was now clear about one thing. The priests and

the matthadheesh were sanctifying the shrine they stood in – preparing for something extraordinary. Something other-worldly.

Something supernatural.

·‖ॐ‖·

Vidyut had never been to this part of the matth. In fact, he did not even know such winding alleys and hallways existed in the raakshasa-khannd. Dwarka Shastri had led him into a dark pathway right behind the dominating bust of Lord Kaal Bhairava. Vidyut was surprised to see a concealed entrance behind the splendid statue. This doorway was not visible from any spot in the mandir.

They were now walking in and turning into almost a maze of stone corridors led by Balvanta, who illuminated the dark passageways with the flame of his tall wicker-torch. The incantation of mantras and tolling of cymbals continued in the Bhairava mandir precinct, now sounding a little muffled. Vidyut could make out that the dark corridors were slowly spiraling downwards, taking them deeper and deeper into the basement of the raakshasa-khannd. Dwarka Shastri continued the intonation as he walked, while Purohit ji and Govardhan sprinkled the consecrated ash and flowers at every step.

In the gradually dimming light, Vidyut noticed something. The devta turned to Damini, who was right by his side, and silently pointed to the walls and ceiling of the pathways that were more like tunnels now.

Damini could not understand what Vidyut was trying to say. She raised her eyebrows, expressing her bafflement.

'The stones are turning darker with every few steps,' he murmured.

'And…?' Damini whispered back.

'They are turning black.'

·||ॐ||·

It was a long walk. Several minutes had passed and they were still negotiating the underground stone maze, somewhere deep inside the Dev-Raakshasa matth. Balvanta, Purohit ji and the matthadheesh himself appeared quite surefooted. Vidyut thought to himself.

Looks as if they have travelled this serpentine path several times.

Serpentine.

Vidyut had no idea how close he was to the fantastic reality that awaited them!

'Baba, all three of them, Romi, Bala and then Trijat said the Order has kept me alive for all these years. If I am such a threat to them, if I am the prophesied devta who is going to stand in the way of their grand design, why did they not kill me much earlier? If they could plant Bala in my company, in my house years ago, if they could eliminate international leaders and military dictators at will, if they could trigger civil wars and fund revolutions – why didn't they just eliminate me when I was a child? Or even after that?'

'I was expecting this question from you, Vidyut,' replied Dwarka Shastri, without turning around. He knew the acoustics of the tunnels would make sure that every word he spoke would reach his brilliant great grandson, along with everyone else in the small delegation that was making its way towards the underbelly of the raakshasa-khannd. Each one of them was a trusted pillar of the matth, and of the war against the sinister Order.

'The answer is simple, Vidyut – the secret of the Black Temple cannot be unlocked without you. Or to put it in other words, you are the only one who can unearth and unveil the divine secret. All your ancestors, including Kartikeya, were tortured or killed because the Order wanted to track down the location of the Black Temple. But you...you were most precious to them. You still are!'

·‖ॐ‖·

They walked a few more paces in silence, the distant chanting of the Rudra-Path still tearing through the thick stone walls.

'Hard as that is to believe, Baba, if that is the case then why did Romi, then Bala and then Trijat try to kill me?' asked Vidyut.

Naina responded on the matthadheesh's behalf.

'None of them were going to kill you, Vidyut. They were going to injure you grievously, capture you...and keep you alive till this moment...till the Rohini Nakshatra. You think

Romi, who was the world's deadliest and most sophisticated assassin, would simply miss his target when you were so close to him? Would Bala, a trained ex-Army commando, have missed a shot from point blank range? Why did Trijat Kapaalik tie you in chains, when he could have easily killed you in your unconscious state? Think about it.'

Before Vidyut could even ponder over what Naina had just explained, the ground shook violently. Damini grabbed Vidyut's arm, petrified, as clouds of grey dust fell from the low ceiling of the dark alleyway. It was once again the rumble that they had felt a day ago, sitting in the matthadheesh's verandah.

Only this time, it emanated from somewhere or something much closer.

The Marshes Surrounding the Great Ark, Aryavarta, 1698 BCE

'THEY ARE COMING...'

The meeting had been going on for two hours now...most of it in cold, heavy silence, disturbed every now and then by the loud clap of thunder. The unavoidable prospect of facing Nara-Munda now loomed menacingly in the room. With no solution in sight.

'As the *guptachar-dal* of Harappa had informed all of us members of the city-council, Nara-Munda's hide cannot be penetrated easily by regular swords, arrows or spears. Even the most well-timed, most speeding arrow gives him only a superficial flesh wound. They say he has so much brute strength that a full-blooded punch from him fractures the skull of a horse! Tearing open the chest bones and rib-cages of his fallen foes with his bare claws, only to eat their hearts while they were still beating, is not infrequent for this savage half-human, half-beast.'

There was pin drop silence in the room as Somdutt uttered these last, menacing words.

For all her valiance and courage, the beautiful Satrupa could not hold her tears back. She burst into a loud sob giving her angst away, as all the men in the room swallowed lumps of fear in their throats.

Manu was no less afraid than anyone else present there. He was no less terrified even at the thought of coming face to face with this living legend of a monster. But it is in times of starkest adversity that a true leader of men stands tall - rising above material greed, above individual preservation, and even above the fears of grave personal loss. It was not for nothing that the magnificent Matsya had chosen Satyavrata Manu to be the future king and guardian of the human race.

'I will face him, O great architect of Harappa,' announced Manu.

'No, you will not!' screamed Tara instantly, as she paced across the room towards Manu.

For a very brief moment Manu was more afraid of the beauty charging at him than he was of even Nara-Munda.

·||ॐ||·

'What is the matter with you, O son of Surya??' she questioned Satyavrata, now standing inches away from him, staring into his eyes imploringly. She breathed heavily, filled with anger and dread.

'Satrupa is right, Satyavrata,' intervened Somdutt. 'We all know of and admire your valiance. We saw you overpower not just Ranga but hundreds of bestial adversaries in the months that followed. But this time it is different. Nara-Munda is equal to ten Ranga's taken together. There is no prudence in attempting the impossible, O son of Surya.'

Manu turned to the chief architect of the Ark.

'The impossible...? What do you mean, Somdutt ji? Are you declaring the result of the duel even before it is fought? Do you remember similar predictions being made when I battled the dreaded bandit warlord Kankoli in his own stronghold? Did I not quash the bestial Senapati of Dholavira when he attempted to sabotage the eviction of the city? I was unarmed when I fought and defeated the daitya attack on our caravan...'

Satyavrata Manu was not talking to Somdutt or to anyone else present in the room. He was speaking to himself... strengthening his will from the inside, drowning his mortal fear in words of self-praise – only so he could garner the courage he needed to face the demon Nara-Munda.

But that is not how his words came across to the people in the room.

Somdutt sighed. For the first time in about a year that he had known and worked with Manu closely, he noticed a hint of conceit in the young priest-king.

'Look Manu, it is not valor to jump into a battle that one is fated to lose. Let us think of some other…'

'Why are you mincing words, Somdutt ji? Just say what you want to say clearly!' snapped Manu.

Somdutt lost his cool as well. As far as he was concerned, Manu was behaving like a petulant child, unwilling to see the reality as it was. The great architect treated Manu like a son, and could not let his beloved child walk into the jaws of certain death. He decided to abandon all tact and make this young man face the truth.

The architect of Harappa glared into Manu's eyes and spoke with an uncharacteristically high pitch.

'If you fight the giant cannibal one to one, he will slaughter you and consume your flesh while it is still warm!'

·||ॐ||·

Satyavrata Manu rested sunk into a camp chair made of wood and leather. He sat bending forward, his forehead buried into his hands, his fingers pushing back his long hair from falling over his face.

He was not afraid. Neither was he upset with Somdutt for his plain-speak moments ago. He was simply, deeply worried. If *he* could not combat and defeat Nara-Munda, who else would? This one factor could change the course of history. Was the human race going to welcome the new dawn beyond pralay as a free, liberated and civilized people? Or as slaves and fodder for a savage, barbaric cult?

Somdutt felt miserable. He felt he had irreparably demoralized the only man who stood between mankind and extinction. Tara's heart cringed at seeing her man in this broken state. But she was relieved. Maybe this last outburst from Somdutt ji would make Manu change his mind and keep him away from the suicidal duel he was planning to embark upon.

It was only Dhruv who understood what Manu was really going through. As a childhood friend and as someone who had studied Manu's mind and heart to the remotest depths, the splendid archer stepped forward and put his hand on Satyavrata's shoulder.

'We can overpower him, Manu. We can kill him. But you are not going to like what I am about to suggest,' said Dhruv.

Everyone in the cold, windy chamber was listening intently. What Dhruv was going to recommend could mean the difference between victory and death.

'Go on...' replied Manu, without looking up.

'The only way we can slay the beast is if twenty of our best warriors surround him simultaneously. I will lead the assault myself.'

Manu looked up in a start. He could not believe his trusted, most reliable friend had just suggested the route of cowardice.

'You disappoint me, Dhruv. An extraordinary warrior like you proposing such a...'

Even before Manu could complete his sentence, a soldier of the fish-tribe darted into the war-room, slamming the door open, let alone knocking.

The soldier was panting heavily, both due to the long sprint up to the meeting chamber, as well as from near-panic at what he had beheld from the watch tower of the Ark.

He could utter just a few words, but they conveyed the message.

'They are coming, Satyavrata...a sea of them.'

Banaras, 2017

IT IS TIME I MET THE DEVTA...

The Maschera Bianca looked up from his breakfast plate of fresh fruit and Greek yoghurt as Aslam Biker walked into his presidential suite's posh dining room.

'Good morning, Maschera,' mumbled a nervous Aslam.

The White Mask smiled politely. He looked nothing like the petrifying ghost he had appeared to be the previous night at the hotel's health club. His slick expression was back. His expensive cologne filled the room. His gelled blonde hair and his disarming smile both beamed across the long table.

The cruelest man in the world asked in the most endearing manner.

'What news of the devta's movement, Aslam, my friend? Have they left for the mountains yet?'

The Mumbai don was relieved to see the mask in his usual, civil and stylish self.

'No, Maschera. They are all still there. Still in the Dev-Raakshasa matth.'

The Mask's face turned pensive.

'This is very strange. They should have left for Kedarnath by now. Something is not right...'

·||ॐ||·

The big screens came to life.

Secured by the most sophisticated encryption technology money could buy, this video call connected the three most powerful men in the world.

Each time they conferred digitally or in person, something changed dramatically in the course of world history. A civil war, a lethal epidemic, a series of assassinations, a major terrorist attack, a nuclear power-plant leak, a passenger aircraft lost mid-air...

These three men were the supreme Overlords of the New World Order.

One of them was something more than that.

·||ॐ||·

'They are still here, your holiness,' said the Maschera. He sat at the far end of a long conference table facing the two screens.

The Big Man from Rome was not pleased. He had expected better news.

Frank Stonefellar felt like he was hit by an express train. The implication of failure now meant a horrible end for the Order and everything it stood for. On the other hand, victory meant absolute global control and unquestioned sovereignty over the entire human race. The stakes were never higher.

'But...but they should have left by now. The dangerous constellation will light up the night sky in a few hours. How will they make sure the *devvtuh* reaches that mountain shrine in time??' demanded the Big Man.

'Something is not adding up here, Maschera,' said the Stonefellar scion from the other LED screen, his voice cold as ice. 'Kedarnath is the last Black Temple. The devta *must* enter it tonight. It is a millennia old prophecy...'

'Unless...' hissed the White Mask.

After a moment's pause, Frank Stonefellar asked matter-of-factly, 'Unless what, Maschera?' He knew what was at stake, but his tone was unwavering. He was not a supreme Overlord of the world's most powerful secret brotherhood just like that.

'Unless...Kedarnath is not the last Black Temple after all!' said the White Mask, his green eyes staring into the screens across his long table.

·||ॐ||·

The possibility of the shrewd Dwarka Shastri having out-witted them was not too remote. The old fox had done it several times before. But this time the Order was confident they had zeroed down on the last Black Temple. For years the secret lay buried in the Kedarnath shrine in Uttarakhand. The prophecy was to be fulfilled in the heart of this holy sanctum.

Their plan was simple. They were going to wait till the Ro-hini Nakshatra appeared and the foretold hour arrived. As preordained for millennia, the devta would be taken there. The brotherhood would wait for Vidyut to unfurl the secret of the Black Temple. After which they would eliminate the last devta of planet earth and acquire the secret they had been hunting for over centuries.

But now it was evident that something had changed last minute. If Vidyut was still inside the Dev-Raakshasa matth, only hours away from the sacred constellation – how would he reach Kedarnath in time for the prophecy to be realized?

'Ha…Ha…Ha…!'

The White Mask burst out laughing, getting up from his chair and throwing his head back.

The two men on the screen just watched quietly. They knew the Mask had bumped into something unexpected. They had seen such a reaction from him before. It also told them that the Mask already had the next step planned.

The Maschera Bianca kept guffawing, shaking his head in self-admonishment. After a minute, he started to calm down, wiping the water in his eyes with a neat handkerchief.

He then turned to the screens and spoke with the finesse of a corporate CEO.

'Gentlemen, I don't know how, but the secret has been removed from Kedarnath, from under our very noses. It has now reached where it was destined to reach – the last Black Temple.'

This was an update that the Overlords were not going to take lightly. The Big Man's face twitched with fury. Frank Stonefellar swallowed a lump of extreme rage. But none of them could express their anger to the Maschera's face.

Finally, the Stonefellar scion spoke with calculated irritation.

'You assured us that your man in India would not let us down, Maschera.'

'Yes, I did…yes, I did…' replied the Mask, as he abruptly switched off the screens with the remote control in front of him and ended the call.

He sat in silence for a few minutes, assessing the situation. This was the final hour.

It is time I met the devta…

The Marshes Surrounding the Great Ark, Aryavarta, 1698 BCE

ANTIM YUDDHA – PART I

It was a sight that could freeze the blood of even the most fearless of men.

An army so vast had never marched on planet earth before. And would never tread on it again. It was a militia of a size that was beyond the imagination of even writers and poets of the greatest wars. This congregation of fighters was several times larger in number than the armies that had gathered for *Dasarajna*, the great ancient battle of the Ten Kings. That men could gather and walk together in such vast numbers was unthinkable for anyone alive in Aryavarta.

With dry mouths and pounding hearts, the Generals of the

Ark watched their enemy approach like a lumbering serpent strangling them slowly from all ten directions. They were awestruck with the sight. Millions of torches glowed like a river of light from a radius of a few miles away. The frontal legions of daitya and brigand forces were now perhaps just an hour's ride away from the great Ark. But the final waves of this approaching colossus of an army were not visible. The enemy military was so massive, that it stretched beyond what the naked eye could behold.

The messenger who had darted into the war-room was right.

This was truly a sea, a typhoon charging at the Ark. To drown it.

In blood.

·‖ॐ‖·

'How…how many do you think they are, Satyavrata?' blurted Prachanda, not believing what he was seeing.

Manu stood like a statue at the highest deck of the Ark, rain drenching him and his fellowship from head to toe. In the darkness of the night, the torches of the daitya legions spread out in front of his eyes like a blanket of light covering the entire earth. They were indeed immeasurable.

'Looks like *all* the bandit tribes from here to the Vindhyas have joined forces with Nara-Munda. The scouts say that the great flood will strike the final swathes of *bhoomi* in a matter of days. Every last man, woman and child left on this part of the planet knows one thing for sure now,' said Dhruv, not taking his eyes away from the crawling ocean of cannibals even for a second.

'And what is that, Dhruv?' asked Somdutt.

Dhruv paused for a moment, drew out a glistening arrow from his quiver and placed it on his mighty bow.

'That the Ark is the last hope for survival. And that it must be stolen.

Be prepared, O defenders of the Ark. The enemy is going to fight till death.'

With these words Dhruv lit the head of the specially crafted arrow from the flame of a burning torch nearby, and shot the blazing arrow far high into the sky, as a signal to his troops.

He had declared the war open.

·||卐||·

The battle-cry of the bandit mobs was bloodcurdling.

They had now approached close enough to be heard by the fighters and residents of the great boat. They shouted themselves hoarse in unison, tens of thousands of them, and sounded more menacing than the screams of burning hell.

They were savage, skilled, hysterical, and most of all...desperate.

'Do you notice, Dhruv,' said Manu, 'that this entire forward assault does not have a single daitya soldier?'

Dhruv chuckled.

'I expected this, Manu. The scoundrel Nara-Munda will get the brigands slaughtered first, use them to weaken our defenses, and then attack us with his massive daitya contingent to annex the Ark.'

·||卐||·

'Waaaiit…' commanded Tara.

Nine thousand bows around the entire circumference of the great Ark's top decks were ready to fire their first volley of arrows.

Another three thousand supremely skilled archers waited, crouching behind the railings of the lower decks.

The growling front row of the bandit warlords' militias now broke ranks and charged towards the Ark on foot. They had waited for over an hour to incite a response from the defenders of the great vessel. But nothing had moved. Losing patience and in the heat of the gigantic assault, they picked up their twisted blades and their climbing hooks, and dashed towards the wooden colossus on foot.

Several anxious moments passed and the panting attackers came as close as a thousand steps away from the Ark.

It was now that the beautiful Tara submitted a silent prayer to Durga, and roared like a lioness.

'Nooowwww!'

THWACK!

Half a moment.

THWACK!

Half a moment.

THWACK!

The dazzling speed at which the able archers of the Damini Sena drew their arrows, placed them on their bows and shot them towards the desired targets was incredible. Over twenty thousand arrows were in flight within a matter of a couple of seconds.

The war for the Ark and the Earth had begun.

THE BLACK TEMPLE

'Where are we headed, Baba? It has been several minutes since we have been walking…'

Damini could not hold herself back. She was both terribly nervous as well as uncontrollably excited. The energy of the mantra-chanting in the Bhairava-mandir was captivating. The hidden doorway, the mysterious alleys, the inexplicable rumbling and the prospect of a divine constellation that appeared once in a thousand years…everything was making her nerves palpitate.

It was now that the grand old man turned. He smiled at Damini, glanced at Vidyut and turned back, walking deeper into the labyrinth of black stone purposefully.

'Do you know why Bhairava is revered and worshipped, biti-ya?' asked the matthadheesh, his voice echoing in the narrow lanes.

'Err...not really, Baba...sorry,' replied Damini, looking at Vidyut, grimacing sweetly and biting her tongue. She was embarrassed at her lack of knowledge about something that the grandmaster might have expected her to know.

Vidyut grinned. He loved her so much!

'He is worshipped because he is the all-powerful *dwaarpaal* or gate-keeper of the God of Gods, Lord Shiva Himself,' explained the matthadheesh.

'Ji, Baba...' replied Damini. She had no idea what to make of what Dwarka Shastri had just explained.

'It is only through him, Damini, that one can get to *Neelkantha* Shiva.'

It was like lightning that the truth now hit Vidyut. The Bhairava-mandir, the intonation of Rudra-Path, the hidden doorway, the Rohini-Nakshatra, the tunnels made of black rock, the unexplained rumbling...and now Dwarka Shastri hinting at them reaching Lord Shiva through His dwaarpaal.

Why did it not strike me before?

The last Black Temple is not somewhere far. It is here...in Kashi.

It lies buried deep under the Dev-Raakshasa matth itself!

·||ॐ||·

A few more minutes passed and the matth convoy now reached a shadowy end that led to a spiraling, stone-cut stairway. The stairs went further deep into a dark cellar.

Before starting to climb down the steep, twisted staircase, Purohit ji turned to speak to the group that followed Dwarka Shastri and him.

'What you all are about to witness is something you would have never imagined even in your wildest dreams. Just bear in mind that, no matter how fearsome the sight you are about to behold, you are the chosen few who are getting this sacred opportunity. Once you step down this stairway, your lives, your souls, your journey over births and rebirths... nothing will remain the same.'

Everyone was listening silently. A strange force emanating from deep down the cavern was beginning to overpower their senses. None of them were afraid. They were simply eager to play their respective roles in shaping the future of the human race.

They were ready.

·‖卐‖·

Vidyut, Damini and everyone else in the group was dumbfounded as they surveyed the magnificent Black Temple that enveloped them.

The rough, rock-cut ceiling appeared as if it were built thousands of years ago. The figurines sculpted right into the black stone walls were breathtakingly intricate and beautiful.

The sheer size of this magnificent shrine was awe inspiring. It was hard for Balvanta, Naina, Sonu, Govardhan and the other priests to believe that such a massive Black Temple lay buried right under the precinct of the Dev-Raakshasa matth. They had lived in the monastery for years and yet none of them had any knowledge about the existence of this splendid temple.

Dwarka Shastri permitted Vidyut some time to study the gigantic basement shrine, even as he instructed the sadhus accompanying them to begin the sacred rituals. A glorious statue of Lord Shiva stood in the center of the temple. The priests lit a ceremonial fire at the foot of Shiva and commenced the Rudra-Path once again. Upon the direction from his father, Sonu lit the scores of wicker-torches that lined the temple walls one after the other. Slowly, the entire precinct began to glow in the orange light of the flames.

'What I am about to share with you now will be very hard for you to believe, Vidyut. But keep the faith, my son. Every word I tell you is the truth.'

'Yes, Baba. This sanctum is anyway inexplicably holy, as if it has been touched by the Lord Himself. I have been fortunate to have visited almost all the holy temples of Lord Shiva across India. I have had the *darshana* of Lord Rudra across all the twelve *jyotirlinga* shrines. I have been to several blessed temples of Kashi also over the last few days. But never have I felt divinity as strongly as I feel here. There is something very different, very overwhelming here, Baba.'

The grand old man smiled.

'Not something, Vidyut.

Someone.'

The Marshes Surrounding the Great Ark, Aryavarta, 1698 BCE

ANTIM YUDDHA – PART II

The beast stood a mile away from the great Ark, observing the progress of the assault. Nara-Munda was stunned to see the rain of arrows that was wreaking havoc on his forward legions. He had expected fierce resistance alright, but never in the innumerable battles that he had participated in had he witnessed such a severe, lethal deployment of archers.

He was not overly worried, however, given that the entire first wave comprised warriors from the bandit tribes. He could not care less about the loss of life they were suffering. For him they were nothing more than a human shield, meant only to press forward the attack. He was not planning to take any of them on the Ark anyway. Whoever survived from the brigand troops was to be executed before the Ark was washed aloft by the gigantic waves of pralay.

'This cannot go on, my lord,' said Doonda, the daitya senapati. 'The Ark-men seem to have an infinite supply of arrows. Clearly, they have been preparing for this war more rigorously than we had imagined.'

'Hmmm…' growled Nara-Munda, as he observed hundreds of bandit fighters falling prey in an instant to the next barrage of sharp metal.

'Soon the bandits will all be dead, O mighty chieftain. Our daityas will be in the direct line of fire thereafter.'

'Or maybe not…' said Nara-Munda, as he turned and smiled crookedly at Doonda, baring his blood-stained fangs.

The daitya senapati knew instantly that the giant fiend had come up with some cruel, ingenious plan.

·||ॐ||·

'They are getting slaughtered, Manu!' cried Somdutt with glee, unable to hide his excitement at the early success of the Damini Sena archers. They were watching the proceedings from a high deck of the great vessel.

'We are cutting them down by the thousands. Not one enemy soldier has been able to plant a hook onto the Ark,' added Prachanda.

Even a battle veteran like him had not seen arrows deployed at this unimaginable scale. Not an inch of the marshes surrounding the Ark was left untargeted. The arrows shot from the bows of the Damini-Sena competed in numbers with the scathing raindrops.

Manu kept silent. Deep inside he was delighted to see the dominance of the Ark archers over the savage enemy. But this was all too easy. And that thought was troubling the young priest-king. Nara-Munda was not one to let this on-slaught continue.

'They are retreating!' exclaimed one of the Ark soldiers, pointing towards the battle lines.

All the spectators on the great boat pinned themselves against the wooden railing of the observation deck to get a clear sight of the battlefield. The soldier was right. Having lost thousands over a matter of hours, the attackers were falling back.

'Relieve the Damini-Sena and get Dhruv's bowmen to take position,' Satyavrata Manu shouted his orders. 'Ask the kitchens to serve the valiant ladies a hot meal. Several of them have splayed their fingers while pulling the bowstring for hours together. Their hands are bleeding profusely. Get them to the *vaidya* immediately! The night guard should re-main sharp and alert. This war is just getting started. Tomor-row the daityas will attack with double the fury and definitely new tactics.'

Manu could not even imagine what the daityas were going to come up with the next day.

Even now he underestimated the brutality of Nara-Munda.

·‖卐‖·

'In the pitch darkness of the stormy night, the daityas are taking away the dead and the wounded,' said Tara, as they sat over the day's progress.

Everyone in the room was deeply satisfied with the proceedings of the first few hours of battle. Countless bandit warriors lay dead, pierced by the deadly arrows of the Damini-Sena. The casualties were so heavy that some in the room hoped the war was already over. Who would come back the next morning to face this blizzard of pointed copper once again?

'The daityas do not care one bit about the brigands, Tara,' responded Dhruv.

'Then why are they taking the dead and the injured away? I presumed it was to perform the last rites of the demised and to treat the wounded...'

'They are not taking away men, Tara. They are taking away meat. The massive daitya army will feed on the dead.'

Tara felt she would throw up. Even the thought of what Dhruv had just explained made her nauseous.

'Tomorrow they will not be so vulnerable. Having seen our firepower today, they will spend the night preparing a defense system. It could be stronger, thicker armor for their men...' said Manu, thinking aloud.

'That seems unlikely, Manu. Even if they begin to organize such armor, given their mammoth numbers that exercise would take weeks, if not months,' replied Dhruv. 'They do not have that kind of time. The deluge will strike any day now.'

'You are right, brother. But they will come back with something…God knows what.'

Banaras, 2017

THE SERPENT KING

'Pundit Bhairava Shastri, the founder and builder of the Dev-Raakshasa matth, was a visionary. He could predict that the last Black Temple would be hunted for more than any other. He also knew that the Order would go to any extent to acquire the secret of the Black Temple during or immediately after the Rohini Nakshatra of this year of the *Shak-Samvata* or Hindu calendar.'

The matthadheesh was taking Vidyut and Damini around the underground Black Temple.

'For several years Kedarnath was the temple that hid the secret. But the Order was close on our heels and soon discovered that the holy shrine in the hills of Rudraprayag held what they had been seeking for centuries. The sinister brotherhood had then entrusted a Mumbai based gang-lord named Aslam Biker to keep an eye on Kedarnath.'

'Aslam Biker? God! He is quite a notorious criminal, running drug cartels and illegal arms trade. Who would have imagined that even he would be associated to the New World Order?' exclaimed Damini. She was a journalist. She knew all about Aslam Biker.

'Yes, the same dreaded gangster. He is in Varanasi these days, by the way. Anyhow, we moved the secret from Kedarnath back in June 2013, under the cover of the devastating floods that had hit the mountain-state. The head-priest of the mandir, Mahant Bhavaanishankar, worked closely with Naina, and the divine secret was shifted to the Dev-Raakshasa matth, here in Banaras. This underground temple was built in the year 1253 AD to serve as Kaliyuga's last Black Temple. Today it will fulfill its destiny along with you, Vidyut.'

·||ॐ||·

'NAAAAGG...'

Damini was struck with mortal fear as she felt she heard the temple's black caves hiss.

'Did you hear that, Vidyut?' she asked, as she grabbed the devta's sleeve, almost choking with fear.

'Yes, I did, Damini,' he replied. He was equally stunned.

They had now reached the opening of a broad, long tunnel that led to an even darker section of the Black Temple.

Vidyut could feel a magnetic pull emanating from deep down the tunnel. He felt like every cell in his body was rejoicing, tearing to reach whatever lay hidden at the end of this black, mysterious corridor.

'NAAAAAAAGGG...'

Once again, the hollow cavern was filled with a chilling hiss. This time it was even louder. An unknown force was announcing the presence of something exceptionally powerful.

'You wait here with Balvanta and Naina, bitiya,' Dwarka Shastri instructed Damini, stroking her head lovingly in a blessing. 'As Vidyut's eternal spiritual companion, your presence here at the Black Temple is vital. But for now, it is best you wait in front of the Shiva statue. Here on it is a journey that the devta needs to traverse alone.'

'Ji, Baba...' replied Damini, even as Naina put a reassuring arm around her.

·||ॐ||·

'You might think it is hypnosis. What you are about to see could well be a very profound hypnotic conjuration. The ancient sage you are about to meet is one of the most accomplished yogis in the world. His power of the mind and the spirit over the body is nearly supernatural. They say he is thousands of years old and has never left the planet since the time of the Matsya avatar almost four thousand years ago,' explained Dwarka Shastri, as they made their way towards the celestial guest that awaited them.

In the darkness Vidyut first noticed the green shimmer some distance away. He was experiencing an inexplicable feeling of fear combined with devotion. As if he knew the visitor from another place, another time.

Slowly, the scores of king cobras slithering across the floor and ceiling caught the devta's eye. Vidyut stopped in his stride, as he looked at his Baba in shock.

'These are cobras, Baba...we must not risk it,' he said, cringing at the sight of the gleaming black reptiles.

'They will not harm us, Vidyut. They accompany our divine guest. I have been coming here every night for a week now, beta. Trust me.'

They proceeded slowly and finally reached the stone-cut enclosure that housed their unusual guest.

·||࿗||·

He appeared to be human, but of extraordinary size. He sat crouched in the center of the stone cave, which glowed in a soothing green from the brilliant texture of the visitor's skin. In the darkness of the Black Temple, Vidyut noticed something bizarre.

The crouching man's face was bent between his knees. It was covered with long white tresses of hair, and his body was covered with scales! Splendid serpent-scales that dazzled in glittering shades of blue and green. Even though the sight was starkly unnatural, Vidyut was not afraid. Something inside him was urging him to fall at the feet of this astonishing visitor. The entire Black Temple seemed to have come alive under the overpowering, magical, cosmic spell of this serpent-man!

The grand old matthadheesh now folded his hands and spoke with unhidden devoutness.

'Darshan dein, Sarpa-Raaj!'

'Show yourself and bless us, O Serpent-King!'

The gigantic man stirred. The radiance of his skin seemed to turn even more brilliant. What happened next was something that made Vidyut dizzy with disbelief.

The celestial visitor seemed to grow in size, the glow emitting from his body now almost blinding in its luminosity. The devta could not believe his eyes as in the blur of the brilliant blue-green light he felt he saw the giant serpent-man's head splitting into several heads.

Not heads, in fact.

Hoods.

The primordial serpent now appeared over twenty feet in height, as its glorious ten-hooded reptilian head erupted into the darkness of the cave-temple in a dazzling glimmer.

For Vidyut it was all a dream.

What Dwarka Shastri said next, that echoed like they were coming from a far distance, were words that the devta had never thought he or any human would ever hear.

'Swaagatam, Naag-Raj!'

'Welcome, O Emperor of Snakes!'

'Swaagatam, Shesh-Naag!'

'Welcome, Shesh-Naag!'

The Marshes Surrounding the Great Ark, Aryavarta, 1698 BCE

'BEFORE THEY BEGIN TO CLIMB THE ARK, WE MUST CLIMB DOWN'

Even though it was supposedly the hours well after dawn, black clouds continued to cover the Sun completely. Just like each day of the several months that had passed since Harappa fell, Aryavarta was enveloped in darkness. Streaks of the sky visible beyond the cloud cover appeared blood red...as if preparing for what was about to unfold on the earth below. Merciless rain continued to pour, only with much greater force. Such incessant cloudburst was an evident harbinger of the chilling reality.

The colossal flood waves were now just days away.

Pralay was coming to swallow the marshes.

And with that, all of known earth would drown in the great deluge.

The daityas were now getting desperate. They had to take the Ark, or it was clear that every single one of them would perish. It was now a battle of survival for the barbarians, and no act of cruelty was beyond them.

·‖ॐ‖·

The daityas were back. Once again in fearsome numbers. From a distance, it was not visible as to who led the attack, but the ghastly battle cries made it clear that it was the daityas themselves leading the frontal assault.

They were positioned a mile away, not moving. Then something strange happened. One rider galloped out from the multitudes of daityas and rode alone towards the Ark. Tara looked enquiringly at Manu, asking if the rider should be stopped by her archers.

Manu shook his head.

'Let him come. He might be a messenger.'

As the rider came closer, everyone atop the Ark noticed something odd. Clearly an expert horseman, the daitya warrior galloped with the reins held between his teeth. He held big, smoking torches in both his hands.

Satyavrata Manu and Tara were on high decks and could not see the rider clearly. He now came within a few paces of the Ark and stopped. As if displaying himself and inviting an arrow, he strode along the Ark staring into the eyes of the archers on the lowest deck. No arrow was fired.

He then turned and waved his torches at his daitya forces. Twenty more riders broke ranks and began galloping towards the Ark.

Manu and Tara could not understand what was happening.

'He is not a messenger. Why is Dhruv not shooting down the daityas who are riding towards us?' said Manu, unable to grasp what the cannibals were up to.

He did not have to wait long.

Dhruv came running towards Manu. He had climbed several levels to bring this bizarre news himself.

'They have made armors, Manu. But not what we had expected.'

'What do you mean, Dhruv?'

'All these daityas have living, crying infants strapped on to them.'

·||ॐ||·

'They are children of the thousands of bandits who fell yesterday,' explained Dhruv. 'The daitya fighters have each strapped on a child in front of their torsos, thus fashioning the most shameless form of a human shield. They were testing us. First, with one rider. Then with twenty. Now they know we will not fire our volleys. This has an ominous implication for us, Manu.'

'The scoundrels!' yelled Manu, slamming his fist into the wooden railing he stood against. 'The stinking cowards!'

'This renders our entire Damini-Sena dormant, Manu. We cannot shoot a single arrow now, lest we should hit a child.'

'What about your archers, Dhruv? They are all supremely trained and are three thousand in number. Can they not take out the enemy one by one, without hurting any of the infants?'

'That would be a bad idea, Satyavrata. They are moving targets. Taking headshots from such a distance, that too in this rainy environment would be impossible.'

That things would change so dramatically overnight was something Manu had never expected. But then, even in his wildest thought he could never stoop to the level that the daityas had so readily, blatantly fallen to.

·‖卐‖·

'There is one saving grace in all this, Manu,' said Tara, who had been quietly observing the enemy troops.

'And what is that?' asked Manu, hoping to hear something that could save the day.

He was not disappointed.

'Do you notice there are no bandit banners in the armies that surround us?' asked Tara.

Manu turned his gaze to the enemy. Tara was right.

'But Tara, the visibility is poor and the bandit forces may have been rested after the massive numbers that succumbed yesterday,' said Manu.

'I do not think so, Manu. No matter how savage the brigands from the badlands are, none of them would permit the daityas to use the children of their dead fellowmen in this manner.'

Everyone listening to Tara pondered over what she was saying. She continued.

'With a large section of their ablest warriors dead, the bandit tribes are of little use to Nara-Munda. The daityas have probably slaughtered all the remaining bandits in the darkness of the night. And that means we have a significantly lesser number of enemies to combat.'

If what Tara was saying turned out to be true, the scale would tilt back somewhat in favor of the defenders of the Ark.

Manu did not want to depend on it, but he nodded vigorously at what Tara had said, hoping for the best. He turned to Dhruv.

'It is up to us then, Dhruv. You, me and king Prachanda need to lead our infantry out to the battlefield and face the man-eaters head on.

Before they begin to climb the Ark, we must climb down.'

Banaras, 2017

SHESHNAAG

Vidyut sat in a daze in front of the Shiva statue.

He had fallen to his knees upon the magnificent sight he had just beheld. He had folded his hands and bowed his head, unable to lock eyes with the ethereal, the supernatural radiance of the primordial serpent's yellow and black eyeballs – ten pairs of them!

It was as if the divine naag wanted Vidyut to see his true form only momentarily. Seconds later the gigantic, ten-hooded reptile had slowly, magically begun to shrink in size, his blue-green aura slowly subsiding. When finally Vidyut had raised his head to look at him, Sheshnaag had transformed into an old sadhu, sitting in deep penance. He looked hundreds of years of age, his crumpled skin still resembling that of a snake. Even from his sitting posture the devta could tell that the serpent-king was unusually tall and powerfully built.

'Your darshana for today is complete, Vidyut. The mighty Sheshnaag will summon you again soon,' Dwarka Shastri had whispered into the devta's ears, before they touched the serpent-king's feet and took leave of him.

As Vidyut trudged back to the central sanctum of the Black Temple, he was speechless. He had experienced the most transcendental spiritual elation of his life.

Little did he know that it was just the beginning.

·‖卐‖·

'Some sadhus from the Himalayas claim that Sheshnaag has been consistently spotted by sages practicing penance in the highest peaks of the mountains. They say he has been seen from a distance by several hermits ever since the *Mahaparin-irvaan* of the Buddha. He has most commonly been sighted in the area surrounding the Sheshnaag Lake, that falls on the way to the holy Amarnath temple of Lord Shiva, about thirty-two kilometers from Pahalgam.'

Vidyut was listening to every word, but he looked as if he was still in a trance.

The others sitting around were in a shocked state of their own. They could not believe they were actually listening to a discussion around Sheshnaag, the eternal companion of Lord Vishnu Himself! They knew that in the era of Lord Rama, his brother Lakshman was believed to be an incarnation of the immortal serpent. When Vishnu had arrived as the Krishna avatar, his older brother Balram was none other than an avatar of Sheshnaag.

And here they were, being told by the great matthadheesh that the divine serpent from the mythical tales now resided in the Dev-Raakshasa matth...just a few paces away from where they sat.

'So, *this* is the secret of the Black Temple!' deduced Damini suddenly. 'This is what the Order has been after for centuries? Sheshnaag! They want to kill him because someone as indescribably powerful and indestructible as him can stand in the way of their nefarious ambitions?!'

The others turned to the grand old man, their eyes wide in anticipation. Damini had to be right. Sheshnaag had to be the secret of the Black Temple.

'Speak please, Baba...is Sheshnaag the secret of the Black Temple?' urged Naina.

Dwarka Shastri gave an amused look to all of them.

'Of course not.'

·॥ॐ॥·

Purohit ji sat with a *maha-panchanng* or the Sanatana astrological calendar spread out in front of him.

After studying it for a couple of minutes, he looked up at Dwarka Shastri.

'It has started, gurudev...the Rohini Nakshatra has begun.'

Just as he completed this sentence, the muffled sound of hundreds of *shankha* or conches could be heard by everyone in the Black Temple. Even though they were deep down in the underbelly of the earth, surrounded by walls made of black stone, the potent and melodious hoot from conches being blown into by hundreds of priests across the city of Kashi could not be stopped.

'What is this, Baba? Where is this *shankha-naad* coming from?' asked Vidyut.

Dwarka Shastri, Purohit ji and several other of the matth priests now produced conches of their own. The other sadhus picked up the cymbals and the worship-bells.

'The holy hour has arrived, O devta! Remember your ancestors! Fold your hands in veneration of all your forefathers – Vivasvan Pujari, Satyavrata Manu, Advait Shastri, Durgadas Shastri, Bhairava Shastri, Markandeya Shastri and your father, Kartikeya Shastri!

They all fought and bled so that you could stand here on this holiest of days – and do what the universe has sent you to do!'

The Marshes Surrounding the Great Ark, Aryavarta, 1698 BCE

ANTIM YUDDHA – PART III

The decks of the Ark were now clanging heavily with the rustle of armor and weapons. Tens of thousands of defenders of the great Ark were preparing to launch a frontal counterattack against the daitya aggressors. Each one of them knew that even after the perishing of the bandit legions, they were still outnumbered three to one.

'The Damini Sena can be of great service even now, Tara,' said Manu, as a helper fastened the hooks of his heavy armor behind his waist.

'We are ready to fight, Manu,' replied Tara. 'My warriors are second to none.'

'Yes, Tara, I know. Which is why they need to be held back as reserves, as the Ark's last line of defense. If we fall to the daitya swords, they will storm the Ark. That is when the Damini Sena will fight to protect the innocent residents of the great boat. But until then, there is something they can do.'

'And what is that?'

'The daityas that get slain or wounded by our soldiers, will still have infants tied to them. The little ones, if not rescued in time, will get trampled under the hooves of the cavalry from both sides. As we make our way into the heart of the daitya army, fighters from the Damini Sena should rescue all the infants and bring them to the safety of the boat.'

'You really are the chosen one, Satyavrata,' said Somdutt, who was also tightening his armor just a few paces away and could hear what Manu had just advised Tara.

'Only you can think of the safety of even your enemy's children, that too in the face of such extreme adversity. Matsya made no mistake, O son of Surya. Someone like you shall always have the blessings of Lord Pashupati!'

·||卐||·

'No way am I letting you descend into that bloodbath, Somdutt ji.'

It was only when Somdutt spoke the kind words to Manu that the young priest-king noticed the great architect putting on armor. He was determined not to let his late father's loyal friend face the heat of the daitya attack. While Somdutt was also an accomplished warrior, somewhere deep-down Manu knew the aging architect was no match for the ferocity of the cannibals.

The daityas were more vicious and more skilled than any enemy he had seen before.

'That is no place for you, Somdutt ji. We need you. The Ark needs you! Heaven forbid if something were to happen to you, we would be all but orphaned!' insisted Satyavrata.

'Yes, Somdutt ji, please do not climb down into the hellfire that awaits us. As you have seen, these beasts are unpredictable. They can stoop to any level. Do not endanger yourself,' added Dhruv, who was equally concerned looking at Somdutt prepare for battle.

The wise architect raised his hand, gesturing to his man-at-arms to stop working on his armor. He turned to the two handsome men, the two men he knew were the future of mankind.

'Look, Manu, I sincerely appreciate your concern for my well-being. But when I saw your father last, when I witnessed you riding away from the battlefield with Sanjna in your arms, I promised myself that I will protect you till my last breath. If you think I am going to let you jump into that madness alone, you are mistaken.'

'But, Somdutt ji...'

'That is all, Satyavrata. We are wasting precious time. The enemy is at the gates. Their soldiers are already beginning to climb to the first deck. We must leave now. Just remember this, Manu...I love you like a son.'

The wise old man was not willing to listen. Manu did not say anything more.

That is the problem, Somdutt ji. I too love you like a father.

·‖ॐ‖·

The scale and fierceness of the counter-strike by the defenders of the Ark was unexpected even for the mighty daityas. They were awestruck as they saw thousands of Harappan soldiers sliding down innumerable ropes from the highest decks of the colossus of a boat. The upper echelons of the Ark were not even visible beyond the black clouds. The fighters of the Ark seemed to be flying down straight from the heavens!

The clash of metal was heart-wrenching, as without waiting for their feet to hit the ground, hundreds of Harappan soldiers launched themselves from the high walls of the Ark directly into the multitudes of the daitya warriors, swords drawn.

It was brutal combat right from the first instant. The daityas used everything as weapons. Swords, spears, machetes, daggers, animal claws, poison darts, their own nails, limbs and teeth. For the Harappan soldiers it was like fighting a pack of rabid wolves rather than human beings.

The next to reinforce the Ark fighters was the asura contingent led by Prachanda. They used ladders made of rope and vine to climb down the vessel and join the blood-fight below.

And then, like meteors screaming down the sky, two fierce warriors struck the daitya formation. While the trained Harappan soldiers had dived off the Ark walls ten or fifteen arms high up from the ground, these two magnificent men seemed to have hurled themselves into the enemy troops from over forty arms in the air.

Both held tall and broad battle shields, using the cover of which they crashed into the spears, armors and swords of the daityas from above, crushing several of them upon their landing. Both warriors rolled forward to use the momentum to tear further deep into the cannibals' battle lines.

One of them held a splendid bow. He had four quivers full of arrows strapped to himself, one each on his two thighs and two across his back. He was the known world's most feared archer.

He was Dhruv.

The other warrior was clad in a shining armor made from bronze and leather. His long hair was matted and tied in a single braid. He held a shield and a long-sword in his hands, while two menacing short-swords hung from both sides of his waist. He was the man who had never lost a battle. He was the fighter every daitya wanted to avoid. He was the man Nara-Munda was waiting for.

He was Manu.

Two lions had pounced upon a cackle of hyenas.

Banaras, 2017

THE STATUE OF RUDRA

'All of Kashi is rejoicing, Baba!'

Sonu came clambering down the tricky stairway. He had been sent all the way out to the matth terrace by his father, the wise Purohit ji, to observe the night sky. But he came back with much more.

He came closer, panting, but very pleased.

'The Nakshatra sparkles in the sky just as you had told me. But there is more. The entire city joins us in this holy hour, Baba! Thousands of temples are performing the aarti of Lord Vishnu. Holy yajna pits billow sacred smoke from hundreds of monasteries. Hundreds of priests have gathered at the ghaat of the holy Ganga to perform a late-night worship. The whole of Kashi is welcoming the Rohini Nakshatra, Baba!'

Dwarka Shastri closed his eyes and thanked the Lord.

'They are not welcoming the Nakshatra. They are welcoming He who is going to arrive.'

·‖ॐ‖·

'But, Baba, how can so many people know about this Nakshatra? I was under the impression that it would have been kept under wraps. Do they all know about the secret, Baba?'

'No, Vidyut. But a message had been sent out to them from the Dev-Raakshasa matth. These are the same holy men who had assisted me in the battle of exorcism with the Big Man from Rome, when he had attempted to possess your soul. I sent them the word. They know something divine is about to occur. But only Sheshnaag, Purohit and I know what it is exactly. And in moments from now, you will know too, my son.'

With this the matthadheesh raised his shankha to his lips and blew into it with great force. The other sadhus joined him with conches, cymbals and bells. Incense sticks were lit, camphor lamps decorated around the Shiva statue and once again a powerful chanting of mantras began.

This time Vidyut noticed it was not the Rudra-Path. He focused again on the words of the chanting -

| | Shantakaram Bhujagashayanam

Padmanabham Suresham;

Vishvadharam Gaganasadrisham

Meghavarnam Shubhangam... | |

Vidyut recognized the powerful mantra immediately.

The Vishnu Shantakaram Mantra! The mantra that drives away fear, granting the reciter valor, courage and victory.

Damini came and stood next to her devta. The atmosphere of the Black Temple was now pulsating with spiritual energy. The resounding echo of the multiple shankha, the roaring chanting of the Vishnu Shantakaram Mantra, the clanging cymbals and chiming bells, the fragrance of marigold and camphor...the Black Temple reverberated with infectious, dizzying, captivating energy!

While the other priests continued their intonations, Dwarka Shastri walked up to Vidyut. He had to come close to the devta's ear and shout at the top of his voice, to be audible above the mesmerizing din of the cave-temple.

'Come, Vidyut...it is time!' he said, and held his great grand-son's wrist.

·||卐||·

Dwarka Shastri led the way, taking Vidyut by his arm right to the marvelous stone sculpture of Lord Shiva that stood in the center of the sanctum. The statue was now surrounded by bright lamps of camphor and glowed in a pious light.

The matthadheesh offered a short prayer to Rudra. Almost instantly with one swoop he pulled out the heavy copper *trishul* or trident of Shiva, that stood planted into the stony ground.

A moment later a peculiar, grinding noise could be heard from somewhere behind the enormous statue of Neelkantha Shiva. It was more of a faint rumble that only Vidyut and Dwarka Shastri could hear amidst the deafening noise of the chanting. The trishul being pulled out had triggered a series of hidden gears, levers and pulleys.

To everyone's awe, the Shiva statue moved. In a smooth circular movement, the massive stone sculpture turned around a full one hundred and eighty degrees, with the back of Shiva now facing the central sanctum. After a few moments, the rear of the statue of Shiva parted from the center, from its shoulders to the waist of the seated deity. Decoupling several plates of stone that ran down the body of Shiva like a spinal cord made of rock, a vertical cavity appeared within the hollow of the statue.

And there it glowed in a brilliant blue, frightening verses of the Garuda Purana engraved all over its length, gleaming just like the ancient messenger of death that it was.

The great sword.

The Ratna-Maru!

॥ॐ॥

Vidyut's face reflected the blue aura of the sword that he stood facing. The Ratna-Maru was encased vertically, along the entire height of Shiva's torso. Its bejeweled handle was now within the devta's reach. He felt an urge to draw out the weapon from its stone casing.

'This is a celestial sword, Vidyut. It was blessed by divine galactic forces when it was being wielded by the great Vivasvan Pujari during his last battle with the asuras. Thereafter it was passed on to his son, the immortal priest-king, Satyavrata Manu. The sword was the great Ark's most precious cargo when pralay struck and did not recede for nearly two years. For three and a half millennia thereafter, this cosmic weapon has been protected by our bloodline.

It is an indomitable weapon, Vidyut. Anyone who wields it, will be unbeatable, invincible. However, there is a rider – the sword chooses its master and not the other way around.'

The priests continued with their holy intonations. Damini, Naina, Balvanta, Purohit ji, Govardhan and Sonu now gathered around the devta.

'And you think it will choose me, Baba?' asked Vidyut, unsure of what he was expected to do.

'Maybe it will, Vidyut. Maybe it will not. But that does not really matter. The great sword is not destined for you, my son...' answered the matthadheesh.

Vidyut was embarrassed for a second. For all the burden of

being the last devta that had been laid upon him over the few trying weeks, this last statement from Dwarka Shastri was quite a dampener!

Dwarka Shastri now turned to his great grandson, with an expression of disbelief.

'You still haven't understood the secret of the Black Temple, have you, Vidyut?'

The devta gave a blank expression. The grand old man burst into a short laugh, once again displaying his mild exasperation at his beloved Vidyut's ignorance.

Dwarka Shastri asked simply.

'You have read the scriptures, Vidyut.

Don't you know *who* is supposed to be the ultimate master of the Ratna-Maru?'

The Marshes Surrounding the Great Ark, Aryavarta, 1698 BCE

RIDERS OF THE FISH-TRIBE

It was mayhem.

The second day's battle between the defenders of the Ark and the man-eating daityas was a bloodbath that shook even the heart of prithvi. Never had she witnessed her children spill each other's blood with such pitiless insanity.

The daityas pounced five to one, like a pack of hungry hounds. While one stabbed, the other two grabbed the arms and legs of the opponent. Even as the fourth man tried to claw out the eyes of the enemy, the fifth one attacked the body with his teeth, beginning to devour the foe.

Even though the Harappan warriors and the asuras were a formidable force, the sheer number and unconventional battle style of the daityas was winning the ground for the cannibals. While the daityas perished in the hundreds, the defenders of the Ark were losing soldiers by the thousands.

'There is no way we can go on like this, Manu!' yelled Dhruv, as he sent an arrow tearing through the lungs of an attacking man-eater.

'Let's fight and see this day through, Dhruv...this is only the beginning!' replied Manu, panting and surveying the violent chaos all around him. He could see his soldiers falling from their horses, only to be consumed alive by a dozen pouncing daityas in a jiffy.

'If this goes on for a few more hours, there will be no beginning and no end, Manu!' shouted Dhruv, trying to make Manu see the grave reality.

The leader of the Ark relented. He knew Dhruv was right. But he also knew, it was too early to call in their elite troops.

'Okay, Dhruv...do it!'

The ace bowman nodded and pulled out an arrow with a rounded head. He rubbed it against the rough ground and the arrow lit up in a red flame. Dhruv shot it in the air, towards the Ark.

It was a signal.

Tara saw the red streak in the sky. She too was surprised at this early deployment, and instantly understood that they were losing the battle.

She was stationed at the lowest deck. The tigress of the Ark turned to one of the commanders of the Damini Sena and shouted her orders.

'Now!'

Moments later, the daityas froze at what they saw and heard. Massive platforms of thick timber began to open up at the bottom of the Ark. Sections of the Ark's bottommost hull were being lowered using powerful chains, to reveal massive hidden chambers. To the frightened trepidation of the cannibals, each chamber was filled with hundreds of cavalry of the Ark's most elite troops.

The mighty fish-folk!

·||ૐ||·

They rode like a tornado, destroying everything that stood in their way. The earth shook under their hooves as they galloped in their typical, synchronized, almost choreographed manner.

The fish-folk were unstoppable. Their swords were made of alloys that no one had seen before. Their battle-shields glinted each time thunder struck, blinding the enemy. Within minutes it appeared as if the tide of the battle had suddenly turned. Daitya heads flew in the air after being decapitated by the precise slicing blows of the army of the fish tribe. The fish-folk then split ranks and charged into the cannibal military in five different directions, attacking the center as well as the flanks.

This sudden change in the complexion of the war spurred on the Harappan soldiers as well as the asuras. The armies of the Ark attacked with renewed vigor. Even now the Ark forces were outnumbered, but it appeared like the advent of the fish-folk would soon alter the equation.

'GRRRAAAAAAHHH...!'

Suddenly, in the middle of the raging battle, something snarled as if ten lions roared together. From a distance what they saw, sent a chill down the spines of Manu, Dhruv, Somdutt and Prachanda.

Nara-Munda roared like an otherworldly fiend, his head thrown back, his hands outstretched, his elbows bent, his massive biceps bursting and his fingers twisted into claws.

'UURRRGGGGGRRRAAAAAAAAAAAA....AAAHHHH!'

He roared again, this time even more monstrously, as his head moved to look around at the enemy.

Thousands of hearts stopped and blood froze in veins. Amidst the soldiers from both sides, he stood out like a colossal titan, towering even above the riders. As his second growl tore through the battlefield, the fighting stopped for a few moments. Warriors from both sides remembered their Gods.

·||卐||·

Manu and Dhruv exchanged glances. Even though they had heard several ominous legends and folklore about the emperor of the dark forests, none of them had imagined him to be as unnaturally grisly as he now looked.

'I had told you so, Satyavrata. This is not a man. This is pure evil incarnated in a body rejected even by hell! We must surround him. We must kill him!'

'No, Dhruv! Whoever he is, whatever he is...he is the leader of our enemy. And he deserves to be fought with honor.'

'Honor? Did you just say honor? For a man who fronts helpless, orphaned infants in the face of arrows? For a man who slaughters his allies in their sleep? You want to fight such a scoundrel within the boundaries of honor, Satyavrata Manu??' retorted Dhruv irritably, stunned at the stubborn idealism of his friend and king.

Manu was quiet, as he observed his near-invincible foe from a distance.

He drew his sword, and before charging towards where Nara-Munda stood like an oak, he turned to Dhruv.

'Promise me, Dhruv...no matter what happens, you will not intervene in my duel with the king of the cannibals.'

'But Manu...' protested Dhruv.

Manu reiterated his instructions.

'Remember, Dhruv...no matter what.'

Banaras, 2017

'PADAARPANAM KURU, PRABHU!'

Vidyut stood there bewildered, drawn by the power of the blue sword that glittered as if it had lightning embedded deep in its ominous blade.

In the moments that passed, the devta strained his brain to see if he had heard of the Ratna-Maru anywhere.

To no avail.

'Sorry, Baba...I am unable to recall if I have read about this mighty weapon anywhere. Please do enlighten us. Who is this sword meant to reach? Why has this secret of the Black Temple been hidden for so many centuries?'

Dwarka Shastri shook his head, still looking straight into his great grandson's eyes, still not ready to accept that Vidyut had not deciphered the truth till now.

'This sword is not the secret of the Black Temple, Vidyut.

That is!'

Everyone turned to see where the grandmaster's finger was pointing.

It was towards a significantly lesser impressive object that lay mounted on a nearly decomposed wooden stand at the bottom of the Shiva statue's cavity, right below the gleaming Ratna-Maru.

·||ॐ||·

Vidyut and his fellowship observed the object carefully, not daring to touch it just yet.

'Go on, my son. Only you should lift it, Vidyut. Only the last devta of planet earth is prophesied to unfurl mankind's most precious secret.'

Dwarka Shastri invited Vidyut to pick-up the strange object from its wooden stand.

Something made the devta fold his hand in veneration to the object as he stepped forward and raised it in his hands. As soon as his fingers touched the crooked structure, a piercing scream tore through Vidyut's eardrums. As if an ancient dragon had shrieked into his mind and soul. No one else heard a thing.

Vidyut stretched his arms suddenly, to distance the object from himself.

'What happened, Vidyut?' enquired the matthadheesh.

'I...I can't say, Baba. It felt like a primordial sea-monster roared deep inside my heart...'

They now studied the piece carefully. Each one of them was in a beautiful daze just looking at it. Something within the crooked article seemed to exalt their spirit, cleanse their souls.

'It is a horn of a giant beast, it seems,' said Damini, her voice breaking with unexplained devotion.

'Yes...but it also looks like a twisted, mammoth sea-shell. It appears to be the horn of an aquatic monster!' exclaimed Vidyut, not believing what he was saying himself.

'You are right, Vidyut. This was a gift from Matsya to Satyavrata Manu. It was the siren or blow-horn that the ancient priest-king had used to summon the Lord for help – when the great Ark was all but devoured by pralay.'

·‖卐‖·

'Look inside the crooked sea-horn, beta,' urged Dwarka Shastri.

He then turned around and gestured to everyone else to step back and give space to the devta.

Vidyut did not have to look hard. He glanced into the interi-

or of the horn and immediately spotted a scroll – rolled and placed at the core. He pulled it out.

The scroll was yellow-brown in color. It appeared to be older than anything that Vidyut had ever set eyes upon. It was made of a material that the devta had never felt. It was also the most powerful object Vidyut had ever beheld. It seemed to be speaking to the devta.

'This is an ancient scroll that has been passed on from generation to generation for over 3,700 years, Vidyut. It was re-written in the Harappan script by our great ancestor, Satyavrata Manu, which he did upon the instructions of none other than Matsya Himself!' pronounced the grandmaster of the Dev-Raakshasa matth.

Vidyut was in a trance. He now felt very intensely that he was a part of the prehistoric legend. Holding the scroll in his hand, for the first time in his life, the devta felt exactly like what they had been saying he was.

Half-human, half-God!

·||ॐ||·

'You must read the ancient scroll, Vidyut. It is time, my son...'

'But, Baba...you said it is in Harappan calligraphy. Let alone me, no one in history has been able to decrypt this primeval script,' said the devta, hesitantly.

The deafening chanting of mantras and clashing of cymbals continued unabated. The priests and sadhus now appeared to be in a frenzy, rejoicing the holiest hour of the whole of Kaliyuga. Dwarka Shastri once again raised his shankha, and spoke in a loud, reverberating voice -

'Open it, read it and uncover the secret for the glory and goodness of mankind!

The scroll shall reveal itself to you, O devta! It is foretold!

Read it, and welcome the new dawn!

Read it, and put an end to the Curse of the Blood River!

Read it, O mighty devta, and unveil the ancient secret of the Black Temple!'

Dwarka Shastri now broke down himself, stretched out his arms as if imploring to a divine force, and screamed with unabashed devotion –

'Padaarpanam kuru, Prabhu!'

The entranced priests and sadhus of the Dev-Raakshasa matth repeated after him in loud unison –

'Padaarpanam kuru, Prabhu!'

'Present yourself, Oh Lord of Lords!'

Vidyut was burning with such divine, transcendent vitality that he had never experienced before. He felt One with God.

True to the primordial prophecy, in line with the holy hour of the Rohini Nakshtara, the last devta on planet earth... unfolded the ancient scroll.

The Marshes Surrounding the Great Ark, Aryavarta, 1698 BCE

GANDHAK!

The Ark decks served as vast, makeshift hospices, as the sickbay of the great boat could not accommodate the uncountable wounded. Cries of the fallen, amputated and mutilated soldiers rendered standing anywhere nearby impossible. While after the surprise attack of the fish-folk the equation for the second day had changed, enough men had already been lost by then.

Day-one belonged to the Arkers. Day-two was swept by the daityas.

Everyone could tell that the battle would not last beyond the third day.

The next time the adversaries came face to face, would be the decisive battle. This war was going to find its winner tomorrow. Moreover, having witnessed the battle prowess and lunatic cruelty of the daityas on the battlefield, Manu knew that if they fell the next day, the Damini Sena would not be able to defend the Ark against the mighty daityas for more than perhaps a couple of hours.

Even the thought of the thousands of men, women and children of the Ark falling into the gruesome hands of Nara-Munda was making the priest-king bilious, more anxious than he had ever been. To top it all, two things were now against the forces of the Ark.

The surprise factor of the fish-folk was gone. The daityas would be prepared for them the next day.

And the soldiers of the Ark had beheld Nara-Munda in all his macabre glory. Consequently, their morale was in their boots.

No one was saying anything to the leaders of the Ark.

But the murmurs were clear.

Nara-Munda was invincible.

·||ॐ||·

They stood half a mile away from each other.

The growling, howling, flesh-hungry daityas on one side.

The wounded, vastly outnumbered, gritty troops of the Ark

on the other.

This was the last day. Of the last war. Before the great deluge swallowed everything. Flood waters had now reached the marshes around the great boat. Both armies stood in knee-deep water. The indication was clear.

Pralay was hours away.

The roar of the catastrophic waves was now within earshot. Wind speed had increased exponentially, as an ominous messenger of the hurtling water-mountains that had already decimated almost all of Aryavarta.

Both armies were willing to fight to the death. Not because they wanted to defend a kingdom or enthrone a king. Not because they were patriotic or because they wanted to loot and plunder.

The men of both sides had their children, their wives and their aging parents behind them. Defeat was not an option now. Because defeat would mean not just their own end, but the certain death of their loved ones.

And that was the supreme, frantic motivation that drove both armies to the hilt.

This was going to be an unprecedented bloodbath.

·||❁||·

Upon directions from Somdutt, one column of the fish-folk riders turned towards Nara-Munda.

The Arkers had convened hours before this day's confrontation with one singular objective – to stop Nara-Munda. In the order of the warfare they faced, one beast like Nara-Munda could change the course of the war. He could tear open defense columns singlehandedly, he could kill commanders of the great vessel at will, he sent shivers down the defenders' spines and offered a giddy sense of confidence to his own cannibal fighters. His barbaric method of battle paralyzed the limbs and froze the souls of his foes.

Manu, Tara, Dhruv, Somdutt and Prachanda knew this beyond doubt – if Nara-Munda lived through that day, the Ark would be lost forever.

·‖卐‖·

He was visible from miles away. Ripping open soldiers of the Ark, flinging them into the air, biting away heads, crushing men under his elephantine heels. The ground around him was nothing more than a sickening pit of dead human filth, reeking with the stench of fresh blood.

The fish-folk column of riders galloped towards the emperor of the dark forests, with the singular mission of challenging him and finishing him. They had seldom been beaten in the past. But even the select riders of the fish-tribe had underestimated the brute strength and dexterity of the cannibal-chieftain.

As they succeeded in singling him out and surrounding him, the fiend broke into an outraged laugh...slapping his own head in an insane display of fearlessness. In the next moment, his exultant face suddenly turned barbaric, and from under the arm-deep water they all stood in, he produced the long, smoothened trunk of a tall tree!

·||ॐ||·

It was beyond the imagination of the Ark commanders to see someone twirl an oaken tree like a regular staff. Nara-Munda's veins throbbed on his muscular girth, as he swung the long tree stalk like a toothpick. In one sweeping stroke, he struck twenty riders of the fish-folk. Chests and ribs fractured in moments. Skulls and shoulder-blades of the warriors of the fish-tribe were crushed to powder.

In the minutes that passed, the king of the cannibals wreaked havoc in the fish-folk regiments. His bizarre weapon of choice crushed the craniums of horses just the way it shattered the armor of the sea-folk.

It was soon clear to everyone. It was written with the ink of the fish-folk's blood.

The demon Nara-Munda was the harbinger of hell.

He was the future king of the great Ark.

He was the future lord of the Earth.

·||ॐ||·

'Gandhak ki jwaala ko ye bhi nahin rok paayega, Dhruv...'

'Even he will not be able to stand in the way of the destructive flames of gandhak, Dhruv...'

Dhruv was now smeared in blood, part from his own wounds and the rest from the ruptured arteries of the daityas who had fallen prey to the archer's sword and arrows.

The two magnificent men, who had together pulled mankind along on the road to survival for over a year, were now distressed beyond measure. They had no choice left but to turn to the ultimate weapon that He had left them with.

The weapon of mass destruction that Matsya had left them with.

Gandhak.

Banaras, 2017

'HE IS HERE...'

Vidyut felt he was travelling through space, through time, through galaxies, across births and deaths, wars and famines, revolutions and renaissance, meeting saint and satan, families and fortunes. He seemed to be dying several times, coming alive in different worlds, he remembered the fragrance of many mothers, the kiss of many lovers, the laughter of his children, the angst of his lost loved ones. He remembered happy homes and somber graveyards, the courts of kings and the huts of hermits.

His chosen soul was scattered across the universe, beyond the realm of time, worlds and distances.

And it was all happening since he had laid eyes on the prophetic letters written in the holy scroll he held in his trembling hands.

'I...I... cannot make out anything, Baba...' he gasped.

Dwarka Shastri could not hear his beloved great grandson's words in the din of the prayer-chants. But he understood. He gestured with his eyes, urging the devta to look harder, look closer.

'Read from the eyes of your soul, Vidyut...'

The matthadheesh had not said anything. But Vidyut heard these words in his mind.

The grand old man was communicating with the devta mentally!

·‖卐‖·

Vidyut looked at the scroll again, feeling nearly dizzy with the spiritual energy that was overtaking him completely.

Strange sights flashed in his mind like lightning. He saw a gigantic deluge swallowing a magnificent city. He could see the faint smile of a dying woman, struck down by arrows. He found himself surrounded by scores of gnarling warriors, covered in ash. A merry family enjoying a feast of *pooris* and *kheer* together. A ravishing dancing-girl stepping out in a splendid mansion. He saw three blind black-magicians incanting demonic verses in a haunting cave. A man yelling *'Ride to the East...find the Black Temple'*. A hollow mountain, with a gigantic statue of Shiva. He saw himself falling from a cliff, shooting arrows amidst mountains made of brick and bronze. He saw himself drenched in blood, sweat and spit, being tortured by a delirious crowd in a prehistoric arena. A courtroom with guffawing judges. A clay seal with a one-horned bull. The screams of men in dungeons worse than a grave. A raging blue fire. A gigantic boat, beyond human conception. Two Portuguese executioners with steel fangs. A mighty Roman emperor.

And then he saw *Him*.

A face more handsome than he could ever imagine...laughing joyfully. An indescribable man with the golden-blue skin of a fish! Vidyut saw the magnificent fish-man in the black cave-temple of Shiva, making fun of him like an inseparable friend. Over a bonfire, eating a meal of poha like family. Pronouncing the onset of a great deluge, 'PRALAY...ESH-HYATI...!', like a hard mentor. He then saw the blue fish-man, perched atop a high rock, standing tall against screaming skies, glowing like the prophet of prophets.

The last devta opened his eyes. He looked at the ancient scroll.

Tears flowed down his eyes as the words magically came to

life.

It all made sense now to the devta.

After 3,700 years since this day was foretold...

...Vidyut had unveiled the secret of the Black Temple.

·||ॐ||·

He was now on his knees, bowed before the statue of Lord Shiva. The devta was weeping uncontrollably, and yet lost in a meditative trance.

Kashi had now erupted in celebration. They did not know what or who they were welcoming, but the Rohini Nakshatra was now at its peak, and the holy men of Banaras knew the Dev-Raakshasa matth was rejoicing...after centuries!

And that meant only one thing.

The savior had arrived!

Damini could not stay away from Vidyut anymore. She decided to go to him, to hold him, to share his burden. As soon as she stepped forward, something froze her steps. Out of nowhere an extremely old yet mystical looking yogi stood in front of Vidyut. He was both fearsome and benevolent. Damini gasped as she noticed his skin. It was like that of a serpent!

But her fear evaporated when she saw the strange, gigantic, scaled man brush his hand on Vidyut's head, in profound love and blessings. The snake-man's eyes were tender, like he was caressing his own child.

'Come here, bitiya...' said Dwarka Shastri, now looking visibly exhausted, yet supremely contented.

His life's work was done.

·‖卐‖·

'He is here, Damini...He is here...' said Vidyut into his soulmate's ears, as she held him close.

'Yes, Vidyut...it's okay...tell me when you can...' Damini replied. For her, the well-being of Vidyut was more important than the most prized secret of the universe.

'Why did I not grasp this sooner, Damini...?' continued the devta, his head bowed, tears flowing at the feet of Shiva. Damini's arms were still wrapped around her devta.

'Grasp what, Vidyut...? Who is here, my love...?' she asked. She could sense that Vidyut wanted to share the secret of the Black Temple with her.

'He is here, Damini...moments ago...at the peak of the holy constellation...

Vishnu...'

The beautiful Damini was unable to understand what Vidyut was saying. She asked him again, softly.

'Who is here, my devta? What is the secret of the Black Temple, Vidyut?'

Vidyut looked up at her. His eyes appeared to be different. They were...enlightened!

He responded in the very few words that could escape his lips.

'*Kalki*...

Dreaded by the sinners, awaited by the virtuous...the tenth avatar of Vishnu has arrived, Damini.

The Kalki avatar is born.'

The Marshes Surrounding the Great Ark, Aryavarta, 1698 BCE

TRUCE

No one on living prithvi had witnessed so much fire before.

Everything was burning. The cannibal soldiers were in flames. Their horses were being smoldered. Swords of alloy were melting. The heat was comparable to that of the Sun, as most of them imagined it to be.

The dark, stormy, night had lit up as if stars from the heavens exploded on earth every few moments. The daityas were petrified and were running amok in the chaos that was unfolding on the battle field. They had never seen this rain of fire before. Not even the Ark soldiers and commanders had witnessed such infernal mayhem. It was something bizarre, something unbelievable.

Barrels of fire were flying out from the Ark decks and streaked across the night-sky, exploding with earsplitting bangs in the heart of the daitya regiments, charring hundreds of them within moments. Nara-Munda and his war-general Doonda stood paralyzed for a while, unable to comprehend what was going on. How could such great balls of hell-fire fly out of the great Ark one after the other, burning down their troops and routing their formations?

In a matter of an hour or less, the battle scales once again tilted and were now poised right back in balance.

For now, this was anybody's war.

And one game-changing fact was evident to the defenders of the Ark.

They were very afraid of fire.

The daityas were unexpectedly, unusually afraid of fire!

Matsya had known this. He had blessed the Ark with gand-hak or fire-powder that no one across Aryavarta had ever even heard of. He had trained Manu and Dhruv on building gigantic catapults that could fire barrels filled with gandhak far into enemy lines.

This was the first time Matsya had saved the great Ark and all its inhabitants.

But not the last.

·‖卐‖·

It did not take the titanic emperor of the dark forests much time to first compose himself, and then work himself back into his typical, furious bloodthirst. In his fearsome voice, that seemed to combine the roar of lions with the trumpet of wild tuskers, he summoned his army of man-eaters to fight back.

The forces charged at one another once again, this time with renewed frenzy. The clash of metal, of sword on sword, of spear on armor, of axes on battle-shields, was deafening.

'Let us send a messenger to Nara-Munda, with a truce proposal,' said Manu to Somdutt, who was mounted on his horse right next to Manu's, as they surveyed the burning and bleeding battleground.

'What?' intervened Dhruv, who stood next to Satyavrata Manu's steed. 'Are you out of your mind, Manu? You want to negotiate a truce with that monster?!'

'Look, Dhruv, my friend, I know it is lunacy to expect any civilized response from that beast. But no matter what the situation is, we must give peace a chance. At this time, he is rattled by the storm of fire gandhak has inflicted on his men. This might be our only chance. If he agrees to a peaceful settlement, we can save thousands of human lives, including those of the daityas and their families.'

Dhruv knew Manu was right. Even now their chances of winning this war were slim. A peace solution could end this nightmare right away. But he was far from being convinced.

He knew Nara-Munda was not a man of amity or reason. He was not a man at all.

On the other hand, Somdutt found great value in Manu's proposition. He spoke in support of the priest-king.

'With the bandits gone and half of the daitya army decimated, their numbers have hugely dwindled. We have lost thousands as well. Under these new circumstances, we can accommodate the remaining daityas on the great boat.'

Dhruv now walked around Manu's horse and stood facing the two mounted men. His exasperation was evident.

'Accommodate them? Did I hear you say accommodate, Somdutt ji?'

Both Somdutt and Manu were quiet. Dhruv continued, trying his best to convince his two fellow-Arkers on the futility of the truce effort, as well as about the ramifications of having daityas on the great ship.

'Have you forgotten, O wise Somdutt ji? *They are cannibals!* he shouted, amazed that his simple logic was not hitting home. 'They eat people like you and me! What you are saying sounds like offering shelter to a pack of wild dogs in a barn of hapless calves!'

·||ॐ||·

The three men went silent. Dhruv paced up and down in front of the horses of Manu and Somdutt, waiting for their decision, looking at the proceedings of the battle.

'I have thought of it,' Manu spoke after a few minutes of

careful consideration.

'We will offer Nara-Munda refuge for the women, children and the wounded in the main Ark. As for his combat forces, they will need to surrender their arms and agree to be housed in the Ark prisons. This way we will save our own people, save the innocent women and children of the daityas, and also keep the daitya fighters incarcerated. In return, the daityas get to live through pralay, if the giant Ark indeed survives it.'

Somdutt turned to Manu and nodded in consent. Dhruv looked away, unable to swallow this seemingly disastrous decision.

·||࿗||·

After much deliberation, it was decided that Somdutt would approach the daitya-king. Despite resistance from Manu, Dhruv and Prachanda, the wise architect had insisted that he should be the messenger and negotiator of peace. Anyone smaller in stature did not stand a chance. Nara-Munda was not going to lend an ear to anyone less influential.

To Dhruv's surprise, Nara-Munda had agreed to talk. Both armies had pulled back and now stood in panting, bleeding formations facing each other. Somewhere deep down, every soul present on the field, in the daitya camp and atop the Ark, was hoping for peace. The battle so far had been more vicious and more devastating than anyone had bargained for. Too many men had died painful deaths in too short a time. Thousands lay moaning and writhing in unbearable suffering. The great flood was knocking at their doors.

Everyone was hoping that the talk between Somdutt and Nara-Munda would put an end to this war.

Nara-Munda walked out into the field, lumbering like the monster he was. He was not carrying any weapons. To everyone's great surprise, ten children, nothing more than eight or nine years of age, accompanied him. Such a gentle gesture of goodwill and harmony was totally unexpected from the emperor of the daityas.

Somdutt, who was now walking out to meet the cannibal-sovereign, turned and smiled hopefully at Dhruv. Nara-Munda had come with children.

Peace finally had a chance.

But both Manu and Somdutt had forgotten.

They had forgotten the curse of the Blood River!

"The Gods will never release you from your hateful destiny. The serpents of violence and bloodshed will never loosen their stranglehold on mankind, which shall kill and destroy each other...! Never shall carnage and butchery leave your side. This is my curse, O fallen devta! Humankind shall hear the shrieks of boundless suffering till the end of time!

I CURSE YOU! I CURSE YOU ALL!"

Banaras, 2017

'THEY ARE COMING FOR YOU, VIDYUT'

They sat around the ritual fire at the feet of Lord Shiva. Vidyut, Damini, Dwarka Shastri and, towering above all of them by a tall margin, the fearsome Sheshnaag. Naina, Purohit ji, Sonu, Balvanta and Govardhan sat a few steps away, their hands folded in veneration. Several other trusted sadhus of the matth also sat in silence, their eyes closed. Each one present in the Black Temple was now lost in the love and omnipotence of the holy avatar.

Vidyut had the ancient scroll in his hands. The brief yet priceless information inscribed on the scroll of Matsya and Manu was now etched into Vidyut's soul. He now understood why the New World Order had spent centuries looking for this secret.

Dwarka Shastri and Sheshnaag had been submitting *aahuti* or offerings into the flames of worship, chanting mantras that even accomplished yogis and taantrics like Vidyut and Purohit ji had never heard of. These were secret, advanced *shlokas* that only two very old men in the world had the knowledge of. And they were both sitting around the ritual fire. The mantras were so powerful that it seemed as if the divine words rose with the camphor laden smoke of the pit-fire, and were going straight up to *Vaikuntha*, the celestial abode of Lord Vishnu.

·‖卐‖·

'Offer the holy scroll to *agni* now, Vidyut,' instructed Dwarka Shastri.

Vidyut hesitated. In the few minutes that he had held it in his hands, the devta seemed to have forged a deep bond with the scroll and the golden words transcribed on it.

'This is where it needs to go now, Vidyut...back to where it came from. Only you now know the secret of the Black Temple, Vidyut. In fact, you *are* the secret of the Black Temple now!'

Damini was very confused. She had seen Vidyut break down in extreme devotion and utter the name Kalki. But she was not clear exactly what was written in the script. The matthadheesh could see the perplexed expression on Damini's face.

'Damini deserves to know what the scroll has been hiding in its mysterious words for millennia, Vidyut.'

Vidyut nodded. He smiled and turned to the love of his life. He was mentally wondering if Damini will believe what he was going to tell her.

'As I told you, Damini, the divine, the awaited avatar of Lord Vishnu, the Kalki avatar has been born minutes ago, some-where far from here. The prophesied Rohini Nakshatra was nothing but the time of Lord Kalki's descent on earth.'

The beautiful journalist from Delhi was mesmerized as she heard these words. She had heard of Kalki, the tenth avatar of Vishnu, who was ordained to arrive on earth when the sins and sinners of Kaliyuga reach the zenith of depravity. But she could not believe she was now a part of that divine occurrence.

'So that is what the scroll says, the time of Lord Kalki's birth?'

Vidyut grinned and replied, 'Yes, that...and something more.'

Damini raised her eyebrows gently, urging Vidyut to com-plete.

'What more, Vidyut?' she asked.

'The scroll not only has the time of Kalki's birth, Damini...

...it also has the exact place of His birth.

I now know where He is!'

·||ॐ||·

It was nearly dawn as they made their way out of the Black Temple, bidding farewell to Sheshnaag after seeking his blessings. The mystical, all-powerful serpent-king was not going to stay on in the basement of the Bhairava mandir for long. His presence was needed at his master's side. He had waited for two thousand years for this prophesied day.

As they sat on the terrace of Dwarka Shastri's cottage, they could hear the familiar sounds of a typical Kashi morning. Sonu brought tea for everyone, as they sat on chairs that were laid out around a low center table. The grand old man was visibly exhausted, nearly out of breath with fatigue. And yet he had the most gratified look on his face. But he knew his work was not yet done.

Or to be precise, Vidyut's work was not yet done.

A few sips of hot tea and a few biscuits seemed to have worked wonders for everyone after the long, high-octane and spiritually amplifying night behind them.

'Balvanta, get all fighters of the matth to double the perimeter guard of the monastery. You inspect every gate, every parapet personally. Naina, take Damini with you and keeping her safe will be your duty. She should not be in Vidyut's vicinity now, not for some time at least.'

Balvanta bowed to the grand old man and left immediately to carry out the orders he had received. Sonu followed him, prepared to fight another battle for his devta.

'What now, Baba? Do you think the Order will come after me?'

Dwarka Shastri turned to Vidyut with amazement.

'Do I *think* they will come after you, did you say, Vidyut? I am surprised you ask this question. Know this, my son...the secret of the Black Temple that the Order wants at any cost, now lays buried in your heart.

So have no doubt in your mind.

They are coming for you, Vidyut.'

·‖卐‖·

'Constantine knew about the Kalki avatar. A king as all-powerful as him had the world's most accomplished mystics as his counsels. He firmly believed that just like the divine messengers, prophets and avatars of the past, the advent of Lord Kalki was a certainty. He also knew that the exact place and time of the holy manifestation was hidden in the Black Temple. The reason he commissioned the New World Order was because he thought he was going to make the world a better place, thus helping Kalki in bringing justice, happiness and everlasting peace to the human race. He grossly miscalculated. In trying to be an able servant to the Lord, he created the worst monster in the history of man.'

Everyone around the great Dwarka Shastri was listening to him, as he unpeeled the final layer of intrigue over the Black Temple.

'Like I have explained before, the secret brotherhood of the

New World Order has a deep understanding of ethereal and spiritual matters. They have the most terrifying devil-worshippers at their service. They have their own mystics, exorcists and black magicians. Very early in their journey they were cautioned by these distorted occult practitioners about the coming of Kalki and the end of Kaliyuga. The supreme Overlords of the Order were told in no uncertain terms that the *only* force that could stop them was Kalki. They were also advised that Kalki would be born in the brilliant, holy constellation that has just passed, and that if He is allowed to cross the age of thirteen, the end of the Order is definite. So, while the secret society created wars, planted dictators, unleashed epidemics and controlled world economy over the centuries, their primary quest was always to find the secret of the Black Temple and know for sure where the avatar would be born. It was to obtain the secret scroll that they waged war with the Dev-Raakshasa matth, relentlessly, unstoppably.'

Vidyut knew now that the war was far from over. In fact, the real war would now begin.

'Baba, what is it that the Order wants now? Why will they come after Vidyut? Despite hundreds of years of bloodshed and violence, the Kalki avatar is already here. Won't they just accept defeat?' asked Naina.

'You don't seem to have fully understood the Order, Naina,' replied the grandmaster. 'They will never back down. They comprise the world's most capable, most ambitious and by far the most dangerous men.

They will try what King Herod tried when Christ was born.

They will attempt what the demon emperor Kansa attempted when Krishna arrived on the planet.

They will do everything in their power to kill Kalki...while he is still an infant.'

·‖ ॐ ‖·

Out of nowhere Naina's mobile phone began vibrating.

She took it out and looked bewildered.

'This is odd. No one has this phone number except Mahant Bhavaanishankar, and he is not due to call,' she said to the others as she took the call.

Her face froze within moments. In less than thirty seconds she put the phone down. The caller had disconnected.

She ground her teeth as she spoke.

'It was Professor Tripathi, or the one-eyed goblin Brahmanand. He was laughing hysterically.'

Everyone was stunned. Vidyut shut his eyes, not wanting to hear what Naina was about to say. Against everyone's advice it was he who had decided to let Brahmanand go.

Naina spoke with chilling calm.

'Mahant Bhavaanishankar is dead.

Someone called the White Mask has invited Vidyut to the ghaats this afternoon.'

The Marshes Surrounding the Great Ark, Aryavarta, 1698 BCE

THE ERA OF KALI

They were beyond earshot, about three hundred paces from where Manu, Dhruv and Prachanda were keenly watching the proceedings, prayers in their hearts. Somdutt was face to face with the giant ghost of a man. The little daitya children stood around the pillar-like legs of Nara-Munda, unaware of what was going on.

It seemed to be going well. Somdutt was speaking fearlessly, gesticulating his arms around, clearly trying to convey to the cannibal-king what further destruction and bloodshed awaited both the sides if the war for the Ark was not halted immediately. To everyone's surprise and even some groans of relieved disbelief, both armies and their commanders saw the mighty Nara-Munda fold his hands and bow to the wise architect.

Was the war finally over? With so much loss of life and thousands of wounded struggling to prevent their lesions from festering poisonously under the incessant rain, soldiers from both sides looked on hopefully.

Everyone wanted peace.

·‖卐‖·

It was with a great sense of elation that Somdutt turned back to his own troops and comrades. Even from the distance Manu could see a smile on the wise architect's face. Nara-Munda had accepted the truce proposal!

Both sides of soldiers began rattling their weapons and armors in support of this decision. The forces of the Ark raised their swords and spears in salutation to Somdutt's fearless effort as he began to walk back to his camp. The chief architect of Harappa, the most loyal friend of Vivasvan Pujari and a beloved father-figure for Manu, waved at his men with a sigh of relief.

Everyone wanted peace.

Except the emperor of the man-eaters.

In one swooping motion, as swift as that of a cobra, the mammoth monster lunged forward. Even before the onlookers could bat an eyelid, Nara-Munda had lifted Somdutt from the back of his neck. Using just his left hand to raise the wise old man high up for everyone to see, the fiend growled in lunatic rage!

'You want peace??' he roared looking at the troops of the Ark, displaying the hanging man in cruel mockery.

'You want peace??' he growled again, this time turning to his own soldiers, his eyes bloodshot with insanity.

He then turned slowly to look straight at the king of the Ark, Satyavrata Manu.

By now the captured architect had drawn his dagger and was swinging it in futility, trying to reach the cannibal's arm with his blade.

His struggle did not even make Nara-Munda flinch. The beast was still looking at Manu, who was being held back by Dhruv and Prachanda from dashing into the field, to rescue the architect of the Ark.

'You want peace, Satyavrata Manu?' roared the towering monster for the third time.

In the very next moment, Nara-Munda turned Somdutt like a rabbit, brought him close and bit into the old man's neck with his giant jaws. In a nerve-wracking, tearing action, he ripped out Somdutt's throat with his ghastly fangs.

As he chomped and ate Somdutt's bleeding entrails raw, he threw the thrashing body of the still-alive emissary of peace on the ground.

The ten children that accompanied Nara-Munda were starving after days of rationed eating. Today they had been promised a treat by the demon. Like a cackle of young hyenas, they pounced on the bleeding architect all at once.

In front of the thousands of troops, in front of the residents of the Ark, right in the face of Manu, Dhruv and Prachanda, the chief architect of Harappa was eaten alive.

·||ॐ||·

'Surround him! Surround the dastardly scoundrel! Dhruv... send in your best men!' cried Satyavrata Manu, his voice hoarse with anguish and hate!

He was still being held back by ten of his men, including Dhruv. They knew Manu was now ridden with indescribable sorrow and punishing regret. If they left him be, he would dash towards Nara-Munda — and perhaps towards certain defeat and death. It was his decision to let Somdutt take the message of peace to the vicious cannibal. Dhruv had counselled him against it, and yet he had gone ahead. His burning desire for harmony had made him risk it. It made him blind to reason.

No one in the Ark forces had ever witnessed such a macabre sight of inhumanity. Nara-Munda had crossed all boundaries of sadism, stretched all limits of brutality. Manu was now clear that this fiend had to be wiped out from the face of the earth. No Matter what it took. No matter how many rules of honor had to be twisted and broken.

Sobbing heavily and unable to breath, Manu turned to his closest friend and ally.

'We have to kill him, Dhruv. Bring the ropes. Get the best fighters. You and I will lead them, and we will destroy this behemoth of evil – no matter what it takes! We stab him from the back, we encircle him, we tie his hands and we chop him to pieces!'

With none other than the pious, the magnificent, the righteous Satyavrata Manu himself abandoning idealism in its purest form...the age of violence, deceit and strife was heralded.

The era of Kali had begun.

Kaliyuga had begun!

Banaras, 2017

SHAITAAN!

The five-star hotel was in a frenzy. Uttar Pradesh police had cordoned off the premises of the luxury resort and every staffer was being questioned. Around noon that day a housekeeping lady had discovered a dead body in one of the rooms.

It was a gruesome murder. The body had been perforated with a pointed object over thirty-five times, including the temples and eyes. The press had also reached the spot, given the profile of the murdered man. He was the notorious Mumbai don – Aslam Biker. The initial investigations had revealed that the pointed object used as a killing device was most likely a common screwdriver.

In exchange for the wealth, arms and protection they provided him, Aslam Biker had been entrusted by the Order with a vital duty. He was to ensure that if the secret of the Black Temple moved from the shrine of Kedarnath to any other location, it had to be tracked.

But the gangster had failed in his duty. The secret had been shifted successfully from Kedarnath to a new, unknown Black Temple, without the knowledge of the Order. Aslam Biker had let them down.

And anyone failing the White Mask met with the same fatal fate.

·||ॐ||·

'You have got to be kidding me, Vidyut!' exclaimed Damini.

It was for the first time in Dwarka Shastri's presence that Damini had lost her cool. Vidyut was adamant that he would go and meet this White Mask.

'Baba, please knock some sense into this man's head. He knows he is now the prime target for the murderous brotherhood. You told us how they will go to any extent to capture Vidyut and extract the coordinates of the Lord's birthplace. Then how can he even think of stepping out of the matth?'

Before Dwarka Shastri could intervene, the devta spoke.

'Try to understand what I am doing, Damini. Whoever this man is, he is behind the killing of Mahant Bhavaanishankar. He is probably also the killer of Aslam Biker, as we read in the newspapers this morning. Brahmanand too is serving his will. Clearly, this White Mask is someone very influential in the secret brotherhood's hierarchy. The Order will come after me one way or another anyway. At least by coming face to face with this man, I will know who the enemy is! Till how long can we fight an invisible foe? Till when can I hide from an adversary who we do not even know and cannot even see?'

'But, Vidyut...' protested Damini, pressing her throbbing forehead with her hand.

'Let me go, love. This man has reached Banaras. He knows I am within the walls of the matth. If he can kill someone as accomplished as Mahant Bhavaanishankar as well as a big Mumbai don, the guards of the matth will not stop him.'

Vidyut kissed Damini on the forehead.

'I have to go, Damini. Nothing will happen to me.

Bhagvaan Kalki has arrived now. He will protect us.'

·||ॐ||·

The grandmaster of the Dev-Raakshasa matth blessed Vidyut, as the devta bowed to touch the feet of his Baba.

'Remember, Vidyut, this man is different from the others like Romi Pereira, the daakinis, the mercenaries or even Trijat Kapaalik and Brahmanand. I did not want to speak in front of Damini, but the White Mask, or the Maschera Bianca as he is called, is something disturbing.'

Vidyut noticed that his Baba had used the term *something* and not *someone* to describe the Maschera Bianca.

'Baba, Naina mentioned to me that Mahant Bhavaanishankar said something about Lucifer or the devil himself walking in Kashi. I also saw a terrifying statue of Satan at the *yajna-shaala* of the Masaan-raja. Is the White Mask an incarnate of Lucifer himself, Baba?'

'No, Vidyut. He is not Lucifer. And we are not sure if Lucifer and *Shaitaan* (Satan) are the same force. The scriptures are not clear. Several of our clansmen believe the Mask is the devil or Shaitaan himself. Mahant Bhavaanishankar was one of those believers. But I am certain he is not.

When, heaven forbid, Shaitaan arrives, the whole world will know, Vidyut. He carries the dark forces of the entire cosmos with him. And neither you nor even the mighty Sheshnaag will be able to stand in his way. We pray to the universe that it does not happen before Kalki is ready to take him on.'

The devta remembered the gigantic bust of Lucifer he had seen amidst the dead bodies and ritual pits of the Mritak-naath, Trijat Kapaalik.

'Then who is this White Mask, Baba?'

Dwarka Shastri's face showed a glimpse of grave worry for the first time.

'The Maschera Bianca is Shaitaan's messenger, Vidyut. For want of a better description, let me say he is...

...half-human, half-demon!'

·||ॐ||·

His white shirt of fine, expensive linen fluttered against his ribbed built.

The Maschera looked nothing less than a Hollywood movie star.

Vidyut stood at the steps of the holy Ganga, wearing his black t-shirt, which caressed his equally chiseled physique.

The devta looked every bit the God that he was!

The colors of the two men's shirts were starkly in contrast with the cosmic powers they represented.

'Hello, Vidyut,' said the Maschera, suave as ever, a glowing smile adorning his face.

The devta was not Aslam Biker. He did not ease his guard at the evidently shrewd presentation of the Mask.

'What do I call you, my friend?' asked Vidyut, as the two shook hands.

'Well, I am most certain you already know what I am called, Vidyut,' replied the Mask, taking off his sunglasses and looking at Vidyut with those legendary green eyes.

The devta did not relent.

'I don't speak to people without knowing their names.'

The White Mask laughed merrily. He folded his glasses and put them in his pocket. He pulled up his pink designer trousers as he sat down on the stairs of the ghaat. He gestured to Vidyut to join him, much like once Romi and the devta had shared the stony seat.

'You know, Vidyut...in another time, you could have called me Winston. Or Joseph. Or even Adolf.

But for now, it is Maschera for you...my friend.'

The Marshes Surrounding the Great Ark, Aryavarta, 1698 BCE

ANTIM YUDDHA – PART IV

Manu's eyes glistened like embers, fraught with tears and venom.

Dhruv had never seen his friend in this barbaric form before. Satyavrata Manu had transformed into a killing monster, hacking down any daitya warrior who stood between him and Nara-Munda.

Both the armies were once again attacking each other fiercely with their blades, spears, fists and teeth. With the last hope for peace lying in shreds with the body of the unfortunate architect, men from both sides were now baying for each other's blood. The rumble of the great deluge was growing louder with every passing minute. Wind speed was now almost a tornado, making it hard for the fighters to even maintain balance.

It was clear now. It was a matter of a couple of hours at most. Those who would climb the Ark in time would live to see another day. Those who miss the boat will get washed away like insects under the great waves of pralay.

·‖卐‖·

As the priest-king of the Ark made his way towards the cannibal monster, Dhruv and his men closed in as well. They had Manu's permission now. They were going to surround the emperor of the dark forests and make him pay for all his sins. Each of Dhruv's riders carried a rope noose. They knew that as long as Nara-Munda's hands and legs were free, it was impossible to vanquish the beast. He had the strength of ten men, and he had to be captured before being sent to his maker.

Dhruv was the first one to ride like a whirlwind around the giant beast. Before Nara-Munda could raise his oaken staff to toss Dhruv off his horse like a toy, Dhruv swung the rope-noose by his side to gain momentum and flung it around the beast's neck and shoulders.

Even as Nara-Munda grappled with what was happening, five other nooses were thrown over him. The riders of Dhruv were now encircling the cannibal and tightening the grip of the ropes. Within moments the expert warriors sent a volley of vine-chords with metallic bearings tied at their ends flying at the man-eater's ankles. In not more than a few seconds, they had trapped Nara-Munda in a web of ropes and chords, right from his shoulders to his feet.

For a moment, the eyes of the Arkers twinkled. Nara-Munda seemed to lumber around under the screaming wind and roaring thunder, unable to move his limbs.

But that twinkle came and left in the same moment.

·‖ॐ‖·

Nara-Munda was quiet for a few blinks of the eye because he was summoning all his bestial strength.

To the dismay and shock of Dhruv's riders, Nara-Munda broke his gigantic, muscular legs free from the vine-chords as if the bondages were made of cotton thread.

The demon then roared again, sending ripples of fear down the spine of every man that stood on the battlefield. Using the madness of his dragon-like snarl to work himself into a frenzy yet again, Nara-Munda grabbed the ropes that bound him. Taking four or five ropes together in his giant grip, he pulled them with unhuman strength. In the next moment, a dozen of Dhruv's riders were being twirled and dragged around on the bloody marshland. Nara-Munda was stronger than a wild tusker!

Frustrated with this failed attempt, Dhruv decided to take on the fiend himself. He jumped off his galloping horse and walked up to the cannibal, his sword drawn. The demon grinned like a goblin as he saw Dhruv approaching. As the brilliant archer came near, Nara-Munda bent down slowly to pick up a gleaming, gigantic axe. Dhruv had no real plan in mind that would defeat the cruel man-eater. He also knew his sword would not withstand even one blow of the cannibal's axe. He was going in nevertheless.

Then suddenly, from right behind him, Dhruv heard a voice. His favorite voice in times like these.

'Haul me, Dhruv!'

The archer turned to see Satyavrata Manu charging like a wounded lion, short swords dancing in both his hands. He screamed again.

'Haul me...!'

Dhruv instantly bent and made a cup of his hands. Manu strode right into Dhruv, put one foot on his friend's hands, another on his shoulder and launched himself upon Nara-Munda, high up in the air.

Everyone watching was stunned to see the bravado of the son of Surya. Manu flew against the black and red sky for a few feet, and tore one of his short swords deep into the beast's shoulder. The merciless titan grunted aloud in agony. It was the first wound inflicted on Nara-Munda during the entire war.

Dhruv saw his king and friend leap like a fearless young panther. For him time froze for a moment.

The future of humankind, the builder and defender of the great Ark, the very magnificent Satyavrata Manu was going into battle!

Banaras, 2017

DEV-RAAKSHASA

'Cigarette?'

Vidyut noticed the Maschera was offering him an Indian brand of tobacco. The Mask saw the devta's eyes and smiled.

'Your friend Bala used to send me a carton of these, every month. It is a shame no cigarette in Europe can match the flavor of this Indian brand.'

Vidyut was seething with anger. He knew that the Maschera Bianca was taunting him. Bala was nothing more than a toy for the Mask. It was unbearable for Vidyut to think about how the Order had infiltrated his life years ago. How they had played with his work, his home, his emotions...and even now this green-eyed man sat next to Vidyut, remorselessly.

349

Fearlessly.

'What do you want, Maschera? Why are we here?'

The White Mask laughed. He lit his cigarette and blew out the smoke in a smooth, silken manner from a little gap between his lips. He then turned to Vidyut, still smiling.

'I want to make you a billionaire, Vidyut. I want you to marry Damini. Have beautiful children. I want you to live a long, happy life. That is what I want, devta.'

It was now Vidyut's turn to laugh. He found the Maschera's offer very amusing. He knew they were wasting time. And it had stung him like a bee to hear Damini's name from his vile mouth.

'That is very generous of you,' said Vidyut. 'And what, may I ask, do you seek in return?'

The Mask grinned, looked away towards the far end of the holy Ganga and took another drag from his cigarette.

They both knew what the Mask wanted.

·||ॐ||·

'You cannot blame me for trying, can you, Vidyut? Although I knew my offer of a king's life would not deviate you from your destiny.'

Vidyut was listening. He wanted to know more about this man. He wanted to understand what works in the mind of someone as ruthless as the White Mask.

'Tell me, Vidyut. I saw thousands of devotees at the Kashi Vishu…'

'Kashi Vishwanath,' Vidyut assisted him.

'Yes, that. I saw an ocean of people there, worshipping, chanting, bending…basically consumed by their devotion. But most of them were indescribably poor. They were suffering beyond endurance. They were shriveled, diseased, grieving, penniless…and yet they bowed to your God like misery meant nothing to them. Why?'

'*Your* God?' asked Vidyut, his eyebrows raised enquiringly. 'In that case, who is *your* God, Maschera?'

The Mask laughed and shook his head.

'It amazes me how little you understand these things, and yet you are willing to sacrifice your life for them! Do you not see, Vidyut - good and evil, God and Satan, light and darkness… they are all creations of the same power that wants billions of human beings to suffer all their lives, bow each day of their miserable existence to their so-called God and finally die hoping to meet their maker? Is this what your God has to offer – pain, loss, tears, grief, illness…death?'

The White Mask was speaking with uncanny conviction. Perhaps the same mindless fanaticism that propels evil to spread terror and violence in the name of religion. In the name of God. The same destructive, inhuman and foolish conviction.

'I don't know what God has to offer. But I know about your final solution, Maschera. Culling down billions of people…

mercilessly, systematically? Is that what you have to offer as an alternative?'

·||࿕||·

'Human beings deserve to be culled because a majority of them are the biggest fools in the entire universe. You bring children into this world knowing well that this is a place for suffering, disease and hate.

You establish worthless institutions like marriage, and both man and woman spend the rest of their lives pretending to be pious, lusting for other men and women.

Today you say human culling is wrong. Less than a hundred years from now when dying of thirst, heat and disease these very seven billion people will turn into man-eating zombies – hungry for flesh because they will have nothing else left to eat. Thirsty for blood because there will be nothing else left to drink! Where will your God be then, devta?

Don't you see, Vidyut? YOU are the evil. Your God is the greatest of the dark forces – veiled under a fake, glowing white light. Whereas WE are the truth, the virtuous…and the future!

What makes a stone so powerful? Or a shrine? Or a book or an idol? It is you – you humans! You venerate these lifeless objects and transfer your cosmic, collective spiritual energy by the millions for hundreds of years – and naturally, the stone becomes divine. And then it uses the very power it has accumulated from you – to govern you! To give you pain, sorrow and malicious tendencies in the garb of free will!'

The Mask took out another cigarette and lit it in a rush. He took a deep drag, inhaled the smoke and kept it inside for a few seconds. He then shrugged to Vidyut, keen to hear the devta's response. But before Vidyut could say anything, the Maschera added a chilling appendage, his cold, green eyes glowering down at the devta.

'Leave Kashi today, Vidyut.

I have killed too many young men like you. I don't want to add your name to the list.'

·||卐||·

Vidyut had not failed to observe how the Mask was referring to humans as 'you humans'. As if he himself was not one at all.

The devta felt compelled to respond.

'I pity you, Maschera Bianca or whatever you call yourself. It is you who seems to be completely oblivious to the splendor of the human spirit. We bring children to this world not for them to suffer pain and disease, but for them to live and love! For them to bask in the boundless benevolence of God – the cradle of a mother's lap, the fingers of a father's hand, the unforgettable touch of a lover, the fire of ambition, the triumph of achievement, the caress of a cool breeze, the peace of a temple, the laughter of sons and daughters, the carefree abandon of friendship...*this* is why we want our children with us.

You make me laugh when you speak about marriage with such pathetic patronizing. Agreed men and women cannot just switch off their instinctive desires. Yet a majority of them spend their entire lives devoted to their partners, deeply in love – so much love that it is enough to outweigh their banal cravings. And that is the greatest testimony to the sacredness of the institution. Togetherness that creates soulmates for journeys far beyond just this life, is more precious than your dark being can ever comprehend.

Yes, we make shrines. Yes, we shower our Gods with our purest sentiments. Those are just humble ways to build a channel, to feel His presence within the limited senses we have as humans. But as the scriptures say, "*Aham Brahmmasmi*" or "I am Brahmma" or simply - "God resides within me" - is the simplest way to understand the cosmic connection between each individual and the Lord. Every man or woman who walks on this planet is a living shrine of the Almighty. You say He governs us. Nothing could be farther from the truth. God has never intervened in the way we choose to live, and yet He watches over us as we laugh, cry, struggle, resolve and rejoice. He loves the atheists as much as He looks after the pastors.

As for seven billion human beings turning into flesh-eating rogues...you should not worry too much. Several naysayers and doomsday soothsayers like you have come and gone – underestimating the resilience of the human race. You see, we are still here. While challenges of climate change have been created by us, it is we who are now harnessing the power of the Sun and the wind to light up our cities. While we have, no doubt, polluted our air and our oceans, it is us now manufacturing green cars and constructing green buildings to fight back. Why, it is the magnificent men of our species who are now taking the giant leap to inhabit even the planet Mars, and transform us into a multi-planetary civilization!

We are here for good, Maschera.

Leave us alone.

And tell your Overlord brethren the same.'

·||ॐ||·

The meeting between the *Dev* and the *Raakshasa* was over.

Vidyut got up to leave as the Maschera Bianca sat looking far into the horizon, his teeth clenched.

Before the devta turned to leave, he added a chilling appendage, his brown eyes locked with those of the demon.

'Leave Kashi today, Maschera.

I have never killed a human being in my life. Don't make me change that.'

Vidyut turned and walked away along the Ganga, climbing the steps of the ghaat slowly. He could not help but think about his last statement.

If this green-eyed monster is not human...it will not be wrong to punish him for his sins.

In his own currency.

The Marshes Surrounding the Great Ark, Aryavarta, 1698 BCE

NARA-BALI

The rest of the battle slowly came to a standstill.

Warriors from both sides watched the bloody contest with bated breath. This duel between man and man-eater was going to be the decisive battle of the war for the Ark and the Earth.

Tara stood atop the Ark deck, trembling with fear. She had seen what Nara-Munda could do. She was witness to the gruesome fate of the great architect. She had seen how the cannibal-king had crushed the riders of the fish-tribe. Her heart had stopped when he had dragged twelve horsemen from their mounts in one go. And now her Manu, her beloved Manu was battling the fiend singlehandedly.

She closed her eyes and prayed to the One she knew would never let any harm come to Satyavrata.

She prayed to Matsya.

·‖ॐ‖·

After momentarily staggering with his shoulder wound, Nara-Munda had recovered, more enraged than before. He lifted and flung Manu away. The might of the giant was such that Manu fell twenty feet away from him. But the moment his body touched the ground, Manu scrambled up and was on his feet, charging head-on again towards the monster.

As Manu came closer to his gigantic adversary, the canni-bal-king smashed his colossal foot like a battering ram into Manu's chest and abdomen. Once again, the son of Surya flew back several feet, unable to breath as an outcome of the crushing impact. But once again, as soon as his body landed on the marshy ground was he up and charging at the giant.

Manu was fighting like a wounded tiger against a wild mam-moth tusker. Not backing down, not retreating, not afraid!

The third time Manu charged at the man-eater, he succeeded in dodging a massive axe attack and slashed the monster's knee with his short sword. Satyavrata Manu's blade-strike was so accurate that it would have sliced off any other man's leg into two. But Nara-Munda's hide was like rhino leather. He only suffered an inch-deep gash. The giant gnarled, as Manu pranced around him waiting for the next opportunity to pounce.

·‖卐‖·

Both Nara-Munda and Manu were out of breath, panting and sweating heavily under the rainy night. They had been fighting for what seemed like eternity. The cannibal emperor had suffered several wounds at the hands of the young priest-king, but none fatal enough. He was nowhere close to being vanquished.

With every passing minute, Manu was running out of moves, ideas and breath. In his desperation, he committed his first mistake. In an attempt to reach the fiend's jugular, Manu came within hitting range of the titan's arm. Nara-Munda did not miss his chance and struck the defender of the Ark with a mighty fist blow. The smashing hit was enough to fracture a wall. Manu instantly spat blood and crashed down to his knees. His world went black as he felt a giant hand grab his long hair.

Pulling him by his hair, Nara-Munda dragged Manu around the field in a circle for everyone to see. Tara broke into heavy tears as she picked her sword and ran towards the rope ladder dropping from the Ark deck's thick wooden railing. She was held back by several fighters of the Damini Sena, who were now bracing themselves for a full and final attack on the great boat.

The beast then threw Manu a few steps away from himself. He turned to first look triumphantly at his own soldiers. In their response, the daityas roared to cheer for their invincible sovereign, raising their weapons in celebration of victory. Thereafter Nara-Munda looked at the Ark defenders with cruel, prophetic eyes, indicating coldly what fate awaited them. He then slowly walked towards the son of Surya. In his usual style, the monster raised his gigantic, muscular leg and pressed it against Manu's head.

He guffawed like a giant goblin before increasing the pressure on the fallen warrior's face.

He was going to crush Manu's skull to pulp.

·‖ॐ‖·

The colossus did not know what tore through his leg. The fool had forgotten who he was fighting. In his premature celebrations, he had forgotten that the son of Vivasvan Pujari was wounded. He was not dead.

Still squashed under the monster's foot, Manu had pulled out his dagger. Drawing on every last ounce of strength left in him, he had dug the blade deep into Nara-Munda's calf. Within moments Manu ripped through the giant's pillar of a leg, the fiend's calf muscle hanging out, his fibula bone exposed.

Nara-Munda screamed in unbearable agony. As the beast stuttered in shock and intense pain, Satyavrata Manu sprung back to his feet. While he was indeed shaken by the brutal assault from the cannibal's fist, the son of Surya was not unconscious as he was being dragged. The defender of the Ark was waiting for the right time to claw back into the fight.

The giant was now swinging his axe madly, growling like a wild beast, unable to maintain his balance. Satyavrata Manu once again began to walk around the bleeding man-eater. This time it was a slow walk. The king of the Ark could not forget the gruesome sight of Somdutt being ripped to pieces. He was clear in his mind. This brute deserved no mercy.

As the monster turned and swung his axe in a futile attempt to strike the priest-king, Manu broke into a sudden sprint. Before the fiend could realize what was happening, Manu had climbed up on the cannibal's massive shoulders from behind.

'This is for my father's last friend, Nara-Munda! This is for the architect of Harappa! This is for Pundit Somdutt!' screamed Manu into the demon's ears.

In the next moment, the son of Surya stabbed the daitya in the neck with his short sword, twisting and pushing the blade deep, shredding open the cannibal's throat.

Somdutt's ghastly killing had been avenged with an equally brutal end.

Blood sprayed out of Nara-Munda's jugular like a fountain, as the gigantic monster crumbled to his knees. The cannibal was now certain to bleed to death. Even though he was still seething with rage, Manu decided to end the fiend's suffering.

Lifting the dark emperor's own battle-axe, Manu swung the heavy blade in one precise move. That was the end of the daitya king.

Nara-Munda's huge head flung in the air, as his headless body crashed into the slushy mud.

·||ॐ||·

Another monster appeared as one monster fell.

'Imprison the daityas! And fall back to the Ark! Fall baaaaac-ck!' yelled Manu to his army.

Tearing through the stormy clouds, silencing the thunder in its wake, covering half the sky under its devastating curtain... it appeared.

Pralay!

The calamitous waves of the great deluge were hurtling towards the Ark.

Banaras, 2017

DEADLIEST ASSASSINS IN HISTORY

'They are here, Vidyut dada!'

The Order wasted no time. They knew that the secret of the Black Temple, the exact birthplace of the Kalki avatar, the names of His mortal parents...everything was now buried in the heart of the devta. The ancient scroll had been burnt in the holy fire during the Rohini Nakshatra.

The secret brotherhood was left with no other alternative. Their survival and their vision of the New World Order depended on finding and murdering the infant Kalki. They were repeating the mistakes and the desperate bids made by tyrants of the past. Kansa, the demon-king of Mathura, endeavored to kill all infants born when Lord Krishna arrived on earth. Emperor Herod of Judea tried the same when Jesus Christ stepped on the planet. And now the Order was attempting a similar depravity.

Vidyut *was* the secret of the Black Temple now!

The Order was clear.

Vidyut had to be captured. He had to be tortured. The information he had was to be extracted at all cost. And the Kalki avatar had to be extinguished in the cradle itself!

Sonu had knocked at Vidyut's door well after midnight.

'You will not believe this, dada...but they are attacking the matth,' he whispered, as the devta opened the door.

'Where is everyone?' asked Vidyut. 'And how many of them are attacking?'

Sonu took a deep breath to calm himself down before responding.

'We cannot say, dada. They are...'

He appeared lost for words. Vidyut looked into his eyes.

'They are what, Sonu?'

'I don't know what to say, Vidyut dada. But they are dressed in black clothes and they move as stealthily as a cobra, vanishing into thin air upon being spotted! Their faces are covered revealing only their eyes, and they carry strange looking weapons. Three of the matth's night guard have been found dead on the terrace, their throats slit from behind.'

Vidyut now grabbed Sonu's arm and dashed towards the wing where Damini and Naina were staying. He knew instantly what the Maschera's attackers were, and it was very bad news.

They were the deadliest warriors and assassins in the history of the world.

Ninjas.

·‖卐‖·

'By now Sheshnaag would have reached the Lord, so Kalki will be safe at least for the time being,' said Naina.

They were now huddled inside the large meeting hall in the basement of the matth, all doors bolted with heavy iron paddles and each entrance guarded by a dozen fighters of the monastery. Several warriors of the matth had been killed within a few minutes of the Ninja attack. Dwarka Shastri, Vidyut, Balvanta and Naina had rushed to get all inhabitants and fighters of the matth into the temporary protection of the hall.

The residents, young students and children of the Dev-Raakshasa hermitage were terrified. They were not weaklings by any measure. Nor were they new to the world of warfare and violence. But the battle-tactics of these black ghost-fighters was something none of them had ever seen or heard of before. The stealth attackers were slowly extinguishing and destroying every source of light of the monastery – every bulb, every tube-light, every sodium vapor lamp and even the earthen diyas placed for worship. Gradually the entire matth was engulfed in a blanket of complete darkness. Telephone lines were cut and mobile signals jammed using cutting-edge telecom technology. There was no doubt in Dwarka Shastri's mind that the all-powerful secret brotherhood would have bought off the local authorities as well, making sure they looked away from the matth for the next few hours, no matter what happened. In other words, the matthadheesh and his devoted followers knew one thing for sure.

Tonight, they were on their own.

·||ॐ||·

'You are right, Naina bitiya...that is one silver lining,' replied the grand old man. 'I am glad that the divine serpent-king is there by the Lord's side. But now Vidyut and Damini need to be protected with everything we have!'

Everyone nodded in agreement, though not totally sure of what needed to be done next. After a minute's silence, that felt like a year to the commune gathered in the basement hall, Dwarka Shastri turned to Balvanta and Vidyut, desperately seeking answers. He knew they could not combat an enemy they did not even understand.

'What are these wicked attackers who kill dishonorably from the back, Vidyut? Who are these sinister assassins, Balvanta? I have never seen such surreptitious methods before!' exclaimed the grand old man, trying to grope for defense and counter-attack measures.

Vidyut was about to quickly tell his great grandfather and every fighter of the matth present about the lethal Ninjas, when he noticed dark shadows crawl across the ventilator windows of the basement.

'They are here, Baba...' whispered Vidyut. 'We cannot all stay in here. They will eventually break in. They can even be brutally reckless and use some kind of a nerve gas. Their mobile jammers are just a small indicator of their sophisticated methods. The White Mask will not hesitate to murder every man, woman and child of the matth, if that serves his need.'

'Who are these people, Vidyut?' asked Damini, her eyes wide with terror.

'They are Ninjas, Damini. A medieval cult of assassins that originated in Japan. Considered inferior to the *Samurai* because of their brutality and deceitful methods, the Ninja battle-art travelled to the West during the 19th century. They are the deadliest assassins to have ever existed.'

The chilling silence came back again, as several people broke into cold sweat.

'So...so what does this mean, Vidyut?' asked Balvanta.

'It means that if you thought the mercenaries that came with Romi Pereira were skilled fighters...

...then the Ninjas are virtually unbeatable.'

The Great Deluge, 1698 BCE

'MA...AATTSYA!'

'They are all going to die...' mumbled Manu to himself. 'And I will die with them.'

These desperate souls, these young men and women, the infants, the old and the destitute, this entire collective I promised to protect forever, will be crushed like ants.

Manu now realized the ghastly reality of his daring enterprise fully for the first time. Till this horrifying moment of truth, he had been way too immersed in carrying out the bizarre yet fateful commandment of the mystical Master of the ocean-tribe.

The fiery young leader of this nearly deranged, ragtag architectural force froze as he saw the gigantic vessel tilt beyond the endurance of the twenty thousand jute chords and tree-vines holding it aloft. The violent, monstrous waves of the river-sea were pounding on the biggest ship mankind had ever built. And the vicious flood was going to sink it.

Does the murderous deluge know what irreplaceable cargo this last boat carries?

·‖卐‖·

That the final, universally destructive flood was incoming was not hard to tell. The dark, reddish-purple clouds, that appeared like some insane celestial painter had dyed the skies with the color of stale blood, enveloped all of known earth. The maddening roar of *Indra's* thunder and the unnatural tempest of violently lashing rain had now announced the apocalypse, or the final end. Droplets the size of tiger fangs were falling from the skies, transforming into a piercing shower of agonizing water-arrows as they struck Manu and his devoted followers. Every drop hitting the skin of the *Manu-Shishyas* or *Manushyas* was like an invisible spear penetrating through. What this militia of valiant men and women was trying to tug and balance on the furious waters was not a regular boat anyway.

It was the *last* boat. Not the last boat from a harbor. Not the last boat of a fleet. Not the last vessel to leave a port for the season or a sailor rowing away for the night.

It was the last boat for creation itself. It was the Nauka where Prithvi herself was going to take refuge. Along with the seeds of all her flock.

It was the great warrior, priest, ascetic, philosopher and king Manu's ultimate deliverance.

It was his ark.

Manu's Ark.

·॥ॐ॥·

The fearless struggle of over one hundred thousand men and women against a vessel, the expanse of which even the Gods could not imagine, was a spectacle that had never been seen before on the planet. And would never be seen after, even till the end of time. Manu's gigantic ark was the size of a glorious city. But its purpose was the noblest that mankind could ever fathom.

It was a doorway. The only bridge of continuity. From the decaying, ancient world…to the new dawn of resurrection. It embodied a fierce contest between Armageddon at the behest of nature and the survival instinct of man. Humanity was not going to perish without a fight that even the heavens would remember. But despite this heroic endeavor, a lot was going to be lost. Eons of precious and irreplaceable wisdom acquired by the human race was not going to pass through this portal of sorts between different universes, even though it was all going to unfold on the same planet. Ancient alchemy, medicine, aviation, occult, architecture, weaponry and spirituality were all going to disappear forever, drowning in the aftermath of the great deluge, to the bottom of the mighty oceans in spate.

And yet the Ark was the last ray of hope for life, as Aryavarta knew it. Much as we are dumbfounded by God's profound conceptions like the stars, the galaxies and the constellations being the symbols of his divine workmanship, the greatest of the Lord's creations is undoubtedly – *life*. The magnificent, the resilient…life. Beings that feel pain, give birth, weep tears and love boundlessly. Beings that mirror the image of the Gods themselves. And it was *this* creation that needed to be saved.

Above all.

·‖卐‖·

The thick, twisted and drenched ropes and vines were now cutting into the arms, necks and flesh of Manu's militia. The tearing force exerted by the ropes harnessing the toppling boat as big as a floating city, was breaking their fingers, dislocating their shoulders and ripping into their forearms and biceps. Men, women and children fought on alike against the formidable onslaught of the unimaginable weight of their adversary. They were all made of destructible blood and bones, whereas the Nauka was made of heavy wood, reinforced copper and rock-stone – so enormous that the people pulling the ropes in the water could not even get a glimpse of the mast of this massive vessel, even if they looked straight up at the grotesque skies.

The Nauka was taller than Mount Sumeru and wider than the gory field that had hosted the Dasarajna or the decisive ancient Battle of the Ten Kings.

Manu was getting increasingly desperate. He pulled out the crooked seashell blow-horn that had been given to him as signaling gear, only to be used when caught in the midst of the worst calamity. And that time had come. Nothing could be darker than the imminent and painful demise of his devoted people. Manu wiped his face with his leather wristguard, took a deep breath and blew into the horn, which shrieked out in its horrendous and maddening call, nearly splitting open the stormy skies.

Standing atop a lone and eerie cliff that looked black as coal against the bleeding red sky, Manu covered his eyes against the whipping rain with his open palms, looking far into the misty horizon. He saw nothing. With every passing moment, his despair was growing. He tried hard to hold back his tears of defeat, and once again blew into the twisted horn with all his might. The scream of the blow-horn was like the cry of an angry dragon, and the tens of thousands of Manu's subjects felt needles piercing through their eardrums.

Manu squinted his eyes to ward off the vicious sky-arrows and tried to look far beyond the mountainous waves. He hoped to see the faint silhouette of the One he believed was the true savior.

He saw nothing.

·||ॐ||·

'MA...AATTSYA!' yelled Manu, now darting feverishly on the edge of the protruding cliff that was his observation and control station for the gargantuan undertaking he was overseeing. His tired, afraid and hopeful eyes kept gazing at the far horizon of the devastating deluge. Raindrops lashed on his handsome yet battle-torn face. He was probably crying at the horror he could see enveloping his ambitious enterprise. A sinking realization was making it impossible for him to continue battling this unnatural typhoon.

Had the only person he had ever trusted after his own beloved father, the great Vivasvan Pujari, betrayed him? Had his friend, mentor, counsel, healer…betrayed him?

Had his beloved Matsya betrayed him?

'MAAATTTTSSSYAAAA…ARRGHH!' screamed Manu, looking up at the punishing firmament, his arms outstretched and his lungs ready to explode, as if he wanted the heavens to hear his desperate plea!

And then he saw it. In the endgame flood, riding the oceans' merciless surfs, he saw it.

Lok-naas, the biggest sea-monster that even the mighty creator *Brahma* could have envisaged, raised what looked like its enormous head in the distant waves. It was the first time Manu was witness to the faint outline of the fabled giant-beast.

And there he was, standing fearlessly between the hydra's gleaming eyes.

Matsya.

Banaras, 2017

'EVEN DEATH IS AFRAID OF THE WHITE MASK!'

It was decided. Vidyut, Balvanta and Naina would lead the counter-strike. They were the only ones who stood a chance against the formidable Ninjas. Thirty select fighters from the matth were to follow them from closely behind, armed to the teeth with swords, spears and shotguns. Sonu was entrusted with guarding Damini, Dwarka Shastri, Purohit ji and the rest of the matth's residents, who were to continue taking refuge in the basement. Twenty more warriors of the Dev-Raakshasa monastery stayed behind with Sonu.

'Keep this, Vidyut,' said Balvanta, handing out a gleaming black Beretta 92 semiautomatic pistol to the devta. 'I know you do not approve of my ways of warfare, but this will help you when nothing else works.'

Vidyut shook his head politely, turning down the offer.

'If your blessings are with me, I won't be needing this, Balvanta dada. Baba would never let me step out unarmed and vulnerable now, would he? Besides, I always have you to fall back on.'

With this Vidyut kept his hand on the old warrior's shoulder and smiled. Balvanta felt as if a mountain had been lifted off his chest. His beloved Vidyut had finally forgiven him!

'Come back to me safe and sound, baby,' whispered Damini, as she bid farewell to her devta, her voice heavy with emotion. 'We need to crossover to the other side together, remember?'

'Together,' replied Vidyut, as he touched his forehead to hers lovingly, looking deep into her eyes.

The devta knew he was going to embark upon the toughest battle of his life, one that could mean that he never came back. And what he was worried about most was not the deadly Ninjas. He was gravely concerned about who would arrive after them.

The Maschera Bianca. The Messenger of the Devil.

·||卐||·

It was now the Ninjas' turn to get hurt. Splitting into three different directions, Vidyut, Naina and Balvanta had spread out around the Dev-khannd. Trained martial artists as they were, it did not take the trio much time to get accustomed to fighting in the darkness. As their eyes got more and more tuned to the black shadows moving against the dark corners, they began hitting back. And hitting back hard.

Vidyut dodged a Japanese sword that brushed against his ear and glittered a millimeter away from his eyes. Almost instantly, judging the direction and distance of the attacker, Vidyut smashed his fist into the throat of the Ninja – a perfect Israeli Krav Maga move. The assailant in the well-fitting black robes stopped breathing for several seconds, grabbed his neck with his hands and rolled down a flight of stairs in extreme pain.

Engaging two more Ninja aggressors with equally punishing outcomes, Vidyut came to an open corridor that offered an expansive view of the entire Dev-khannda lawns. What he saw sent a chill down his spine.

Baba!

Dwarka Shastri stood surrounded by seven Ninjas, their swords drawn, their fists raised up to their ears, their elbows raised up to their shoulders - in a typical Ninja offence stance. The old grandmaster looked like an aging lion surrounded by a pack of wild dogs. The matthadheesh could not keep himself hidden when his beloved great grandson was out there, facing a lethal enemy. The great and fearless Dwarka Shastri had decided to step out and offer whatever little assistance his glistening trident and he could offer.

Unfortunately, the 108-year-old mahataantric was up against some of the world's most skilled professional killers.

Their trained swords were going to cut him to pieces in the bat of an eyelid.

·||ॐ||·

The devta crashed into them like an avalanche. The Ninjas did not know what had hit them from above until they saw the devta rolling forward on the grassy ground, only to stop and turn around like a cheetah stalking its prey. Vidyut had leapt straight from the first-floor corridor and pounced on the enemy with debilitating force. His honest eyes were now gleaming with rage and abhorrence. Anyone trying to harm Vidyut's beloved great grandfather became an instant and most hated enemy for him.

And anyone who made the big mistake of being at the receiving end of the devta's wrath - was very unfortunate.

Horribly unfortunate.

Six of the Ninjas charged at Vidyut, while the seventh slashed his sword at the matthadheesh. Even at his ripe old age the great Dwarka Shastri had the dexterity to block the blade with the steel of his trident, as the two weapons clashed with a loud ring. As Vidyut readied himself to take on the half-dozen assassins charging at him, a blinding light, accompanied by the roar of helicopter rotors, washed the entire Dev-khannd in a golden yellow glow.

From the great silver bird that now hung over the Dev-Raakshasa matth, gliding down a metallic chord like an elite commando, descended the black demon with a white face.

His green eyes nearly burning through everything they surveyed, the Maschera Bianca landed on the hallowed ground of the God-Demon clan.

·‖卐‖·

The Mask raised his hand and commanded his black knights to stay put. He walked to the center of the garden-atrium and stood about ten meters away from Vidyut. Naina and Balvanta also came running out as they heard the deafening roar of the chopper.

'You are indeed extraordinary, Vidyut...the Big Man was right!' shouted the Mask, as his Sikorsky bird slowly lifted away from the matth and flew away into the night-sky of Kashi.

The Mask continued.

'I had heard how you had singlehandedly crushed ten trained Russian mercenaries, but I did not expect you to beat even Nin...'

'They were twelve.'

The Maschera was confused.

'Sorry, what?'

'They were twelve of them, the mercenaries...not ten,' said Vidyut defiantly, once again glaring into the green-eyed monster fearlessly.

The Mask laughed, as more Ninjas arrived in the garden

area. Almost at the same time several of the matth's warrior-priests also reached the epicenter of the fight.

'You still have time, Vidyut. Tell me where I will find your omnipotent Kalki. As simple as that, my friend. Even now, I will let you go. I will let the tall old man go. I will let your beautiful woman go. But if you continue being as stubborn as you have been, I will burn down this entire priory, and I will skin every living soul in this monastery alive tonight.'

Vidyut clenched his fists in hate.

'Let them all go, Maschera. Your black knights, my warrior-monks...everyone. Let's sort this between the two of us. You and me. Here and now.'

The Maschera's face changed. Vidyut could not believe what he was seeing. The Italian don's eyes seemed to be getting drained off of all color...and going white.

The white-eyed demon now looked at the Ninjas surrounding Vidyut and nodded. In the very next instant Vidyut felt a throbbing gash on his shoulder. As the devta turned to counter the cowards who had attacked from behind, he felt another sword slice through his thigh. Despite the wounds that tore open his flesh, Vidyut swung in a perfect Jiu Jitsu kick and struck one of the swordsmen on his chin. The man twirled and fell five feet away, propelled by the sheer force of the devta's assault. But the spineless, unannounced attack had taken the devta by a painful surprise. In a blur of unbearable agony and of his own blood flying in the air, Vidyut heard a faint voice. He knew who it was.

'You are a fool, O devta!' said the Maschera Bianca. 'You

fight with those who you cannot vanquish. You lock eyes with me in your misdirected boldness, to show me that you are unafraid. Do you not know, you petulant boy...?

EVEN DEATH IS AFRAID OF THE WHITE MASK!!'

Vidyut tried to jostle his way to where they were, but he was cut down by more *nanchoks* and Japanese scimitars assaulting his body. Unable to maintain consciousness under the fatal barrage of blade and blood, Vidyut stretched out his arm in a futile attempt to reach the grand old man. Only one word escaped his lips in an anguished whisper.

'Babaaaa...aaah!'

The White Mask now stood right behind the matthadheesh.

His eyes were the cold eyes of death.

The Great Deluge, 1698 BCE

LOK-NAAS!

The great Ark was now tilting dangerously, unable to cope with the enormous waves of pralay. The weight of the gigantic boat was more than that of a mountain, and the floating city was on the verge of sinking.

The massive hull of the vessel was being pushed by monstrous waves that exerted the pressure of a million whales. The rain and hail were so severe that several top decks of the Ark were flooded and overflowing. Thousands of men and women worked incessantly to pump the water out, but to no avail. The onslaught of the stormy downpour combined with the lashing waves was inundating the boat.

It seemed to be a matter of minutes now, as panic began to grip the collective of the great Ark. Mothers held on to their children, praying feverishly to Vishnu, begging Him to come to their rescue. Thousands of species of birds and animals now neighed, roared, whined, squawked and trumpeted in chaotic terror. The incarcerated daityas struck their hands, bodies and heads against the bronze bars that held them captive, pleading to be set free from the prison cells that were certain death-traps in the wake of the flooding Ark. Thousands of men and women hung on with ropes on the overturning hull, pulling with all their might against the impossible adversary in a failing attempt to restore the boat to balance. Several unfortunate residents of the Nauka now began to lose their footing and fell screaming down thousands of meters below into the jaws of the yawning typhoon, vanishing like specks of sand in the vicious surfs.

·‖卐‖·

Manu's last vantage point had also been drowned under the deluge and he was back on the Ark after a near-fatal canoe ride, waiting breathlessly as he saw it make its way through the giant waves, advancing towards the sinking wooden city.

The fabled sea-monster really does exist. It is not a legend. And Matsya is its master!

Manu's fantastic delusion was soon cut short by the breathtaking reality.

They were perhaps ten thousand of them. Wearing robes made from glimmering fish-scales, they moved like one single organism. Satyavrata Manu, Satrupa, Dhruv, Prachanda and the rest of the Arkers were stunned as they saw the floating colony approach the great Nauka.

The fish-folk rode the waves in an interwoven network of small boats connected to each other using vines, spread over a couple of miles. The webby structure of light canoes stretching across a vast area made the entire colony virtually unsinkable. They all wore clothes made from fish and serpent skin that glistened against the thunder-flash from miles away. The spearhead of the aquatic colony was Matsya's own boat. A wide raft with a hundred oars on both sides, it had two shining round shields mounted on both edges of the boat's front bow. Used in sea-battles to blind an approaching enemy by reflecting the light of the Sun or the thunder, the massive shields appeared to be the eyes of a mammoth hydra!

This is how the legend of the dreaded sea-monster came to life. The glimmering fish-skin robes of several thousand of the fish-folk, their practiced, sequential movements giving the appearance of a slithering serpent, the front shields gleaming like giant eyes – Lok-Naas was not a living water-beast. It was the floating city of the fish-tribe!

·‖ॐ‖·

What seemed like a million hooks and harpoons flew across from the boats of the fish-tribe. The uncountable projectiles attached themselves to the railings and windows of the Ark's lower decks, all along the great vessel's unimaginable length. The dominance and mastery that the magnificent blue-man and his fish-folk had over the oceans was now becoming evident to Manu and his men. With the ropes of the innumerable hooks and harpoons attached to their agile boats, the marvelous men of the floating colony began to row away from the overturning hull.

Each one of the fish-folk was timing his oars perfectly, using every ounce of strength. An intricate and complex series of sails were erected to assist the effort of the oarsmen. The sails were being maneuvered expertly, harnessing the power of the shrieking wind in favor of the mighty Ark.

It slowly began to work. The combined strength of ten thousand sets of arms and hundreds of surgically engineered sails created a propulsion that would have moved a mountain.

The great Ark rolled sluggishly, before thrashing back to a safer balance, creating enormous, mile-high waves in the process.

Vishnu had answered their prayers.

Mankind was going to survive pralay!

Banaras, 2017

'BABAAAAAA...!'

'We shall meet again, Vidyut, my son...we shall meet again in another life...' gasped Dwarka Shastri, as the Maschera Bianca's weapon of choice tore through the matthadheesh's belly.

By now Vidyut was down on his knees, bleeding from several deep incisions on his body, with the world going either totally blank or flashing as a violent haze in front of his dimming eyes. Blood dripped profusely from his mouth and he was drenched in the cold sweat of extreme agony.

'Baba...' he whispered again, struggling to stay conscious.

But even under the dizzying pain, he seemed to hear the faint yet booming, terrifying voice...as if it came from another universe.

The curse of the Blood River!

Just the manner in which you have watched the divine Sages burn one after the other on this fateful night, fate will watch your lineage perish violently, son after son, generation after generation.

I curse you and your entire bloodline, O fallen devta...

·||卐||·

The second stab from the White Mask ripped through Dwarka Shastri's heart, the red shaft of the long screwdriver protruding from the grand old man's chest like the nail of a crucifixion. The great matthadheesh's mouth spewed blood as he whispered a prayer in preparation to meet his Maker. In this final hour, he was a proud and gratified man. This mahataantric from Kashi was a man who had fulfilled his divine destiny.

In his dying moments, even the old matthadheesh of the Dev-Raakshasa clan seemed to hear the hissing pronouncement of the Blood River, to which he closed his eyes in absolute and devoted submission.

Every single son of your descent will die a death as violent and as horrible as the spectacle today!

I CURSE YOU! AND YOUR ENTIRE BLOODLINE!

THIS CURSE SHALL LAST TILL THE END OF

TIME!

'I will protect you, Baba...' muttered Vidyut, as he summoned every last bit of his strength and determination. Any other man in his place would have succumbed to the pain by now. But Vidyut was not just a man. He was a devta!

He wiped the blood off his face with his hand as he struggled to get back on his feet. But he was too late. When he opened his eyes, and saw what was happening clearly, it was already the end of the great life of the magnificent Dwarka Shastri. In front of Vidyut's eyes, his beloved great grandfather's body was punctured mercilessly by the Maschera's lethal screwdriver.

True to the dark ancient curse, one more splendid son of the Shastri bloodline met a violent, brutal end.

'NOOOOOO...!' screamed Vidyut, unable to bear the anguish of the horror he beheld!

The cruel Mask's eyes were now completely white. He threw the mutilated body of the grandmaster and smiled at Vidyut coldly, inviting the devta to a duel.

·||ॐ||·

Beretta shots rang out in the darkness of the gory night.

Shattered from deep inside at the inhuman killing of their adored matthadheesh, Balvanta and Naina could not contain their fury. Abandoning all thoughts of good and evil, right and wrong, they had opened fire at the Ninjas with their deadly Berettas. Balvanta had aimed for the Maschera Bianca as well, but the Mask had evaded a fatal shot. Balvanta's bullet found its mark on the demon's thigh. While this wound was not going to kill the Mask, it was enough to limit his combat effectiveness.

And that minor difference was enough for Vidyut, who was himself grievously injured, to draw his vengeance.

Vidyut was the embodiment of rage now. Even in his wounded state he pounced on the Maschera. The Mask greeted Vidyut with a powerful fist-blow, that the devta took straight on his jaw. Vidyut's chin split and a bleeding gash appeared almost instantly. The white-eyed monster's punch was brutal. But to the Mask's disbelief, the devta kept coming at him, without flinching even momentarily.

It was Vidyut's turn now. He struck his clenched fist into the steely abdomen of the Italian don. The blow was vicious even for the Mask and he coughed in agony. Vidyut struck again, this time with his knee, and hit the Maschera right into his ribcage. The Mask's bones crackled and he fell on the ground, grimacing under an attack that was more punishing than he had imagined.

But he was the Devil's messenger. He was not going to be vanquished so easily.

In the next moment, the Maschera Bianca sprung up, looking ghastlier than ever. His face carried a strange, macabre scowl. His right hand was tightly clasped around a menacing weapon.

A screwdriver that was still dripping with Shastri blood.

·||ॐ||·

The Maschera Bianca could see Vidyut was losing blood rapidly. Earlier when he had landed in the matth, the Mask did not want the devta to die. But Vidyut was turning out to be a more daunting challenge than the Devil's lieutenant had expected. Reeling under the pain from the devta's blows, the Mask was losing his sense of purpose. His rage was making him forget how important Vidyut's life was to the Order. But more than that, he could see bloodthirst in Vidyut's fiery eyes.

The Mask concluded quickly. Either he kills the devta today. Or Vidyut would not let him leave the matth alive.

'To hell with the avatar, Vidyut...you will die today at my hands, writhing next to your old man's stinking corpse!' hissed the White Mask.

With these words, the demon lunged forward and swung around to land a crushing kick into Vidyut's face. It was a devastating blow. The devta could not stand any longer on his feet and crumbled to the ground, nearly losing consciousness.

The Mask now leapt onto Vidyut and pinned him down. The demon shoved his left forearm into the devta's throat, strangling him slowly. His right hand now held his favorite execution tool, the screwdriver, in stabbing position. He nearly touched the tip of the weapon to Vidyut's eyeball and hissed. His face was just an inch away from the devta's.

'Tell me the place of Kalki's birth, you fool...and I will kill you swiftly. If you still persist, I will take your life more painfully than I took from your old daddy boy...and I will slaughter every single soul...'

Before the demon could complete his cold threat, Vidyut interrupted him.

'I told you Maschera, leave Banaras.'

What Naina, Balvanta, the Ninjas and the warrior-monks of the matth saw next, was something they would never forget.

The Maschera Bianca screamed like a dragon struck by a silver arrow, his head twisting backwards and the veins of his neck ready to explode. His tongue shot out from his mouth due to insufferable pain, even as color began to return into his petrified eyes. Tearing through the monster's entire gut, the devta's clawed hand emerged from the Maschera's back.

'AAAARRGGGGHHH....!' yelled the devta, as he pushed his arm deeper into the demon's belly, remembering the bloodstained body of his beloved Baba.

Vidyut had torn through and through the Mask's body, disemboweling him in the gruesome process. When his blood-smeared fingers and forearm surfaced from behind the demon, they were reinforced with an ancient, concealed weapon of close combat.

Baagh-Nakh!

The same copper-hooks shaped into a claw that the great Manu Pujari had used to defeat the monstrous Ranga. The very same baagh-nakh that Markandeya Shastri had worn when he ripped open the Portuguese killer Agostinho in medieval Goa.

The baagh-nakh was Dwarka Shastri's last gift for his able great grandson. It was the reason why Vidyut had refused the Beretta pistol Balvanta had offered to him.

'AAAAARRRGGGGHHH...!

'YAAARRRGGGHHHH...!'

'BABAAAAAAAA...!'

With his arm still piercing out from the dead demon's body, Vidyut kept screaming, bawling and calling out his Baba's name.

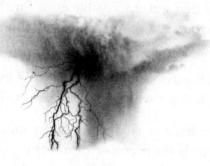

The Great Deluge, 1698 BCE

VIDYUT

'I told you when we first met...those drops of water...I will owe you, Satyavrata!'

Matsya laughed as Manu rushed to hold him in a tight embrace. The blue-man hugged the son of Surya back. It was hard to say who had missed whom more. Did man miss his God? Or did God miss His mortal devotee?

'Why did you leave me and go, Matsya? Why?!' insisted Manu, as he refused to let the leader of the fish-folk go.

'I never left you, Manu. Not for a moment. How can I even exist without you, my friend, my brother? I was watching you. When you evacuated cities without any regard for your own safety, I was there. When you were building this immortal Ark, a feat that was impossible even for the Gods, I was there. When you slew the daitya Nara-Munda, I was there, Manu. I was always there.'

'Then why did you not show yourself, O divine Matsya? Why did you not bless me with your *darshana*, my Lord?'

'*My lord?* You have started using big words I see, *Shri* Satyavrata Manu? Is the presence of a lady in your life bringing about this change? Are you softening up, O mighty warrior?' joked Matsya.

'Well...get ready to get an earful from the woman in my life, Shri Matsya. She is as upset with you as I am, if not more,' replied Manu.

'Okay, now that scares me more than the catastrophic waves of the great flood!' exclaimed the blue man.

The two friends, the lord and his devotee, the avatar of God and the hero among men, laughed like old friends.

·‖卐‖·

'The bestial Ranga, the three black-magicians from Mesopotamia, Ap, Sha, Gun, the beautiful but vile Priyamvada, the demon-king Sura and even Nara-Munda...none of them were even close to the darkness of evil that is about to swallow this planet, Manu. We are entering the era of Kali, when the world will transform into a chaotic mayhem of violence, deceit, intrigue, betrayal, death and destruction. You are taking mankind into a new dawn of survival, no doubt. But what awaits us on the other side of pralay is a world where man will wage war against one another, against mother nature, he will destroy the forests, dry up the rivers, poison the skies and spill blood by using weapons of mass extermination. Nara-Munda killed one man at a time...that too only to ensure his own survival and the survival of his commune. But in Kaliyuga men will wipe out thousands of innocents, women, children...to feed the insatiable lust for a transient throne.'

They stood at a high deck of the Ark, sipping on a delicious wine fermented by the fish-tribe. Matsya had carried it specially for his friend. Tara was also with them. A few days had passed and the maddening storms had given way to slow, incessant rain that was far less cataclysmic. The leaders of the Ark knew that they now had the formidable task of seeing pralay through ahead of them. But they all hoped, they sensed...that the worst was over.

'What is your commandment for us, Matsya? What can Tara and I do to prevent such a dark age?' asked Manu.

Matsya smiled and turned to Manu and Tara, resting his back on the railing of the deck. His face was being splattered with the drizzle. As he took a gulp from his seashell, he looked splendid beyond words.

'You have a lot resting on your shoulders, you two,' said Matsya. 'It is your children and their children who will represent the last ray of hope for mankind.'

Satrupa blushed, as she took a sip of her wine.

'What tells you I will marry this silly boy, Matsya, let alone have children with him?' she taunted Manu naughtily.

The blue prophet of prophets laughed out merrily, thoroughly enjoying Satrupa teasing Manu.

'I agree, don't marry this reckless man, Tara,' added Matsya. 'He is a bit too intense, don't you think?'

All three of them broke into an affectionate laugh that only closest and most trustful of friends share with one another. Both Matsya and Tara knew that she loved Manu more than words could ever describe.

·‖卐‖·

'Protect the Ratna-Maru sword, Satyavrata. Let it pass on from generation to generation, under the protection of your descendants. This cosmic weapon is meant to reach the hands of Lord Vishnu's final avatar that will descend on the planet when evil and depravity cross all limits. You and your bloodline will be its guardians till the Kalki avatar arrives on earth at the peak of Kaliyuga.'

Tara and Manu looked at each other. Even the name of Kalki had moved something in them.

'As you say, Matsya. We will leave no stone unturned in keeping the celestial sword safe. Anything else that we need to do, to save mankind from the dark future that you have just described?'

Matsya shook his head as he looked far into the gigantic waves that the Ark was negotiating.

'You cannot prevent it, Manu. But do not get me wrong. The

dawn beyond the great deluge is also the golden age for humankind in many ways. It is now that men will conquer the skies and fly like birds. It is now that humans will tear into the heart of the oceans and sail undersea chariots. Wealth and wisdom will know no bounds and science will achieve what is incomprehensible today. Man will leap high, even towards touching *Chandra* (Moon) and *Mangal* (Mars). And it is when prosperity and knowledge, poverty and violence, disease and progress reach their zenith...that the Surya of Harappa, the great Vivasvan Pujari will be born again. As one of your descendants, Manu.

He will be the greatest of your bloodline.'

·||ॐ||·

'The scroll of the Black Temple that you have rewritten in the Harappan script, Manu, will be Kaliyuga's greatest secret. Keep it safe. Build Black Temples and guard this precious scroll. Do you know as pralay engulfs all of known Aryavarta and beyond, there is one holy city that remains untouched?'

'Untouched? I thought the great deluge has drowned the entire planet!'

Matsya laughed again, paused for a few moments and closed his eyes. He appeared to be praying to someone before he spoke his next words.

'Who can drown a city that rests on the tip of Shiva's trident, Manu? Who can drown Kashi? Go there once the great flood subsides. Thousands of years from now, it is in the very city of Kashi that your greatest descendant, the *punahrjanma* - reincarnation - of your magnificent father, will unveil the secret of the Black Temple and welcome Kalki to the world. He will be the one to protect Kalki till the avatar turns thirteen and is united with the Ratna-Maru. That is the divine task for which this magnificent man, this devta will be sent to earth.'

There was silence for a few moments. Then Tara turned to Matsya and asked what was in her mind for several minutes now.

'Tell us about this great descendent of ours, Matsya. The one who will unfurl the scroll in Kaliyuga, in Kashi. What will he be like?'

Matsya grinned and gulped down the remaining wine in his glass. In a glimpse of boyish abandon, he tossed the empty shell-glass into the ocean, much to Tara's consternation. Every spoon counted on the Ark.

'What can I say, Tara? He will be extraordinary. He will be a diamond among men. A warrior, a yogi, a lover, a charmer and a leader. He will be half-human, half-God!'

Pausing for a moment, Matsya added to his previous description.

'You might say he will be like the power of lightning.

He will be like... *Vidyut.'*

Banaras, 2017

VIDYUT

The ashes floated on the surface of the sacred waters. It was a fitting end for the marvelous Dwarka Shastri, as his soul departed from this life to another. He had died in the city of *Trayambakeshwar* or the Lord of the Crossover Bridge, Lord Shiva. It was believed that Shiva Himself whispered the mantra of salvation into the ears of anyone dying in Kashi.

Vidyut waited till every last speck of his Baba's remains dissolved into the holy Ganga.

Under the guidance of Purohit ji and the other yogis of the Dev-Raakshasa matth, he had performed the last rites of the great matthadheesh. His cut-up heart wept, as he recollected every small memory. His faint, childhood glimpses of the towering mahataantric in his prime. His first sight of the grandmaster as he had arrived at the matth after over two decades. He remembered how his Baba had fed him lovingly. How Dwarka Shastri believed that it was Vidyut who had protected him against the *Maarkesh* that loomed over his fate.

It was deep sorrow that was consuming Vidyut. After having lost his parents in quick succession while he was still a child, this was the greatest loss the devta had endured in over two decades. Dwarka Shastri was the only family he had. He suddenly felt like an orphan.

Once again.

·‖ॐ‖·

'We should leave now, beta.'

After several minutes had passed, Purohit ji came and tapped the devta on his shoulder.

'Let him leave this realm in peace, Vidyut. The more you grieve, the harder it will be for him to crossover.'

'Yes, Purohit ji...I understand,' replied Vidyut, as he folded his hands in a last salutation to the fading remains of his Baba.

·‖ॐ‖·

'What now, Purohit ji?' asked Vidyut.

They sat on the steps of the Dashashwamedh ghaat, strong

breeze from the holy river brushing against their faces and hair.

'The Order will be compelled to withdraw...at least for a while, Vidyut. By crushing Romi, Trijat and the Maschera in a matter of days, you have inflicted them with heavy set-backs. They will need time to regroup, and they will. They always do. Patience is a virtue they do not lack. But when they do strike back – it will be harder and more vicious than anything we have seen so far.'

Sonu brought them glasses of spicy *aam panna*, a refreshing raw mango drink.

'Thank you, Sonu,' said Vidyut, as he passed a glass of the tangy brew to Purohit ji.

'Without Baba it will be very hard for us to fight them, Puro-hit ji. Who is going to lead us?'

Purohit ji turned to Vidyut with an amused expression on his face.

'Our new matthadheesh will lead us, Vidyut. The successor of the mighty Dwarka Shastri will lead us.

You will lead us, O devta!'

·‖ॐ‖·

'Kalki is not coming for the Hindus alone. He is not coming for the Muslims or the Christians either. Nor for the Sikhs or the Jews. He is coming for all of mankind! Just like the ninth avatar of Lord Vishnu, the Buddha, belonged to everyone, similarly Kalki will defend every pious soul, every righteous human and every innocent individual.'

Vidyut was listening to Purohit ji with deep concentration. After his Baba, it was this brilliant priest that the devta trusted.

'Anyhow, what is your plan now, beta?' asked the wise purohit of the Dev-Raakshasa matth, changing the topic. He knew Vidyut had been through enough.

'Ah...well, I am not totally sure, Purohit ji,' responded the devta. 'I will go back to work and spend a few days setting things in order at my company. Thereafter, I will leave for where the avatar is born, and spend the rest of my years looking after Him, protecting Him. Yes, I have indulged in one luxury. My office will be procuring a super-bike for me. It is one of the most powerful motorcycles in the world. It is being customized as per my specifications. It has a terrific dual-duct engine, because of which my local mechanic Babloo calls the bike Dev-dutt or Dev-das or something! He can never get saying dual-duct right!'

Purohit ji smiled and nodded, as he drank the delicious aam panna. He then asked simply.

'And what about Damini?'

·||ॐ||·

Vidyut and Damini held hands, tighter than ever before. Damini was distraught at listening to her devta's plan. He had decided to devote his entire life to defend Kalki, till the avatar reached the age of thirteen and even after that.

She was trying her best to dissuade him from this perilous and sacrificial life-plan.

'You can look after Him even while you continue working, Vidyut. You just need to spend two days in a week at your company. You can organize a security team for the Lord wherever He is, and visit the place once every...'

'Will you marry me, Damini?'

'You are not getting me, baby...there is a better....'

She stopped as Vidyut's question sank into her.

'Whaa...what did you say, Vidyut?' she asked, praying in her heart that she had heard the words right.

'Marry me please, Damini. I cannot traverse this path without you by my side.'

The beautiful journalist from Delhi could not hold her tears back.

'Yes...yes...a thousand times yes, Vidyut.

I will marry you...you silly boy!'

·||ॐ||·

Vidyut was bidding farewell to everyone at the Dev-Raakshasa matth. Men, women and children of the matth were crying as they saw their devta leave. They all knew without any doubt – Vidyut was the new matthadheesh of the

God-Demon clan.

After he had said his goodbyes to his dear ones like Balvanta, Sonu and Govardhan, the devta came face to face with the most beautiful girl he had known in the world.

'Ooff...why do you do this to me, Nainu?' he said, teasing the stunning beauty that stood in front of him.

'Oh, come on...I am sure every lass from every Gurgaon pub makes your heart flutter, Vidyut,' she replied, rolling her eyes.

She loved him beyond measure. She wanted him today as much as she had ever wanted him before.

Vidyut laughed. But he became serious in a few seconds, as he noticed Naina's eyes were not laughing with him.

'Just know this, Naina, you were the closest I ever came to falling in love...when I shouldn't have.'

Naina gave him a tired smile, typical of beautiful girls when they want to show made-up disdain. But then she realized this was perhaps the last she was seeing him for a long long time.

'Just know this, Vidyut...I love you. And I always will.'

She kissed her devta on the cheek, even as he kissed her back.

·||ॐ||·

As his white and silver tank of a motorbike vroomed to life

under the roar of its extraordinarily powerful engine, and the magnificent Vidyut waved a final farewell to everyone, Purohit ji was reminded of something that had not struck him so far.

He smiled with illimitable happiness as he gestured a good-bye to the last devta of planet Earth.

As per the scriptures, dual-duct or Devdutt was the name of a divine being's earthly ride.

It was supposed to be the vehicle of Kalki.

THE END.

THE BEGINNING...

EPILOGUE

He looked like a ghost on that stormy night.

Hobbling from one grave to another on all four of his limbs, he did not care for the whistling wind and the rain that blew across the medieval cemetery, washing the decaying coffins and broken tombstones. Carrying a small kerosene lamp that he guarded with his life, he seemed to be looking for the right corpse to exhume for his ghoulish black ritual. He did not appear to be human any more, and looked more deceased than alive. His filthy hair was ruffled, falling over his forehead up to his cheek. Soaked wet his body seemed twisted under his deathly white kurta-pajama and his skin was peeling off his demonically aging face. It was all as if he were possessed by some dark, evil force.

He finally saw it from a distance and rushed towards it in mad glee, hopping crookedly on all fours. He brushed the tombstone off mud and rainwater with his oddly bent fingers, just to be sure of the name engraved on the epitaph. Satisfied that he had found the potent sarcophagus mentioned in the dark scriptures, he looked up at the moonless night and growled like a primordial sorcerer, before beginning to dig the grave with his bare hands and dirty fingernails.

As he dug into the slushy grave and threw handfuls of wet earth all around him, he feverishly muttered something, as if communicating with someone far far away. The words that came out from his frothing mouth seemed to be invoking an otherworldly power, summoning it to Earth.

'Rise!' he mumbled like a deranged goblin. 'Tear open the heart of prithvi and rise from its blackest depths!'

His eye flickered under the stormy rain, darting in all directions in complete lunacy.

'RISE, LUCIFER!'

Brahmanand knew only the Devil himself could stop the savior of Kaliyuga.

He was calling Satan to Earth.

TO BE CONTINUED...

TO BE CONTINUED...

ABOUT THE AUTHOR

Vineet is a first-generation entrepreneur. At age 22 he started his company Magnon from a small shed. Today Magnon is among the largest digital agencies in the subcontinent, and part of the Fortune 500 Omnicom Group.

He has led the global top-ten advertising agency TBWA as its India CEO. This made him perhaps the youngest ever CEO of a multinational advertising network in the country.

He has won several entrepreneurship and corporate excellence awards, including the *Entrepreneur of the Year 2016*. He was recently listed among the *100 Most Influential People in India's Digital Ecosystem*.

Vineet's second company talentrack is disrupting the media, entertainment & creative industry in India. It is the fastest-growing online hiring and content-crowdsourcing platform for the sector.

He has written three bestselling management & inspirational books – *Build From Scratch*, *The Street to the Highway* and *The 30 Something CEO*.

His first two fiction novels, *Harappa – Curse of the Blood River* and *Pralay – The Great Deluge*, are both national bestsellers. The books have won rich critical and literary acclaim.

www.VineetBajpai.com
facebook.com/vineet.bajpai
twitter/Vineet_Bajpai
instagram/vineet.bajpai
Write to Vineet at vb@vineetbajpai.com